Some Wandered in the Desert

Jodi Cowles

A Story of the Redeemed

Some Wandered in the Desert by Jodi Cowles

previously published under the title: When Darkness Falls

Editing Services provided by Rebecca Lyles

Cover Design by Raelynn Cramer

Books by Jodi Cowles

Thirst

The Minor Protection Act

for the kind man
{ of great patience }
who won my heart

Kate

"Wake up!"

The voice pierces my sleep-fog, accompanied by a hand shaking my shoulder. I have no idea how long I've been out — three days in transit meant I was comatose the moment she gave me permission to sleep. And even though the urgent tone she's using alerts me on some level that I should pay attention, I struggle to bring my brain back online. I've never done this kind of trip before, and so far, overcoming jet-lag seems akin to trying to focus in a Monday morning staff meeting after a three-day holiday bender.

Her voice is steady, but as my eyes begin to focus I see her movements are anything but. She's driving too fast, steering with her knees, bouncing us across the rough terrain. The motion of her hands grabs my attention, as I try to force sense into what she's doing.

She takes the SIM card out of her phone and cracks it in half, then rolls down the window and tosses both pieces. I watch in groggy fascination as her phone follows the Sim card, then she reaches into the bag between us, pulls out an iPad, and with a mighty heave smashes it onto the dashboard.

This brutal act of technological homicide sends a jolt of adrenaline through me, finally waking me fully. Now my brain begins to categorize her odd behavior and zeroes in on a possible reason — the way she keeps looking in the rear view mirror seems to be the trigger.

I turn to investigate, my view briefly captured by Papis and his wide, wild eyes staring at me. I'd forgotten he was there. Looking further, through the rear window, I see a truck bearing down on us, crammed with men hanging over the cab. They all seem to be yelling, and for a full second or two I try to make out what they're saying, before something clicks and I realize it's sort of irrelevant — the guns they wave illustrate enough of the story.

1

Becca

Stay. Calm.
Oh God.
Take a deep breath.
Oh God!
Remember the training.
OH GOD!

The voices in my head keep up this mantra, repeating every three seconds like a metronome. And there are at least six other voices in there screaming mindless fill-ins whenever there's a moment of silence — crying, praying, and huddling in the proverbial corner repeating *this can't be happening.*

I glance in the rearview mirror. Five hundred yards.

I can see Papis' face in the same mirror, clearly panicking as he mumbles to himself. He and I shared a few words before I woke Kate up, confirming we both thought the same thing about the truck in pursuit. Now he looks like he's about to cry as he fingers the medallion around his neck.

Methodically I destroy my electronics, and in spite of the situation a small part of me cringes as the remains of my much beloved iPad shower onto my lap. Out of the corner of my eye I see Kate turn to look behind her, then I hear her gasp.

Well *that* got her attention. She spins back around with terror in her eyes and I know our time is quickly evaporating.

You have to help her.

The still voice instantly quiets all the others, and I feel momentary thankfulness to have something else to focus on — her terror is much more manageable than my own.

"Kate, I need you to listen to me." I glance over and see that her eyes are lasered in on mine, but I'm not sure how much will get through.

"You need to follow my lead. These are probably not terrorists, probably they're just businessmen. They're probably not going to kill us, they'll just wave their guns and yell a lot. Do what they say. It's probably only about money, so be ready to give them whatever you have."

That's a lot of probablies.

I glance in the mirror again. Three hundred yards.

Kate's eyes are still wild and she's starting to hyperventilate.

Give her a job.

The scarf flapping in her lap gives me an idea.

"Kate. Put your scarf on. Keep it over your head. Try to keep your head covered at all times."

I follow my own advice, rip the scarf off my neck and, one-handed, get it quickly adjusted — a move I could do in my sleep after all these years.

After a pause, she starts moving mechanically. I reach for the bottle of water at my side and take a long sip, knowing it could be a good while before I get another chance. When she finishes with the scarf I hand the bottle over to her, even though the drink I took didn't even begin to touch the dryness in my throat, nearly choking me.

"Now take a drink. Go ahead and finish what's left."

I root around under my seat to find the other bottle I brought and throw it to Papis. He starts drinking wordlessly.

One hundred and fifty yards. The part of my chest housing my frantically beating heart actually hurts. I can't believe my voice sounds so calm to my own ears.

"Okay Kate, they're almost here. Remember, it's probably just business. They'll get in trouble with their bosses for roughing us up without cause, so don't give them cause. Do what they say. Follow my lead. It'll be all right. Just try to keep remembering that our main goal is to stay alive."

Trying to keep her calm has helped me block out a fraction of my own terror, but when I see the truck is only fifty yards away — so close I can see the glimmer of sweat on the driver's forehead — the fresh surge of adrenaline makes my legs go numb.

Oh God, oh God, OH GOD!

What I've told her is true. Usually. But there's always a chance these guys are religiously motivated. Or out for a joy ride instead of a paycheck. In either of those cases there's nothing I could have said that would have prepared her.

Amal

My hands are sweating.

This isn't my first time, not even my fifth. But it's the first time I've been in charge, and the weight of Oumar's expectations feels heavy on my shoulders. I'm only in charge on a trial basis, and the memory of the violent death of our last leader makes my stomach drop.

I wipe my hands one at a time on my pants and keep my gun pointed in the general direction of the car we're chasing, hoping my driver doesn't notice. It wouldn't inspire confidence, and if observing Oumar has taught me anything, it's that this game is about nothing if not confidence.

Something on the rear window of the car flickers in the sun; the sticker the government mandates foreigners to display. We pay a kid to sit at the gas station by the highway out of town and call us when one of them passes without a convoy. Not many do — few are that foolhardy. But every so often when they think the threat has died down, that phone rings again and we're in business.

I wonder who it is this time. My first attempt at kidnapping was Korean Christian missionaries. That was a horrible introduction, Oumar killed every last one after questioning them.

"Korean Christians never pay," he'd said angrily. "They like to suffer; think it gives them a better place in paradise. I am happy to oblige."

As he walked away from their still-twitching bodies he wiped the blood off his long knife, shaking his head at me in disgust — not at the violent act he'd just perpetrated, but at the waste of a golden opportunity for gain.

It was the first time I'd seen my childhood friend for who he had truly become during our time apart, and it frightened me more than I can say. Since then I've wondered if the Oumar I once knew is even still in there, cowering somewhere behind all that violence and anger.

Last year we kidnapped a carload of Spanish engineers. That was a really profitable job, though one died from an infected bullet wound when we shot him trying to escape.

But it wasn't profitable enough for Diadji — at least that's what Oumar said when he explained why he'd shot Moussa, a man who'd given Diadji more than ten years of faithful service.

"As everyone in this business knows," Oumar had spouted, strutting in front of the men as Moussa's body lay still on the ground in front of them, "Spaniards and Italians always pay. Even *one* of them dead means millions fewer in payout for Diadji."

Out of the corner of my eye I see my driver looking at me for direction, and I realize I've let my mind wander too long — something Oumar is always chiding me about — so I raise the gun in my hands, shout "Allahu Akbar" as loud as I can over the lump in my throat, and tell him it's time.

Here we go.

Matt

The ringing phone startles me from the nightmare. Dreaming about Caroline again — big surprise. Fifteen years later, you'd think my subconscious would come up with a new scenario with which to torture me. At least I wasn't yet in the kitchen when the ringing woke me. At least I didn't wake up crying.

The sweat on my chest is already cooling as I fumble around for my phone. I knock it to the floor with sleep-numbed hands and have to feel around for two more rings before I finally find it.

3:12 a.m. and a blocked number. Not uncommon in my line of work. And unfortunately, whatever the hour, it must be answered and swiftly dealt with.

"Hello?" My voice is gravelly, so I clear my throat.

"Hello, is this Matthew Sullivan?"

"Matt," I correct automatically. "Who's this?"

"My name is Amal. I have your sister Rebecca and your colleague Katherine."

Part of my brain is still fighting off the nightmare, while another part is expecting someone from work — or maybe a reporter looking for a comment on some new scandal — so I struggle to make sense of the slightly accented words coming through the phone.

"I'm sorry, what did you say?"

"My name is Amal, Mr. Sullivan. I'm calling from North Africa. I have kidnapped your sister Rebecca Parker and your colleague Katherine Wade. I would appreciate if you would get a pen and write down my terms so that we can discuss them the next time I call."

Chapter 1: Kate

Nouakchott International Airport
2:43 a.m.

I am *not* in Portland anymore!

The Islamic Republic of Mauritania screams in large block letters across the top of the paper I'm clutching tightly in my sweating hand, giving me seventy-two hours' permission to be in the country. I'm surprised at how much of an ominous feeling I have just seeing the words "Islamic Republic."

I've been told I'll have to present myself to the local police station if I stay longer than seventy-two hours, but if all goes well I'll be crossing into Senegal long before that deadline hits.

I'm not usually prone to anxiety, but neither do I habitually pass the wee hours of the night jockeying for position with a planeload of Muslim men taking turns ogling me.

For the first thirty or so minutes of the flight out of Casablanca, I worried over how many men stood in the aisles, chatting animatedly, with no sign of the usual announcement telling them to sit down. Suddenly I realized Arab men congregating probably wasn't the stress point for this flight that it would be in my own country.

No sooner had I had that revelation, then I was truly shocked by a man across the aisle from me surreptitiously lighting up and taking a quick puff, before dousing the cigarette in his coffee cup and smashing it into the sick bag. I was so startled by that episode, that when we finally landed and literally half the plane stood up and started getting into the overhead compartments before we'd even stopped taxiing, I felt a little jaded.

After de-planing I found myself on the open tarmac, with ours the only plane in sight. I noticed one rather lackadaisical guard smoking and, ostensibly, making sure no one skipped passing through immigration which I gathered occurred through the doors of the slightly-weathered building everyone was headed toward.

There were two other women on the flight who I thought I might try to follow, but when I started to get close their male companions boxed me out quite purposefully, as if worried my evident Westernism might rub off.

At least, that's how I interpreted it. It's amazing how active the imagination can get when you understand nothing going on around you and have no one to talk to. Not to mention the countless unsettling scenarios at airports just like this one that I can easily recall to mind, weaned as I was on a steady diet of Jack Ryan and Jack Bauer.

I'm trying to follow the instructions I was given. I didn't wear anything with an obvious American logo. My shoulder-length blonde hair is tied up. The scarf I bought half-price at the Rack is draped casually around my head.

That purchase was easy, but I spent the better part of two days trying to find clothes in Portland that matched the long-and-loose, over-the-tush, guidelines I'd been given.

I'm not making eye contact with men lest they think I'm propositioning them. It's amazing how hard that is — I grew up in the make-eye-contact-so-they-know-you-see-'em part of the world. Plus, it's easy to bump into the guy in front of you when you're looking at your shoes.

I try to keep my eyes down, looking up only when necessary to make sure I'm still moving toward what I hope to be the right booth. I figure I've got a fifty-fifty chance since there are only two lines, but the soldiers with big guns glaring at me don't make me feel extremely confident.

I've seen plenty of guns on TV. But, wow, there's something … I don't know, *louder* maybe … about seeing them up close and personal, especially when the men wielding them have stern faces and are garbed in unfamiliar uniforms in a region known for disappearing people.

The heat is oppressive, but worse still is the press of sweating bodies in an enclosed space because of that heat. I'm used to a culture that spends about a zillion dollars a year in deodorant. I'm also used to a bit more in the way of personal space.

Matt told me I shouldn't need a headscarf right away, but what was the phrase the State Department was always using? *Out of an abundance of caution.* I'm glad I didn't listen and pulled the scarf on as the plane descended.

That's strike two for Matt after the ludicrous routing he sent me on, flying from Portland to Chicago to Washington to Paris, down to Morocco and then over to Mauritania. Hefty layovers in each. The better part of an unendurably long three days. I wonder if he'll earn strike three tonight, or if there'll be a grace period until tomorrow.

The two women I was keeping my eye on are fully covered, and I watch them disappear into a tent which I can only assume is for private screening. I hope they don't think I'll go willingly into one of those!

I can see beyond the bars and soldiers that there's a crowd of people waiting. More women out there, thank goodness, but again all of them fully covered. At least they're not all dressed in black, the fabrics seem to be a wide variety of bright colors and clashing patterns.

Finally I make it to the front of the line. I shift forward and hand over my passport and visa paperwork. The visa briefly sticks to my hand owing to both my stress sweat and the oppressive heat, and I give a small smile to the official as I peel it off.

I've done this before, gone through immigration lines, but never with a soldier armed with a machine gun standing close by. The official looks up and gruffly speaks in what I assume to be Arabic.

How in the world do you answer politely without smiling or making eye contact? I fail on all fronts, but manage to say, "I'm sorry, I only speak English."

He makes what sounds like a derogatory remark to the gun-packing soldier, then turns back to me and says, "Purpose?"

Relieved to have an answer to this question, I boldly say "Tourism," hoping he doesn't see through the bald-faced lie. After all, what is there to visit in the middle of this backwoods, god-forsaken desert? Even Senegal is a step up as far as I could tell from the dossier one of the junior reps prepared for me.

The official finishes whatever security screening he deems appropriate, which mainly seems to consist of snooping at the few stamps I've earned, and clangs his stamp down on a fresh page. He passes it back but doesn't look up, leaving me to wonder what I'm supposed to do next. The soldier next to him takes pity on me and points toward the appropriate exit with the business end of his giant weapon.

I was told to bring only a carry-on, and I'm glad I followed that instruction — I'm hanging onto it for dear life as I begin to scan the room. Almost immediately I catch sight of a pale face that easily stands out among the crowd. I've never seen it in person, but we've said hi a few times over the years on Skype.

I knew I was tense, but I didn't realize just how freaked that little immigration scenario made me until my body literally unclenches as we make eye contact.

She winds her way over to me and I lose track of her as she passes through a group of women hugging and chatting loudly — with her head down and hair covered she fits right in with them. She pops out of the group right in front of me and, with a big smile, says, "Welcome to Mauritania!"

For a second we do that awkward I-don't-really-know-you-so-we-probably-shouldn't-hug dance, but then she leans in and gives me a hug anyway. She reaches down and grabs my carry-on, and says, "Let's get out of here. We can talk in the car."

She turns and heads toward what I can only assume is the exit. I follow as closely as I can, wishing for one of those child leashes Matt and I always make fun of as I lose sight of her a few times in the crowd.

I thought it was hot inside, but when we finally are able to burst through the doors, the fresh air is something akin to what I imagine it feels like inside an oven set to broil. A scrum of taxi drivers start yelling the second they lay eyes on us.

As if!

She waves at a large black man standing beside a car and the taxi drivers melt away, looking for new opportunities. Arriving at the car, she hands him my bag and heads for the drivers' seat. I don't know what the protocol is here, so I start heading for the back seat, but the man heads me off by opening the front passenger seat for me. I give him a small smile and get in.

"Phew," she exhales loudly, "always nice to be back in the car." She looks across at me and smiles as she puts the car in gear. "You made it!"

I laugh a little. "Thank you. I'm so relieved to finally be here. I'm ready to kill your brother — I feel like I've been run over by a truck!"

She gives a little half chuckle. "Believe me I know the feeling."

She doesn't appear at all phased as she dodges taxis and cars and crowds of men to get out of the airport, speaking briefly in a language I don't recognize to another man with a big gun who laughs and raises the barricade.

Just as I would have expected, from all Matt's stories about his heroic, world-tromping, do-gooder sister. It's funny how his description changes based on how he's feeling at the time — sometimes it's an affectionate reference to Super Beck, other times he rolls his eyes in irritation and refers to the size of the stick up her butt. But he never speaks about her without me realizing she's the most important person in his life.

He's sure we'll get on "smashingly" and can bond over our "do gooder" lifestyles. I'm not so sure about that prediction, but a couple weeks at my old pay scale will be extremely helpful in keeping said new lifestyle in the black.

I try looking out the window as we leave, but can't really make anything out in the darkness. Even on what looks to be the main road out of the airport, there isn't much in the way of public lighting; must not be high on the agenda of whoever it is that runs this place.

I feel a slight twinge of concern that I didn't do more research before arriving. It *is* an Islamic Republic after all. I was just too busy doing other things to prepare, I try to justify to myself. Luckily Becca breaks into my thoughts before I can let myself get too worked up.

"We can't head out in the middle of the night, so I'm going to take you to some friends' house to get a couple hours of sleep. But it's best if we get going right at dawn. I'm sorry about that, but it's safer, and you can sleep in the car on the way."

The offer of sleep makes me weak with relief.

. . . .

Sisters Coffee Shop
Portland, Oregon
One week earlier

"You know I chose you over Alex, and of course I did! But I had to give up going to my favorite lunch spot because Alex still eats there every day. You owe me this! Besides, it's right up your new alley, isn't it?"

We're at our favorite hangout, where we meet several times a week to catch up. It's harder than it was when we worked in the same place and met here every day on our walk in. But if it's harder now, well, that just means you work harder to make time. That's what best friends do.

Matt has always been persuasive, but that's not surprising considering what he does for a living. What I used to do. But even bringing to bear all the powers of his extremely experienced and agile silver tongue, he hadn't been able to talk the IRS into allowing a massive write-off for a school for orphans that didn't exactly necessarily exist outside of the imagination of Harry, his major celebrity client. Worse than that, he hadn't been able to talk the IRS agent out of contacting the FBI to investigate further.

Considering Matt works at Stumptown, one of the oldest and most prestigious image management firms in the world, that's actually saying something. I was with him once when he talked a police officer out of arresting him when he was driving us home, open wine cooler in hand and three people, including myself, in the back seat visibly partaking of a joint.

Of course that doesn't sound like such a big accomplishment now that weed is legal, but that doesn't stop him from repeating the story any time he gets a little tipsy.

Knowing the proclivity of IRS agents to supplement their income with an occasional quick tip to TMZ, or one of the countless other gossip sites, Matt knew he was running out of time to get ahead of the story and reframe the little misunderstanding about his client's cross-cultural mis-recollection.

Everyone knows a scandal goes better if the penitent comes forward first, rather than being outed by the press. Then you have control of the narrative rather than reacting and spinning. Enter his brilliant scheme.

"Couldn't you just buzz on over to the tiny, little village in northern Senegal where Harry sends money every month? Harry swears this guy's legit, that he's seen pictures of the Soccer Academy started in his name to take kids off the street and give them an education. Unfortunately the IRS thinks he's full of it, and once the FBI sticks their nose into it we're looking at terrorism implications because of the location and money involved.

"All we need you to do is find the guy and see if there's anything that looks remotely like a school. Or that could be turned into a school with a little creativity. Or some dirt on the guy so we can say he took advantage of Harry's good intentions and swindled him."

He lays it all out at our favorite corner table on the second floor, using the sepulchral tones we always use when discussing clients since he's not technically supposed to share this information with me anymore. He's even talked his do-gooder sister into flying in from Egypt to accompany me.

"I think this is the one Kate, if I can resolve Harry's latest crisis I'll make partner. You know how hard I've been working for that. And I know you could use the money. The truth is, I thought of you immediately. It's a win-win!"

He whips out his phone and says, "just a sec" as he makes a show of checking his email. And even though I know exactly what he's doing — he's the one who taught me use of the "judicious pause" in delicate negotiations — I'm glad he's giving me a minute to think.

I can see the presser if Matt pulls this off — it doesn't take too much imagination, since I was working the account during three of Harry's high-level shenanigans.

He would stand there shamefacedly, explaining how he was duped, how he'd already sent an investigator to find out what in the world could have gone wrong in Africa, what they were going to do to fix it, how embarrassed he was and how deeply regretful. How he'd disappointed his amazing and unendingly supportive fan base and would do anything and everything in his power to re-earn their trust.

Cue tears and swelling exit music, as he receives a supportive hug from his WINO (wife-in-name-only). This particular WINO preferred the company of women, but she'd struck an equitable deal with Harry that made up nicely for the little deception.

Just one of the many heartening facts I'd learned about our famous clients, and one of the many things I didn't miss since I'd left.

Even though I'd resigned and almost everyone at the Stump thought I was a little crazy, they knew me and that I'd do a good job. And no doubt more importantly, as with every employee and ex-employee, my iron-clad non-disclosure agreement is still in force.

Matt said the partners were so desperate not to lose Harry's business that they'd agreed to his plan almost instantly. No wonder, his account fairly prints money and Matt manages a cohort solely focused on keeping up with his frequent misdeeds.

I think Matt's probably right, if he can pull this off, Harry's stock should actually go up a couple of points. And Matt's stock, well — his assessment is no doubt also correct about his promotion. The partners have been dangling the brass ring at him for the last several years.

He looks up from the phone when I sigh, giving me a glimpse of the face of my friend, instead of the smooth account exec trying to convince me. I sigh again, knowing that all of this pondering is kind of irrelevant. What can I do, really? He's my best friend and he needs me.

The few days are a whirlwind. Eight inoculations, including a deeply troubling discussion with the infectious disease specialist about whether the painful and $1,000 rabies series is worth it or not in my case. We decide no.

That discussion is followed by a number of butt-numbingly dull meetings bringing me up to speed on the latest scandal-in-the-making, and then I roll my carry-on through the doors at PDX.

It was hard to get it zipped after fitting in all the items on the "suggested packing list" Becca sent, but I still manage to find a spot for the thick envelope Matt gives me at the airport.

"Reese's. Her favorite," he says sheepishly. Then he smiles and pulls a pair of sunglasses out of his jacket pocket. My eyes widen and his smile grows bigger — he knows I've been coveting these for over a year but unable to justify them on my new salary. "A little advance on a job well done," he says quietly.

We hug for a long time, and then I head through security.

....

Sleeping on a quarter-inch mat reminds me of camping. As does the sand in my sheets. And the flashlight Becca shines in my face to wake me up, whispering "sorry" as she places a cup of what smells like coffee near my head.

I never liked camping.

Her friends seem nice enough, as seen through the eyes of jet-lagged exhaustion. They chat quietly over scrambled eggs and toast that doesn't taste quite right. Becca seems quite perky considering her middle-of-the-night airport run and pours me another cup of coffee before I have to ask for it. Honestly it tastes like a mix of ash and battery acid to my Portland-trained palate, but there's no mistaking the moment the caffeine hits my veins.

By the end of the second cup I'm feeling a bit more like I might live, which is good because Becca says it's time to go.

When we get out to the Land Rover, I'm introduced to Papis, the big black man from last night who is somehow even more intimidating in daylight, until he flashes that huge smile at me again.

Kate tells me he works for her friends, and will be accompanying us across the border. We load up, and I suddenly realize that this is her friends' car, loaned to us for the duration. *Nice* friends.

The sun is just starting to anoint the rolling dunes of the desert as we roll out of Nouakchott. Becca points out the bulldozers as we go by, telling me they run up and down the road every day, pushing back the desert so it doesn't overtake the town.

From what I can see through the rarified vision of my brand-new sunglasses, they're not doing the world any favors with that job. It's just one sand-blasted concrete shack after another on one side of the road, and endless desert on the other. At least the desert boasts the occasional scrub brush and herd of camels, which Becca says they milk. Something about that strikes me as very wrong and I find myself wondering what I cavalierly poured into my coffee this morning.

I'm thinking I should probably get to work, or at least be marginally human and have a conversation with Matt's favorite and only sister, when she offers me a lifeline.

"I don't know what Matt was thinking routing you that way — that's how I would have had to come, mind you, but I'd assumed his pockets were a little deeper."

I manage a grunt that I hope sounds enough like a laugh to pass. "He said it was to avoid anybody following me, but I think one of the interns must have booked it."

"Anyway," she continues, "It'll be a couple hours to the border if everything goes well, so if you want you can try to get a bit more sleep. We'll have plenty of time to chat when you're feeling more human."

And suddenly I don't care about civility or social niceties, or even how fascinating the desert sand looks with the low sun turning it several shades of beautiful. Her words are all the encouragement I need to crash.

I surface every now and then when the car takes an especially large jolt, but it seems like it's been three weeks since I left Portland, not just three days, so it doesn't take much effort to readjust my aching body and slip back into unconsciousness.

Chapter 2: Becca

The vehicle finally slows and I feel my body come to rest painfully against the floor. After hours jolting and rocking across the metal bottom, and what I'm guessing is a poorly-placed tool my hip slams onto any time we bounce, I know I'll be sore tomorrow — but depending on where we are, that may or may not be of much concern.

I hear each of the four car doors slam in turn and it feels like my heart rate multiplies with each one. Oddly enough, getting tossed around for a few hours had focused my brain on the pain instead of on my situation. It had also given me time to remind myself of what I believe to be true, allowing for just the tiniest pebble of rock hard calm to settle in somewhere nice and deep. I wonder how long that calm will last.

I brace myself, rubbing my forehead against the spare tire to settle the blindfold in its proper place. I'd managed to work it off a bit during the drive to try to see something, but I never glimpsed more than the panel on the door. I can't get it quite back in place so a sliver of light still comes through the bottom — hopefully they won't notice.

Though I still feel her pressed up against my back, Kate hasn't made a sound since she stopped crying an hour or so ago. The rag around my mouth wouldn't allow for much more than grunting, and as I didn't suppose that would be encouraging, I didn't even try. I'm sure she feels that we've stopped and expects the same thing I do.

Well, actually, I imagine her expectations might be a bit worse. This is her first time in the region, so she's probably pumped up with reactionary media tales and overblown Hollywood hype. No wonder she was crying.

Not that I wasn't. I just cried less noisily. And in truth, my fear response is more of the vomit variety than tears, but my eyes started leaking again every time the image of Papis ran through my mind. They'd asked where he was from, and when he answered Mauritania, they'd shot him without a second thought. He was worthless to them. The horror of seeing his lifeless body in the dust mixed with an unbearable sadness at knowing how beloved he was of my friends.

I used to love reading spy thrillers, but once I moved to Egypt I found the thrill was gone. Now I'd rather relax with Jane Austen, or something else equidistantly far from my real life. Even still, I've probably got a bit more realistic idea of what's to come than Kate does. Thus another reason for my crying.

The rear door squeals open and I get a glimpse of four skinny black legs and two gun barrels out of my sliver of visibility. At least, I think it's four and two, my vision seems to be blurring in and out.

"Up, up!" they start yelling. I'm not sure what they expect me to do, tied as I am, but I make a few wriggling motions until someone grabs my arm and yanks me forward. I slam into the ground and the wind knocks right out of me. When I can finally breathe, my first gasping inhale takes in about as much dust as air, and I start coughing loudly.

They must yank Kate out with similar chivalry because something heavy crashes to the ground right beside me that I assume is her. Then they leave us alone for a moment while they yell at each other. The adrenaline roaring through every vein makes it difficult, but I try to concentrate on the words.

They're not yelling in Arabic, but I'm not sure what it is beyond that. The one who spoke English is nowhere in sight — Amal, he said his name was when he'd oh-so-calmly informed us he was taking us hostage while his men looked on menacingly.

I know I'm supposed to be noticing details — observe, analyze — instead of giving space to my emotional response, but it's a lot harder than I thought it'd be, way back when I first heard the strategy years ago in a sterile conference room.

From the ground I can't see much more than the thin layer of dust that hovers over everything in view. I see several pairs of dirty feet, some sandaled, and my eyes are drawn to a scrawny chicken that walks calmly right up and over the top of one of those feet before the foot launches it in the air.

"Up, up!" someone yells again and I brace for the "help" that will surely come. Two arms grab each of mine and yank, and suddenly

I'm propelled forward at great speed, trying to churn my legs to keep up. I'm taller than the men helping me, which doesn't add much in the way of assistance.

They steer me right toward the chicken and I stumble to avoid it, then realize I've given away the fact that I can see. Thankfully no one seems to notice my lapse.

I turn my head slightly to the left and see a hut, and suddenly we veer toward it. Someone pushes my head down forcefully while someone else removes the rope from my hands and then shoves me from behind. It's very quick and my arms are dead noodles, so I go headfirst into the dirt without being able to stop myself.

My head is ringing and I'm wondering if my nose is broken when Kate is tossed in and lands on top of me. We're both so stunned it takes a while for us to negotiate an untangling of limbs.

More yelling. And then the door, such as it is, slams shut.

The blood roars through my head, and the noise of men congratulating each other, familiar in any language, recedes. There's even a couple gunshots before an angry voice stops them.

I reach with an unsteady hand to touch my nose, and immediately feel what I assume is warm blood run over my fingers. Slowly, I try to count to thirty, but my mind freezes at eleven. I can't remember what comes next, and for some reason anger rips through my whole body. I sit and tremble for a bit, until finally I remember — twelve!

It feels like a victory. I continue on to thirty, then reach up to take my blindfold off, then the rag from around my mouth.

Dusty straw hut. Dirt floor. About eight feet across. Roundish. Roommate huddled and crying next to me.

I could stand up between the rafters if I wanted, but my head would graze the roof. One door. One unfortunate looking plastic bucket. Two blankets thrown in the corner.

Home sweet home.

....

Cairo, Egypt
One week ago

My brother's face peers at me through the Skype window, even more pixelated than normal.

"I recognize that tone you know — it's the same one you used to use just about ten minutes before we'd get in trouble from one of your schemes."

He laughs, and the screen freezes in the moment he casts his head back, mouth wide open. It's one of the least flattering freezes ever, and I take a screenshot to add to our collection. Such are the vagaries of attempting modern-day communication from a slightly-less-than-modern dot on the map.

We complain about it, naturally, but don't give up our weekly talks for anything. Bedtime for him; bright and early for me. I'm usually sipping from my second cup of coffee while he's often knocking back his second glass of wine.

But for once there's no wine and he seems to be naturally buzzed.

"Oh come on," his disembodied voice continues. "It won't be that hard — all you have to do is babysit my best friend who's actually quite nice as she does a little investigating."

His image unfreezes, and all the pixelation has cleared up for the time being, "six, seven days — two or three weeks tops, and you'll have six months of funding!"

"Don't think I didn't catch that — talking like it's already a done deal instead of in the hypothetical. You taught me that's one of your favorite techniques."

He laughs again, but this time I get to see it in real time. It makes my heart ache. These weekly dates aren't enough, not nearly. But if I'm honest with myself, even his long-promised visit won't fulfill what I'm looking for. What I miss, what I crave, what causes the familiar ache with his name on it to start up somewhere mid-chest, is the closeness we shared in childhood. Us against the world, facing down bullies unafraid because I knew my big brother was standing beside me. I could do anything in those days, meet any challenge and trounce any enemy. Nothing was impossible. Because of him.

But that was a long, long time ago, in a world so distant from the ones either of us live in now that it's hard sometimes to think of it as anything more than a dream.

I'll take what I can get, obviously, but I miss the old Matt.

"I miss you, Matt, when are you going to take that vacation you keep promising me and come over for a visit?"

"Beck, we almost lost the client last time — this guy is a scandal-magnet — and if this goes well and I manage to keep him on the line, it'll be just the push I need to make partner. Once that happens, I assure you, I'll be on the next plane."

"And there's where you dangle the carrot," I laugh, unable to help myself even as I know I'll give in. "You've taught me all your tricks, you can't pull one over on me."

"All right, alright, a'right!" The familiar response of childhood; how he always answered when I called him on his crap. I even miss that.

He tugs at me in these conversations, so much so that I sometimes want to stop calling. I've wondered if the pain would be less severe if it was a once-and-for-all break, rather than this slow burn of distance over the years — but I've never quite worked up the courage to test the theory.

"Look, honestly, you'd be doing me a favor. We're in a major bind, and we need this to stay very quiet. I realize Mauritania and Senegal are outside your area of expertise, but you're a heck of a lot closer to knowing how to maneuver your way through there than anybody I could send from Portland. I want someone I can trust to not sell the story to a tabloid, and I need someone I can trust to take care of Kate. You know how important she is to me."

And with that — sincere, heartfelt vulnerability — he gets me, like always.

. . . .

After a horrifically long night of keeping watch, I'm just starting to drift off as dawn breaks. Suddenly I hear a shout and what sounds like quite a lot of commotion going on outside. I peer out the spy hole I managed to carve out last night by pulling at a few weeds near the door and see Amal stomping about energetically, kicking at the men still on the ground. They don't seem too eager to rise until he points outside the camp and starts yelling louder. When I turn to look where he's pointing I see a car approaching with a large plume of dust billowing out behind it.

This must be the real boss, I think, and my intuition is quickly proven accurate by the way the men start hopping up and dusting off their clothing.

My eyes veer quickly back to Amal to see he's also straightening his shirt, and I could swear he looks a little nervous. Great. I'd just gotten sort of calmed down and here we go again.

I turn and gently kick Kate's foot. I tried to talk to her last night, but she seems to be in textbook shock. She finally fell into an exhausted sleep a couple hours ago, after crying off and on since we arrived.

She wakes slowly, and I hate seeing the moment when she passes from sleep to wakefulness and realizes where she's at. She looks at me with pure panic in her eyes.

"Someone's coming," I say quietly, before returning to my spy hole to see the car has arrived — a black Land Rover quite a bit newer than the beater we'd been driving. The choice of almost everyone with resources in this land — criminal, saint, and everything in between. Amal rushes forward and opens the passenger door, saluting the man who exits.

He's taller than Amal. His shirt is brilliantly white and freshly pressed which must mean they had the AC cranked on high. It won't last long, but it's impressive when everyone around him is considerably more wrinkled.

He smiles and claps Amal on the back. They seem to be exchanging some sort of traditional long string greeting. It looks similar to the one used by my Egyptians, but seems to have more back-and-forths.

I see them look this way and feel a pit open in my stomach. No matter that I invested most of the night in asking the Lord for strength and reminding myself of both His sovereignty and His goodness, my body rebels at the position it's been put in.

"I am a beloved child of God. No one can take that from me." I whisper it, hoping that, aloud, it will find more purchase in my fickle brain than all of last night's silent repetitions.

Amal gestures in our direction, then follows closely behind as the man heads our way.

I look at Kate, "here we go."
Oh God, oh God, oh God.

Chapter 3: Amal

Oumar heads off confidently toward the hut and I hope I don't look as meek as I feel following after him. He had commanded that I await his arrival before speaking to the hostages, but for some reason he'd been held up overnight. He does not offer an explanation for the delay, nor do I expect one.

I hold my breath as he nears the hut, unsure whether he will allow me to go forward with my plan once he sees them. I'd heard the excitement in his voice when I called to tell him we had two American women unaccompanied by male protectors.

As I have off and on all night, I wonder what they were thinking, traveling alone. Their easily removable local man counted only in terms of the cost of the bullet to get rid of him.

Western women never seem to doubt their right to do whatever they want, no matter what part of the world they're striding through, nor how many times their media reports on how badly such striding can go.

Oh no, their motto, *it'll never happen to me. I have rights!*

At least these two weren't out parading half-naked like most of their sisters. I don't think I could have held the men off otherwise, even with Oumar's standing orders.

Oumar opens the flimsy door of the hut with such force that it bounces off the outside wall and flips shut again. He looks quickly at me, but I wouldn't dream of laughing. This Oumar is nothing like the brother of my childhood, and through painful experience, I have learned to tell the difference.

He pulls it open again, this time with less enthusiasm, then leans down and steps through. I take a breath and follow.

It takes a moment for my eyes to adjust before I see them. The brown-haired one who was driving is sitting on the left, looking alert and intelligent and, if possible, unafraid. Her gaze is disturbing somehow, even as she directs it toward my chin.

The blonde on the right is folded in on herself and I can see the tracks of tears down her dusty face. She looks like she's in shock, which will make her the easier one to control.

I wait for Oumar to begin. I know it gives him great pleasure to flex his power over westerners — that they are Americans is even better. His speech will no doubt be long, and it always surprises me how similar his words are to those we heard over and over in childhood. He repeats much of the same religious mumbo jumbo that was used to justify all the horrors visited upon us. This Oumar I will never understand.

He looks at me meaningfully, then begins in a terrible, low voice.

The blonde reacts visibly to his words, inching backward. But the driver continues to watch me, understanding the reason I am here.

"My name is Oumar. I am a soldier for the Fist of Allah, and you are going to be my guests for the time being.

"We have struggled for many years with the oppressive governments in this region, who do not allow us to worship Allah, the compassionate and merciful, as he commands. We are in a holy jihad against the forces of all who oppose his will, but it is an expensive business to be in."

I've heard this speech more times than I would like to remember, and that familiarity allows a part of my mind to wander as the other part mechanically translates.

Will this work? For the millionth time I question myself. This is the first time we've had the chance to try out my ideas, and I've staked not just my life, but everything I hope for the future on the success of this strategy.

Oumar continues, voice rising and tempo increasing, while at the same time taking fewer pauses. But I am used to his style and easily keep up.

"You will provide us with telephone numbers for your family, and we will call them and negotiate your release. Hopefully our negotiations will be fruitful and of short duration, and you will enjoy our hospitality until then. If you provide us no resistance and behave humbly as women ought to before Allah and men, you will not be harmed. Of this, I give you my word."

Here Oumar pauses and looks at me. The next part is crucial and I wait, unsure whether he will stick to the plan.

"I am a man of my word. If you try to escape, or if you do not obey Amal, who is in charge in my absence, I will allow the men to do what they want with you. I tell you with sadness the last woman we kidnapped was not so cooperative and the men unfortunately killed her as they were taking their pleasure with her."

Normally we give instructions to our male captives and leave them to keep their women under control. I'm jittery with nerves, waiting to see how far he will take this. But even Oumar has to answer to someone higher, and he's the one who convinced Diadji that my ideas had value in the first place.

"I tell you this so that you know under what terms you are a guest. I have explained that this is a business and you are a very valuable asset for us. It is not so important to me that you are whole when you are returned to your families, but I do not want to risk the chance that you will be killed. So I ask you to listen to Amal, follow his instructions carefully, and wait patiently before Allah until your family recompenses us for the hospitality which we are so generously providing."

This is one of my tactics — from my research I know that western women are highly susceptible to threats of rape, and even more the sensationalized gang-rape they have been taught to expect every time they see Muslim men gathered together. Threatening that, then offering reasonable care and protection, is part of the cocktail I'm trying to mix to keep them compliant.

The topic has been an interesting intellectual exercise for me over the years, and I have spent much time studying it. For instance, if sexual violation is brought into the picture, the western man is programmed to go blind with rage. He is unable to control his emotional response and thinks he has a chance, brainwashed by a steady diet of action movies where the hero never dies.

I've seen the surprise in their eyes, as I've seen more than one man jump in front of his wife to be killed instantly. I imagine they think it is manly, but I always wonder what he thinks happens after he's gone. In my opinion, it is not manly at all, it is short-sighted cowardice.

In a way, the western man is very similar to our fundamental Muslims and what fuels their honor killings. A woman's virtue is connected to her man's honor, whatever the culture. Our fundamental Muslims kill their women to recover honor; the western man runs unarmed at a man with a gun to recover his, and leaves his woman to suffer the consequences alone.

Sexual violation takes away a western man's reason. The more we can keep him reasonable, thinking of this as a business arrangement, an exchange of goods, the better.

The sexual violation of women seems to me to be key — if we can keep our men in check, we can better control both men and women. We can manage the asset line and have better outcomes. We can use fewer men on each operation, which means fewer errors, and at the same time gives us the flexibility to run operations simultaneously when the opportunity arises.

Time and time again women are the issue — they are killed while being raped, their men are killed trying to protect them, our men who rape must be killed as a warning to the others. All of that equals lost profit. All of that profit could be recovered if we managed the assets better.

And if we had more control and weren't always watching out for escapes, or doubling the guard so half the men were making sure the other half weren't killing the assets, there would be other benefits.

The desert hotline, for one, which is one of our biggest enemies. We've had several operations blown because everyone talks to everyone, news roaring from one town to the next like wildfire, and suddenly the army is upon us.

Less men in the crew means less attention and less gossip, and even a smaller chance of triggering satellite surveillance — all resulting in a more robust bottom line.

I've been formulating these thoughts for years as I operated as Oumar's right-hand man. When he is the Oumar of my childhood, he is receptive to my ideas. When he is Diadji's Oumar, I keep quiet.

A few months ago, in one of his jovial moods, he convinced me to write up a proposal, and then got me an appointment with Diadji — a ruthless, evil-empire kind of criminal, who wanted nothing more than to think of himself as an upright businessman. Diadji liked my ideas and that was that.

Suddenly, before I realized what it might mean to launch from the comfortably theoretical to the practical, I am in charge of a small crew, and can implement my strategies at will. But I never thought I'd be trying them out on just women. It makes me nervous and my mind can't stop calculating the odds.

So here I am, in charge in a world I don't completely understand. I've moved from the intellectual challenge of asset, distribution efficiency and profit margins, to guns and betrayal and men always on the verge of anarchy.

………..

I'm jolted back to reality when Oumar abruptly turns and slams through the door. I can see the blonde is crying again, but the driver seems relieved. It is as I suspected, she is familiar with this scenario. That should be helpful.

I turn to follow Oumar out the door. His white shirt has begun to wrinkle, his brow breaking with sweat, so I know he will soon leave us.

He stops in full view of the men and speaks loudly. "Amal, I believe in you. More importantly, Diadji believes in you. You know that is why he has given you leadership. I am not fully convinced of your strategy, but Diadji is and that is enough. You are in charge. But you must control the men. The orders have been given, but you must enforce them."

He leans in closer and whispers the rest, "Diadji wanted me to tell you that if you fail, I am to make to you the same promise I made to those whores — I will allow the men to do what they want with you."

His words send tremors through my legs, but I manage to keep my voice steady as I reply, "Thank you Oumar. I will not fail you or Diadji."

He takes a few steps toward the car, then stops, and I realize he's waiting for me to open the door. I quickly do and am hit in the face by a blast of AC. His driver kept the car running the whole time! What would it be like to live with such luxury?

He turns toward the men, lifts his arm and yells "Allahu Akbar." They respond in kind and each fire off a couple rounds from their old weapons.

One of Oumar's men gets out to drive the women's Land Rover, and I watch as both cars pull out. I watch until there is only dust in the far distance from where they disappeared. I can feel the stares of the men at my back. All these men with guns.

They follow me now, but they are like wild dogs. They only respect what they fear. Do they sense the fear in me? Or even deadlier, do they sense how much hope I have inside me that this job will be the one that finally sets me free? I haven't been free in nearly twenty five years.

....

Sometimes I try to remember my parents. I lie on my mat and look at the stars and think back as far as I can, but all I am able to see is dust. Dust and sand. My parents sold me to a *marabout,* one of the men responsible for training young boys in religious instruction, and their faces were devoured by the past as I was devoured by my new life.

The *marabout* brought me from my family's hut in a small village, to the one-room concrete block home in Dakar he shared with his students. From there he lived in moderate luxury as he sent us out every morning with stomachs growling. We had a quota, and if we didn't make it, we understood that we shouldn't bother returning — although all we earned for our efforts was a bowl of sandy rice if we were lucky, and a section of the floor where we all slept around his big bed. Those who weren't lucky went to sleep hungry, and the exceptionally unlucky slept in that big bed.

It wasn't much of a home, but neither were my vague memories of my original home. And it was better than trying to make it on the street on your own. At night we'd all huddle together and wait for the *marabout* to yell a bit and then fall asleep drunk.

As far as I could tell, the religious instruction he promised my parents seemed to consist of nothing more than a few curses in the name of Allah as he swiped at us on his way by, and the weekly fiery lecture, the likes of which Oumar was apt to repeat.

Oumar, who had been there all of two weeks before I arrived, was by then a veteran. He took me in, terrified and hungry and crying for my mother. He shared his mat and his bowl of sandy rice. He explained the rules to me and brought me along on his routes. He was my brother.

We tried all kinds of things to make the quota. We begged, we stole, we tried to do little jobs no one wanted. Finally we found some success washing car windshields in front of the American neighborhood. That is, the neighborhood where all the Americans lived. It wasn't walled off or anything, they just preferred living together. Who could blame them? Dakar is a nightmare.

We would stand on the main street where most cars exited the neighborhood and converge on any car that gave even the appearance of slowing. If you could get your dirty rag on the front window and smear it up a bit, they couldn't see to go forward and would usually wait you out while you wiped up. Then they'd roll down the window and a burst of air conditioning would puff out when they threw a few francs at us.

After maybe six years with the *marabout*, with varying success and an already well-developed and entrenched cynicism, my luck finally changed.

A car rolled up with a white woman in the back seat, and for some reason she looked up. She'd been talking to a boy about my age I assumed was her son, and in that moment we locked eyes. I don't know what it was about me that grabbed her — Oumar was pasted to my side as usual, and we were joined by at least a dozen others every day. Never before had I seen her give anything to them. But as we continued to stare at each other something shifted.

Of course I didn't care why, it only mattered that she began to give me a few francs every couple days. I shared them with Oumar for his quota, but no one else.

A couple weeks later I imagine she must have asked around and realized I had to give any money to my *marabout*, because she started giving me the exact amount I owed each night, along with a sandwich in a little plastic bag. It was helpfully cut in half, and Oumar and I usually had it devoured before her car turned the corner down the street.

She cut the crusts off. I never understood that. Years later I asked her about it and she laughed. She said her mother had done it for her, so she always did it for her son John.

I'm not sure what brought it on, but following about eight months of giving me sandwiches a couple times a week, there was another shift. She decided to do something more. I still don't know why she picked me, but she did. One day she opened her car door and said get in.

I'd like to think I wouldn't have left Oumar if he'd been with me, but for the first time in nearly seven years, he'd not been at my side. The night before the *marabout* had come for me, and as I retreated in fear Oumar stepped forward and took my place in the big bed.

He couldn't stand the next morning, which was the only reason he wasn't beside me. But in that moment, when she opened the door to a new life, I chose not to remember. I chose not to remember the nights we'd huddled together, sharing whatever food we could scrape up. I chose not to remember the hours we'd spent dreaming of a different life. I chose not to remember the brother who had kept me alive.

She opened the door, I got in, and I chose never to look back.

Chapter 4: Matt

Stumptown Global
Portland, Oregon

The partners are standing in the corner to my right, arranging themselves unconsciously around Winston, the managing partner. Kate and I call them the ducklings, and used to laugh at how they waddle after Winston wherever he goes.

"When we make partner," we'd promised each other, "no quack-quack!"

They occasionally send furtive glances my way, and continue whispering, while trying not to look stressed. Winston is the only one who can really pull it off — as usual, he looks as carefree as if he's about to walk onto the golf course. But then he's been managing crisis' large and small for almost forty years, ever since he founded Stumptown out of his dorm room at Reed College.

The lawyers and the money men are on the other side of the room, seated at one end of the long mahogany table, whispering and not quite as furtive with their glances. I never realized how long this table is, but I pretend not to notice either group as I sit in the exact middle of the room, staring at the empty chairs across from me.

How many times have I been in this room under different circumstances? This is the room where I made my first pitch, where I sold my first client, where I was given my first solo account. This is the room where I have watched in awe as Winston maneuvers his way through whatever minefield presents itself, and where I hoped to be crowned partner after neatly managing Harry's latest crisis — something that seemed earth-shatteringly important just last night. I'd tossed in bed, thinking through possible outcomes and spins until late into the night. Today the dream I've pursued for the past decade tastes like ash.

Today I find out what is going to happen to my sister. My oldest friend. My only real family. Shared trauma in childhood bonded us in a way most of my friends don't understand, and even though we disagree on some pretty fundamental life issues, I honestly don't know if I'll be able to hold it together if something happens to her. If the last hours are any indication, I'm not even sure I can hold it together until the end of this ordeal, no matter the outcome.

Becca has been the only thing that kept me from disintegrating at different times in our lives, or disappearing altogether into the bottle instead of just maintaining a larger than average alcohol budget. She hasn't been able to stop me from submerging myself in my work, but that's not for lack of trying.

And Kate! What have I done to my best friend? The other reason I've survived the past decade here at the Stump, surrounded by so much that is bizarre and life-sucking. Kate understands this part of my life in a way Becca never will. The complete and utter absorption of it all. The high, the risk, the stakes.

What have I done? I realize my hands have gone numb from how hard I'm clasping them, and slowly release each finger one by one.

We're waiting on the K&R guys — Kidnap & Ransom. I'd never even heard the term before it'd come in Becca's email about suggestions for Kate's visit. I certainly didn't know it was a thriving, multi-national, multi-million dollar industry. One side of a complex and growing new international business model.

It took about an hour this morning for the partners to get back to me with permission to call the K&R company. The 24-hour number they'd given me was answered on the first ring, a soothingly professional voice taking my name and telling me someone would arrive from Chicago within six hours. That meant private jet and trained, on-call staff — no wonder the policy was so expensive.

Becca had given me a couple names, as well as an explanation for why she thought it'd be a good idea, but I trusted her judgement and just skimmed to the list at the bottom of her email. I picked the first one, called up their website and bought a policy. It was expensive, but Harry only balked at the cost to paper over his fiascos when he was not currently in one.

How he ever thought he could get away with a fake school for African orphans in this day and age — but I've learned in my years in image management that there's no end to the size of the bubble these people can live in.

They think everything can be fixed with a phone call — and I can see where they get that opinion as we're often at the other end of that call, marshaling a ten-story office complex and thousands of professionals exercising an expertise honed in countless scandals big and small.

Our three-pronged priority in image management — to minimize the damage, mitigate the loss, and make sure the public falls in love with our clients again as quickly as possible. We have specialists in every field of the spectrum, deeply committed and highly compensated for their absolute discretion.

I'm especially good at it. I've got some of my father in me — his smooth voice, his facility with persuasion, his almost supernatural ability to weave a tale that spellbinds. It makes me an excellent IM hack, though I'm not sure what kind of a person.

I try not to think about the moral implications of my job very often, but when I do, I find the hatred of both myself and my job usually sends me on a weekend bender requiring the occasional Monday morning sick call. But by Tuesday the paycheck and my superior skill at shoveling BS always woo me back to my desk with few regrets.

Two men in custom suits walk past the full pane windows of the conference room, shaking me out of my reveries. They are escorted by Veronica, who has been crying on and off since she heard about my sister. Obviously it's not public knowledge in the building, but as Winston's secretary, she is privy.

I never much cared for Veronica, but I make a mental note to be nicer to her. I always thought she was a bit of a battle-ax, but maybe she's just tired of all the crap we deal with on a day-to-day basis. When she brought in the coffee a few minutes ago I thanked her mechanically, but didn't notice she'd just stood there beside me until Winston coughed. I looked up and caught a glimpse of her eyes welling before she slipped out the door.

The men are big. Though well-made, the suits bulge around their stocky figures. And self-assured. I recognize that walk; my father used to walk that way. I try not to hold their obvious self-confidence against them — I've been fighting against that for years and have it mostly under control, although it used to initiate my gag reflex.

Veronica opens the door and meets my eyes as they brush past her. She nods slightly and looks like she's tearing up again, so I turn away and concentrate on the men.

Winston walks forward, followed by the ducklings, and sticks his hand out confidently. "I'm Winston Fieldcroft, managing partner here at Stumptown. Thanks so much for coming."

They shake hands and the taller man introduces himself, "My name is Ken Foster, I'll be your liaison on the Wade case. I'm sorry to have to meet you under these circumstances."

Preliminaries over, Winston points toward me and I slowly stand, "this is Matthew Sullivan, our point man on this."

"Matt," I say reflexively, as I extend my hand across the table. It's wide enough that it's a bit of a stretch.

"Matt, good to meet you." He points to the other man and says, "This is Javier Mora, my assistant on this."

Assistant my hind end. Unless he means assist-me-in-a-gunfight.

I shake Javier's hand as well, like this is any regular meeting. It's a little surreal.

"Let's get started shall we?" Ken takes control immediately, nodding to the lawyers and the money men. He sits down, pulls a slim leather notepad out of his inside jacket pocket, and flips it open.

I sit back down, and register the fact that Winston sits beside me, rather than taking his normal throne at the end of the table. The ducklings arrange themselves in the seats that remain. It's a fairly large group for such a sensitive matter, but it's a big table.

Ken makes eye contact with me, and his gaze is straightforward and no nonsense. Though his build scares me just a little, I find that I also trust him instinctively.

"Matt, I've got a series of questions for you, and I'm sure you have quite a few questions for me. I have a lot of experience with this process, fortunately or unfortunately, depending on your point of view. I find it's best if we start with a little bit of an introduction to what we're going to be looking at, then I'll take whatever additional questions you have. Are you okay with that?"

I nod numbly, and pick up my pen out of habit. I should be taping this, I think suddenly, then see one of the lawyers stick a recorder in front of Ken.

"It appears Ms. Wade has been taken by the Fist of Allah, a quasi-religious militia that operates almost without opposition in Mauritania, Senegal and Mali. They move around quite a bit, based on where the action is heating up. This is not our first interaction with them. We've had two clients for whom we've successfully negotiated release, and since we share information with the other major K&R firms, we have files on fifteen other kidnappings. They seem to be in the business completely for the money, and rarely kill their captives. Several have died from accidents or failed escape attempts, and a team of scientists was killed outright last year when the Mauritanian government attempted a rescue.

"There has been a major increase in incidents in this region over the last twenty years, but especially in the last five. One reason is the explosion of small groups trying to fund their little revolutions, but I think the larger factor is that some European countries have begun paying out a set ransom per transaction."

His words ebb and flow, and I'm aware enough of my disconnection to be glad that someone is recording this. I'm not sure what I'm capable of taking in at this point.

"Normally this process takes about a year. It's unnecessary, but it's a bit of a power and terror play on their part. I want you to know that we will be with you throughout the process — guiding and advising — as long as this takes. Javier will head out when we finish our meeting here to join the others we have operating in that region.

"And we've found that the Fist is a bit more flexible as an organization. This is a good thing, the shorter duration usually means the client comes out in better physical condition."

He has been methodically scanning the room, but always returning to make eye contact with me. He barely looks at his notebook and I wonder idly how many times he's had to give this speech.

"I'm going to be honest with you, there aren't a lot of women in the files, and this is the first case we've handled of women taken alone. The ones we know of usually come out in worse condition than the men. It's very common for habitual, repetitive sexual assault to happen in these camps. It's not a given, but it's common enough that you need to be aware of the situation, and so you can prepare for Ms. Wade's release. We have a lot of good resources that we can talk about later."

He pauses, no doubt because the blood has just run out of my face to pool somewhere near my stomach, making me violently nauseous.

There's a loud ringing in my ears and I lay my forehead down on the cool surface of the table I've always admired as I try to swallow down the bile that threatens to erupt all over it.

Through the ringing I hear Winston tell Ken what he evidently hadn't been briefed on, that my sister was taken along with the client. Like I'd feel much different if my sister wasn't along, just my best friend of almost twenty years who'd taken the job as a favor to me. But in Winston's defense, I'm not sure he knows how close Kate and I are.

There is a silence in the room, but not a long one, and my breathing starts to return to normal.

"Matt," I hear both anger and what sounds like genuine compassion in his voice, both of which surprise me. "Matt, I apologize. I was not fully briefed on the situation. There is a completely different protocol for family members and I would never have started off this way if I'd known. Do you need another minute?"

Breathe in. Breathe out. Breathe in. Breathe out.

I can hear Becca's voice in my head, calm and steady, talking me down from another attack. So many times in person, and more times in my head, her voice has talked me off the ceiling. I've got to be strong for her now. *Breathe in. Breathe out. Breathe in. Breathe out.*

"No, no I'm all right now. I'm sorry about that. You're right, I want to know the truth so I can be prepared. You can continue."

………..

The meeting goes on for hours, but the only real measure of the passage of time for me is when Veronica brings in lunch menus for us to choose from. One part of my brain notices she brought the Alpha menus, the ones we break out for the best clients. I don't select anything, sure I can't eat, but when she returns a short time later, she sets a grilled cheese sandwich and Dr. Pepper in front of me. She's Winston's secretary for a reason, and probably has a file on each of us with our favorite foods.

I try to get some of it down, chewing methodically and taking a sip to wash down each bite. Regardless, I taste nothing.

The hierarchy in our company is set in stone, and it applies in this crisis as in any other. First Winston asks his questions, then the other ducklings get a shot. Then the lawyers, and finally the money men. Junior account reps take notes frantically, the partners only use pens as props.

Winston's phone vibrates discreetly at least once every five minutes, but to his credit he doesn't check it until our lunches come and we take a ten-minute break.

I wonder if they will ever finish with their questions.

So many topics are mentioned, so much information is thrown at us, that I feel like I'm drowning. Ken talks about how we shouldn't involve either the State Department or the media, explaining that secrecy is the best way, bar none, to do business in these cases.

I feel the collective stress level in the room ratchet down at that statement. We at Stumptown consider ourselves masters of our universe, and we certainly know how to keep our own people quiet, but I can tell it was a worry.

He tells us we need to consider this a business arrangement, a professional exchange of goods and services. The more we can be unemotional, the better. I find myself wondering if he has worked so many jobs he's lost his ability to empathize, when he turns to me again.

"Matt, I understand that this is going to be impossible for you. But the more you can manage your own emotions, the more you can detach, the better. Amal will treat this as a business, and if you can dialogue with him in those terms, it will be better for everyone."

When we finally wrap up, I feel like I've been steamrolled. Winston hugs me on his way out — a first that I normally would have gone straight home to call Kate about, and we would have passed a happy hour analyzing if my chances for advancement had just materially improved.

Ken waits for me at the door as I have to shake the hand and listen to the empty words of each of the ducklings. When I finally get away he pulls me out into the hall and directs us into a corner.

"You're going to have trouble sleeping tonight, but you should at least try. That's why we're meeting later in the morning tomorrow, precisely so you can get some sleep. But I'd like to meet with you before, perhaps for breakfast?"

Veronica walks up and stands at a discreet distance. Ken turns to her and she approaches. "Mr. Foster, I've arranged a room for you and your colleague at the RiverPlace. We've got a driver downstairs who will take you there whenever you're ready."

She withdraws as silently as she came, and Ken turns to me. "How about breakfast at my hotel at 9:00? Would that work for you?"

I nod in agreement, and stumble toward the elevators, wondering if I'll be able to make it home before I pass out.

I know Becca and our Mom visited him once, about a year after he was released from prison and right before Becca moved to Egypt. I think Becca knew I would refuse to go, so she didn't put me on the spot. Mom, of course, never cared about that and went ahead and asked. I'm pretty sure I cursed her out.

I don't know how the visit went — I imagine if he'd fallen to his knees in repentance I would have heard the hallelujah's from three states away. Not surprisingly, there was nothing but silence. Big shock. Repentance was never his strong suit.

When I call, Mom takes it pretty much how I thought she would — within a few moments of the very briefest of explanations, she completely loses it and passes the phone to Aunt Bertie, whom she's lived with almost since the beginning of our return from Guatemala.

We'd lived with grandma and grandpa at first, but that didn't go very well and Bertie had quickly offered an alternative. She had a big house and a bigger heart. Dear Bertie, who held us together those first years, who made our lunches and bought our school clothes and gave us spending money while mom skated around on the third floor like the ghost she was. Is.

Aunt Bertie listens to all the details in her calm and steady way, and we decide together that she won't bring Mom to Portland. Mom does better in her own environment, even without crisis.

Sometimes I think she never really did return from Guatemala with us. Certainly not the Mom I remember. Confident. Strong. Laughing with the ladies at church and joking in fast-flying Spanish. Firm and steady as she held her old Bible in one hand and grabbed some woman's shoulder with the other, giving much-sought after advice. I admired her then.

Just as Bertie and I say goodbye Mom grabs the phone and tearfully demands I call him.

I refuse. She argues. I hold fast. She breaks into noisy tears again and I curse when I hear the click. Actually that's pretty much how our conversations always go.

Chapter 5: Kate

It's been four days. Four days! I don't have very clear memories of the first day or so, so I only know it's been four days because Becca told me.

I haven't slept more than a couple hours at a time. If it's not the chickens that wake me, it's the baby we haven't managed to catch sight of, crying somewhere nearby. Or the donkey braying. Or the rooster that, contrary to the belief instilled in me by a plethora of children's stories, does not only crow at sunrise. Or when I've finally managed to get to sleep, and something crawls across my face and I leap to my feet shrieking and shaking.

And that's only the natural elements. The more frightening are the human incidents that keep me awake — the frequent arguments among the men that often end in shoving matches, or worse, shooting their guns in the air above each other's heads.

I think we both laid awake the first couple nights, wondering if Oumar's promise would hold. There were a *lot* of men out there with only a flimsy door between us. For that matter, the hut itself seems to be made of dried grasses woven around flimsy sticks, so it's not like it would take much effort to come in the back way.

Sometimes the men yell at the pitiful looking woman we've seen a couple times, stuck with cooking the slop we're served at random intervals. She spends an incredible amount of time sweeping the dust in front of the hut, bent in half and using some kind of tree branch in that pointless pursuit. And twice a day one of the men will escort her to our hut so she can empty our toilet bucket, which quite frankly is not often enough due to our both being sicker than dogs from the brown water we've been given.

Becca says it's drink the dirty water and wait for our bodies to adjust, or die, and more than once I've wished I'd chosen the second option. The first couple of times I had to be sick in this tiny room with no screen between us, I couldn't decide what was worse — the humiliation or the stomach cramping. But there is some comfort in knowing *quite well* that Becca is just as miserable as I am in that department.

And surprisingly, over the smells of our sick, I can make out my own particular bouquet, and distinguish it from Becca's. We are, in a word, foul.

I've got some kind of rash from the bite of some bug that is eating me alive — Becca assures me it's not the season for malaria, but then went on to say that will be a problem in another month or so. Just saying that affirmed that she was thinking along the lines of my worst fears, that we would still be here in a month.

And you'd think a little diarrhea and rash wouldn't matter much, what with all the men and guns outside, but since they've left us alone since that first day, the only things to focus on instead of going absolutely bonkers are the physical tortures.

I've cried until my head hurt so bad I had to stop. Repeatedly. My shirt is filthy with crusted snot, as there's nothing else to wipe my nose on.

Amal hasn't returned since the first day when he came back once Oumar left and asked for a phone number. I blurted out Matt's name and number without a thought, the only one I knew by heart.

Becca's eyes bulged — she had a non-family contact all ready to give him — but honestly, how was I to know? Once I'd given him Matt's number she went along with it, but when he left she explained a few things — like how calling her brother in the middle of the night to tell him we'd been kidnapped was not the kindest thing we could have done; that negotiating was statistically best carried out by non-related parties.

Basically, I felt like a big pile of our bucket leftovers.

She'd been quiet for a while, and I continued to berate myself, then she shrugged. "So they're going to call him. That's best for you. You don't ever want them talking to your parents directly. Matt knows that. He'll be a good buffer.

Our conversation was interrupted by loud yelling and a couple gunshots, and she was so startled she spilled the bowl of watery soup she'd been trying to get down. Looking down at the liquid in her lap, she started to laugh.

42

I think I might have looked at her like she'd grown a third head, because she laughed again and said something about how I shouldn't worry about her, she laughs when she's stressed.

But other than the occasional hysterical laugh, she's kept her head remarkably well. It pisses me off. Here I am crying every other minute, and taking turns sitting until my back cramps, then pacing until my legs cramp.

Becca said she's a stress-laugher, unfortunately I'm more of a stress-yeller, or stress-whisperer in this case, since we don't want to draw any extra attention. But it's amazing how poisonous a whisper can sound. And with no one else around, she's getting the brunt of it.

But the more poisonous I am, the calmer she is. Oh I hate that. Matt does that. I'm a bit more, well, drama queen is a term that has been tossed around by friends in the past. I like to think I'm in touch with my emotions, and my emotions are in chaos.

She keeps trying to impart from her vast library of memorized kidnap minutiae. She says it's so we don't have another "snafu" like when I gave out Matt's number.

Though she never says anything, I know she must blame me. I certainly blame myself. I hadn't given one thought to how it would impact Matt, receiving that phone call. I'd been too eager to get this over with, to get some help. Now I think of his face when the call came in and it gives me a physical pain that mixes in with all the others.

Sometimes you'd think Becca was lecturing in front of a class instead of sitting on the opposite side of a hut from her fellow captive. She suggested we sit on opposite sides when I suggested she stunk too badly to sit so close to me. She kept on in the same calm, low voice, so then I had to strain to hear her. And of course I couldn't tell her to talk louder given the subject matter, or come closer given my pride, so I just got angrier.

She's like a machine, spitting out facts no doubt designed to make me a better hostage. I wonder if she feels anything at all.

She's told me about going along, about doing what is asked of us, about how we need to humanize ourselves so the men see us as human beings instead of mere objects for their anti-western vengeance or sexual gratification. Even though I could tell she was phrasing things as clinically as possible, I zoned out when she started talking about that subject — too much for my traumatized brain.

When I zoned back in she was talking about how I needed to figure out what I was willing to die for because I would have to make

43

peace with agreeing to anything up to that point. That was easy — I would rather die than be the eighth wife of some geriatric maharaja.

I'd yelled that one, not out of my usual aggravation, but because the men were hollering at each other again and I figured I could get away with it. She laughed. "Okay, in this part of the world it's only four wives at a time. And the maharaja are from India — I think what you mean is an imam. Or maybe a *marabout*?" Which started another lecture. Yawn.

I'm pretty sure she must have some internal word limit she has to reach each day or she'll explode. And it's a hell of a lot higher than anyone's limit I've run across so far in my life. How in the world do she and Matt get along? He is a great conversationalist, but he's nowhere near as Chatty Cathy as she is.

How has he not mentioned this side of her? How did I not notice? Granted, I never really talked to her before — only the occasional hello in passing when he was talking to her on Skype, but you'd think your best friend would mention if his sister had a wide professorial streak. A little warning would have been nice.

It annoys me that she keeps touching her nose. We don't think it's broken, and every time she touches it she winces, but it seems an almost unconscious movement any more.

I'd also have loved a bit of warning that she was a Jesus freak. I don't have a lot of experience with that particular tribe, growing up in keep-it-weird Portland, but they do leave me with a generally bad taste in my mouth. I always picture women with doilies on their heads, walking behind their men while they shout the rules we should all be following if we know what's good for us.

All Matt ever said was she was religious, but he'd left his religious upbringing after a bad childhood, a subject I learned early on not to delve into.

She keeps talking about how God has things under control, how he'll take care of us, how she has confidence in him. *Blah blah blah*, I'd like to say, but I bite my lip, knowing instinctively I shouldn't antagonize my only ally in this nightmare, no matter how inane some of her chatter.

And really, I think, whatever it takes to cope, man. After what I've been doing the past couple days I realize I don't have much room to talk — her invisible friend is keeping her on more of an even keel than any of my coping mechanisms.

The problem is, her even keel makes me angry — it makes me feel small. I thought I was a strong person, a person of character.

44

Admittedly, I've had a pretty easy life, but it certainly hasn't been a total cake walk either, and I'm horrified to see how quickly I've unravelled.

I thought I was tough, that I'd play a different character if this storyline ever showed up in my movie. I've seen a version of it often enough, and I guess I'd always thought I'd be the heroine. I mean, who imagines themselves as the coward? The weeper? The one who the *real* heroine has to coddle and take care of?

Not that it's not justified for heaven's sake — it's only been four days of sitting in hell, almost seeing the flames licking at my legs!

If I'd been with someone who was less of a machine, maybe I wouldn't feel so bad about myself. It's only in comparison to her that I don't measure up. I hate feeling small and inadequate.

She does seem to know a lot about what's going on, and has no problem sharing it with me. In depth. At length. As previously mentioned.

And when I'd woken up the second morning, I realized she'd given me her blanket. She said her core temperature was higher and she didn't need it. What a liar — I could see her shivering against the wall the next night when I got up, yet again, to use the bucket in the corner.

When she woke up with her blanket on top of her she just looked over at me and smiled. I sleepily asked if her God didn't consider lying a sin, to which she began, "did you know lying is not considered a moral issue in many cultures…"

Last night, we agreed to throw western personal space issues to the wind and combine blankets and body heat. It wasn't much better, but frankly every little bit counts and I started to sleep in slightly longer intervals.

. . . .

"I can't believe how cold it is! I thought we were supposed to be in the desert."

The words are no more out of my mouth than I realize I've given her another entry point for a lecture, and she doesn't disappoint.

"Well you know that's a common fallacy. But in the desert, especially the Sahara, it's the sun that heats the ground, and then the air. So at night the heat all escapes and the temperature drops quite a bit."

I yawn, and lean in a little closer, hoping to drift off while she continues talking. But she stops mid-lecture and I feel her body tense. I hear a scratching coming from the door, but before I can figure out what it might be she's up and at the peephole.

I'm about to ask what's going on when she abruptly starts yelling. "HELP! Amal! You get away from here this instant! HELP!"

She keeps on like that for almost a minute before I hear Amal yelling at her to shut up. He comes to the door and, in direct contradiction to the panicky yelling she's been doing, she calmly explains to him that one of his men was trying to get in our door.

I'd had no idea what was going on up to that point, but I listen as she explains to Amal how she is an engaged woman; how it would bring shame on her fiancé and her father for the men to violate her. This is news to me and I wonder why she hasn't told me in one of her many monologues.

And then my mouth drops as I listen to her explain that her brother has made her responsible for me, his fiancé, and that she could not be responsible for bringing shame on him by having my honor sullied. She prattles on like that, about shame and responsibility and honor, until Amal finally tells her to shut up.

He apologizes for his men, which surprises me, says he'll talk to them, and all of a sudden all we hear is silence. All the yelling has quieted the usual suspects, and the stillness is unbroken for a good five minutes before a donkey brays, the chicken answers, and the nighttime cacophony is off and running.

Becca stays there for a few minutes, then comes back and begins to rearrange our blankets while I just sit and stare at her. Eventually she notices that I'm still upright and asks, "What?"

I whisper just in case Amal is still nearby. "I'm not engaged to your brother! We're just best friends, I'm sure he's told you that."

She laughs a little, and I find I can hear a difference between the genuine article and her stress laugh. "I know that! You're as engaged as I am. This guy I know who works for another NGO in Cairo agreed to be my fiancé one time when we were in a tight spot."

She yawns loudly. "I'll tell you about it sometime, it was pretty funny. Since then he agreed to be my fiancé again if ever the need arose. But you and Matt lived together for heaven's sake, that's enough closeness to pretend engagement. It's something that might protect us. Maybe not, but I thought it was worth a try. Just remember to pine for my brother every now and then."

And with that she rolls over and almost immediately her breathing slows. I lie there looking at the ceiling I can barely make out because of the tiny amount of light that penetrates from the fire outside, wondering how she could lie that easily and calmly. She must have been thinking about it for a while, maybe looking for the opportunity. I'm glad she didn't do it in daylight — my dropped jaw would have given the game away.

Suddenly I feel the strangest sensation. I lift my hand to my mouth and find I'm smiling at the audacity of Becca's incredible whopper. Perhaps with her next to me I'll be able to get through this nightmare.

....

We met at Reed, Matt and I. He came right up to me, introduced himself, and said he'd always wanted to be friends with someone like me.

Alrighty then.

But he was so earnest and likable I decided to give him a chance. He stuck to me like glue, and pretty soon he was the best friend I could have hoped for. Kind. Selfless. Hysterically funny. An excellent jogging or drinking partner, depending on the mood.

Neither of us were particularly interested in the majors we'd chosen, and when one of our most famous alumni — Winston Fieldcroft — gave a guest lecture, we were both hooked. We rode our bikes to our interviews at Stumptown together, and when we were both hired we got blind drunk celebrating.

The next morning, nursing hangovers at a coffee shop near our dreadful affordable student housing apartments, we discussed the plan we'd hatched while drinking. Later that day we started our search for a small apartment in the Pearl. It took a while to find something we could afford on our first-year salaries, but we finally found a place we loved.

Of course we were never there much with our workloads, but we enjoyed living together. We were compatible and happy. Sure, he had black moods and occasional raging binge weekends, but they were pretty rare, and with the childhood he'd once given me the lowlights of, I didn't blame him.

We'd probably still be living together, if I hadn't met Alex a couple years into our arrangement. Matt had laughed at me, joining a gym on a whim, but even though I only went a handful of times, I told him it was worth it because it was where I met Alex. Six months of intense dating, and then Matt graciously moved out and Alex moved in.

But he only moved just around the corner, our incrementally increasing salaries meaning he could afford his own tiny place. We continued to spend most of our waking hours at work, so it didn't change much in terms of time spent together.

We worked side by side at Stumptown for almost twelve years, moving up together, always helping each other out with thorny issues, unlike our other coworkers who were more prone to shark-like behavior. We were a good team, and it benefited both our careers. And then I got mugged.

Chapter 6: Becca

For the first several days talking seems to be the only way to stop Kate from weeping. For crying out loud, I'm obviously aware of what a dreadful situation this is, but does she have to weep at everything? What a drama queen!

I talked about everything I could think of — all the kidnap survival stuff I'd studied, anything about the culture, how to brush your teeth with a wooden stick.

She was leery about that one, but after several days her mouth felt gross enough that she tried it. It's not a bad time waster — you have to chew the stick for several hours a day to be more or less effective.

She seems to have finally settled down a little, which is just in time as I've used more words on her this week than I've probably used in the last six months. My strategy seems to have worked though, she's coming out of her shock little by little.

Last night's attempted break-in may have set her back, I'll have to ask her about it when she wakes up. I'm glad I finally got a chance to try out my idea — it's probably the best shot we have at not getting gang-raped.

I find I can think about the subject now without wanting to go catatonic, like the first couple days. I always waited until Kate was asleep to cry. It seemed right not to scare her, and it gave me some measure of control to make myself wait a little before losing it. But each time she'd fall asleep my mind would inevitably wander to the topic that terrified me above all others, and I'd start shaking, silent tears running down.

Knowing a bit more about this process than Kate does has been helpful in one way, but it can't seem to change my body's normal fight-or-flight response. I am, however, getting somewhat used to the adrenaline spikes and the nausea that follows quickly on its heels.

I guess I'm making progress of my own, laying down what terrifies me.

"Thank you," I whisper to the One responsible for any such progress.

She's not up yet — this is the fifth morning and it seems like she's sleeping as well as I did. The first several nights' lack of sleep finally caught up with both of us.

Five days! I wonder what Amal is thinking. He must have called Matt by now. Poor Matt. I hope he got the K&R policy for Kate, I didn't have a chance to ask him and Kate doesn't know. That would at least give him some room to negotiate and some professionals to help him through it.

Like he's heard me wondering about his strategy, Amal suddenly bangs through the door and startles me out of my reverie.

Kate jerks awake and her eyes widen in panic at seeing him inside.

"Ms. Wade," he orders sternly, "come with me now."

I look over and her fingers, consciously or unconsciously, are digging into her blanket like it would give her any purchase if he decided to drag her.

It's easier to focus on her clenched fingers than on my clenched stomach, but even without that I feel like there's no other choice to make.

"Amal," I venture quietly, "is there something I can help you with?" My voice doesn't tremble as much as I thought it would.

He focuses his eyes on me, thoughtful. "Okay Ms. Parker, I'll take you first."

He turns and leaves as abruptly as he entered.

I start to get up and turn to look at Kate before I leave. And what do you know, her eyes are welling up again. Oh, brother.

"It'll be fine," I try to reassure her. "There's a lot of chatter that goes on with negotiation. Remember, try to follow along unless it's something you can't live with. It'll be all right. And remember, if someone tries to get into the hut, just start screaming bloody murder."

I exit the hut and have to immediately shield my eyes. We haven't been let out since we got here, and although the hut is far from well-structured, it's still dark enough that the unobstructed sun blinds me.

When my eyes adjust somewhat, I see that Amal is standing a few feet away, an armed guard at his side holding a weapon menacingly pointed at me. I'm relieved it's Amal asking for me when I glance momentarily into the eyes of the guard. I wonder if he was the one scratching at our door last night.

As we walk I take in as much as possible, figuring I might as well take advantage of my first chance at recon. There seem to be eight huts of more or less the same size. I see the woman crouched in the dirt in front of a fire, stirring something. She's watching me carefully, but when I make eye contact she looks quickly away. The baby we've heard crying off and on is strapped to her back.

There's one donkey, a chicken, and a rickety looking horse cart sans-horse. I count a dozen men lounging about, besides Amal and our escort, all armed with older weapons. Not that I'm any kind of expert, but they certainly don't look shiny.

Amal leads me to the middle hut and opens the door, then stops and gestures for me to go inside. I register the odd mark of chivalry.

This must be where he stays. There's a desk in the middle with two chairs, and a cot to one side. Looking at the cot, I feel my heartbeat kick into an even higher gear until he points to one of the chairs and then goes behind the desk to sit in the other. He picks up a pen and holds it over some paper, then stares at me for a few moments until I realize he's waiting for me to sit.

"I want to tell you that I am not a violent man by nature. I am educated. I understand your culture. I have spent a lot of time with Americans. I know that it's important to you to understand why this has happened to you, and I will tell you that you are nothing more and nothing less than an asset for us, both valuable and temporary.

"You are a way to feed ourselves and our families. Most of these men have parents to feed, or children; some of them many children and several wives. We have few choices for employment, and this is a very lucrative business.

"If you understand that this is just a job for us, it will go better for you. If you follow the rules, if you do not make trouble, I will try to make this as comfortable for you as possible. I realize it is a stressful situation, but it doesn't have to be any more so than necessity demands."

I feel a stress giggle rising and ruthlessly choke it down. I wonder if he really believes any of this schlock. He's holding two terrorized women at the point of a gun and threatening them with sexual violence, but sure, let's talk about *business*.

"This is my operation and I have been given wide authority by my boss to run this. I have explained to him how Americans think, and offered this as a sort of case study. If our business arrangement is satisfactory, he will let me run more transactions, if not, he will go back to business as usual.

"If I were in your place, I would suggest that you cooperate. Because business as usual does not include the order I have given the men not to touch you. I know it is of particular importance to American women to not experience unwanted sexual advances. It took me a long time to understand this since you walk around in clothing that leaves nothing to the imagination and go to bed with men on the first date — it is a great hypocrisy, but I understand it is a hypocrisy that your system fosters."

I wonder if he realizes he's tapping his pen in time with the words. I recognize the method — he's memorized the speech — and it makes me wonder how many versions preceded this one.

"So I have banned the men from touching you sexually. But please understand, the ban will only remain as long as you cooperate and my operation is moving forward in a positive direction. It is to your benefit to cooperate, and to help your family cooperate in paying the fee in a timely manner."

He lays down his pen and arranges his papers officiously. "Do you understand what I have said?"

I can't believe this. What a lunatic! But on the positive side, if he's for real and can really control his men, this just got a lot easier. I nod my head slowly, not sure if I should say anything.

He nods his, and picks up his pen again.

"Then let us begin. Ms. Rebecca Grace Parker. Born 12/3/80, in Guatemala City. From your passport I see that you live in Cairo. Why is that?"

Here we go, I think. *Keep it simple, keep talking about what you want to talk about.* I memorized the rules, but we'll see how good I am at following them. I take a deep breath and start in.

"I work for a small NGO, a non-governmental organization, that cares for victims of sex trafficking. We take girls off the street and offer them shelter and counseling while they heal, then when they're ready we train them in a marketable skill where they can earn a living in an honest, healthy way. It's very rewarding work, I enjoy it very much. I've been living in Cairo a number of years now. We work with a small staff, mostly Egyptian women. Did you know thousands of girls are sold into slavery every year in Cairo? I think I read that slavery is a problem here in Senegal as well. Is that right?"

I find I'm glad I've been forced to speak this way the last few days with Kate, because this kind of stream-of-consciousness, one-sided rambling is not my style. I can see I've startled him with it, and wonder if maybe I've overdone it a little in my panic, but I know that as long as I keep talking I can keep a modicum of control over what information I give him.

"Yes," he says, and then clears his throat. "I've heard it is an issue here. Now please tell me, how do you receive your funding? I know the government does not care about those girls."

"That's a question I get a lot of the time. We apply for grants from different foundations in Europe and North America. We fundraise from many different sources. I can tell you, we barely have enough in our account to buy milk for the babies some weeks. In fact, I took out a hundred dollars for this trip and left forty-one cents in the account. It's always a challenge, let me tell you, but Allah always provides for us."

He's been making notes in a language I finally recognize as German, which shocks me and I forget the next subject I was going to segue into.

His pen stops and he looks up and meets my gaze before I quickly bounce my eyes away from his.

"So you are a Christian?" He asks gruffly, as they nearly always do. Someday I'm going to answer as I've always wanted to — why is it that your first question after hearing I'm out in the world trying to make it a better place is whether or not I'm a Christian? But of course today is not that day.

"I get that question a lot too Amal. Can I ask you, what do you think a Christian is?"

He looks startled, and I don't know if he's going to answer. Finally, he reels it off as if by rote. "A Christian is the natural and historical enemy of all true followers of Allah. Someone who comes to destroy our culture. Someone who has no morals, who drinks and smokes and steals. A Christian eats pork and profanes the prophet. They practice every form of sexual deviancy and insist upon sending their filth into the rest of the world. They hate Muslims and want to exterminate them."

His voice raises as he goes along, ending with a contemptuous flair.

Exactly, I sigh, at hearing nearly identical versions of the same speech no matter where I go.

"That's pretty much what I thought you'd say. I hear that all the time in Cairo. That's why I asked. So no, Amal, I'm not a Christian in the sense that it's understood today in this part of the world. I follow Issa al Massi, Jesus the Messiah, and He does not condone any of what you just mentioned."

His brow furrows and he sets his pen down. "Someone who follows Jesus is a Christian."

I'm surprised to find that, if I can just close the door a little on the panicked part of my brain, this familiar conversation is just a tiny bit comforting. I've had it any number of times, and it almost always leads somewhere interesting. I can see he's not armed, and especially now that my heart rate has gone down some, I find myself wondering if he's maybe more officious than prone to violence.

"I can see why you'd be confused — that's certainly what it used to mean. But I do not do anything you just listed. And I love Muslims. Especially young girls who have been broken and need to be loved.

"Jesus loved me when I was a young, broken girl, and He says that to love Him you must obey Him. You must love your enemies and pray for those who hurt you. And just as important, you must go on the offensive with love and care for orphans and widows in their distress.

"I love these girls so much I am living away from my family. I make very little money, but it is very fulfilling to love these girls and see them become healed from the trauma that has happened to them."

I'm not sure what land mine I've wandered into, but he seems to be getting angrier the more I talk. I don't know how to segue into anything better, so I stop.

"You Americans," he says with such disgust it seems he can hardly choke it out. "So generous, so kind, so fickle, so forgetful. You give and give, until a new iPhone comes out and you decide you must have it and forget all about us. You have no understanding of the damage you do with all this unthought-through kindness. You come in with your big hearts and big wallets, to our third-world lives, showing us how much better life can be.

"You're so sure of yourselves that you don't think through the consequences of your incomplete charity. You're so sure you will never be conquered, you'll go on forever, and then you move the boundaries of our hope and make us think impossible things are possible. And then something happens, anything, and you revoke the futures you've painted and caused us to hope for."

The brief moment of comfort is long gone. My heart rate spikes and my legs have gone numb again. I don't know how to de-escalate this, but he doesn't pause long enough to give me a chance.

"And what is left for us then? A barren, hopeless, tragic future among our own people. We are left in a position so much worse than if you'd never interfered in the first place. You topple governments when it pleases you. You drop food. You command. You demand. You donate. You interfere. Interfere. Interfere.

"Why can't you just leave us alone? Why do you have to get our hopes up? You shove your worldview into our countries, into our homes. You endlessly preach the good life and what that means — stuff, sex, sex and more stuff. Freedom, liberty, a license to do whatever you want. No one asked you to police the world. No one asked you to send barges of food that inflate the pockets of vicious dictators.

"Your big bleeding hearts. So much damage. Like your country is in such good shape. I can access the internet. I know what the statistics are on your country. I have a sick fascination with it now. I can't believe I ever loved America, it is a diseased member of the world community that needs to be cut off before it brings death to everyone. Guns. Drugs. Sexually transmitted diseases. Debt. Immorality. Pornography. Murder. Addiction.

"The world would all be better off if you would never leave your borders. You wandering doers of wrong, so full of yourselves and your ideas to better the world. In Senegal we know the truth — everyone must take care of their own self, and there is no one who will care for the weak."

He is on his feet, crouched over his desk like he wants to come right over the top of it and rip my throat out. I can barely breathe through the terror that grips me.

Suddenly, he stops and shakes his head, as if to clear it. He draws a steadying breath and slowly sits down. He pushes around the few items on his desk, organizing them into straight lines and right angles. It takes a few moments for his breathing to return to normal, all the while I sit as still as possible.

I don't know how long we sit there, but I do know this is an angry, angry man. I stare at my hands and wait. I can't think of anything except to apologize for my country, but some instinct tells me now is not the time.

"Where were we?"

His tone is so calm and business-like I look up quickly to meet his gaze, then drop it just as quickly.

After a beat he continues, "Tell me, how much are you worth?"

Be careful Beck.

I hear Matt's voice in my head, and wince at the pain it causes. I know I have to walk a fine line here — I'm worth enough to not kill me, but not too much so that I'll be here forever. And I know he's sitting on a hair trigger, which makes it even trickier.

I clear my throat and start slowly, tentatively. "I assume you're talking about money. I have to tell you I'm not worth very much money. My salary is very small. My mother is on disability and lives in a small house in Arizona with my retired aunt. They barely get by on their pensions."

The only sound is the scratching of his pen, then he asks, "What about your fiancé? How much money does he have?"

"Jay works for a smaller NGO than I do. His salary is terrible. He teaches welding to young Egyptian men who don't have any education, helping them find a way to support themselves and their families. He's a wonderful man and will want to have me back, but he doesn't have any money either."

He stops writing and looks up. "So you're telling me no one will pay for you?"

My heart rate spikes, and I rush to backpedal. "I'm not saying that, they'll pay what they can. I'm just telling you my family doesn't have access to the kind of money your boss is probably expecting. I'm hoping we can come to an agreement on something reasonable — that will benefit all of us. I am very valuable to my family, and they will be very interested in helping us find a solution. I'm sure you'll find my brother to be very motivated when you talk to him about how to come to a solution."

He's writing again, maybe wanting to prove how professional he can be. I take the opportunity to look around his office. His cot in the corner has a blanket that looks just like the ones we're using. No pillow. One shirt hanging up behind the bed. I notice a sat-phone sitting in an open box on the floor beside his desk. I recognize the name, and if I'm not mistaken it's military grade. That means encryption. Which means expensive. I feel a pulse of excitement.

I've never had a sat-phone, but some of my UN friends who drip money showed me how they work. If I could get ahold of that for just a couple minutes, I could make a call maybe, get ahold of someone who could help. If I could even just leave the line open long enough for our location to be triangulated.

I don't know that we'll have the opportunity to escape, I haven't been able to observe their movements long enough. But I know I need to be alert to every opportunity. I need to get us prepared. Gather supplies, intel, anything that will help us figure out where we are and where we'd need to go to get away. It's good to keep our brains active and it's good to keep our hopes up.

I know keeping our hopes up is going to be important. Unless I can get Kate rehabbed out of shock, it's going to be a difficult job.

It could be a year, or it could be a whole lot shorter, but they say it's the not knowing that can drive you crazy. You've got to know the averages and prepare yourself mentally and emotionally as best as you can. And pray. And pray. And pray.

I don't have a read on Amal yet. It means something that he apologized last night. That he didn't come in and beat me for my insolence. It means something that he's able to write in German, that his English is slightly accented, but in diction I could close my eyes and almost think I was talking to an American. It also means something that he clearly has a huge chip on his shoulder regarding our country.

But what is his motivation? Can I make him feel compassion for us? Can I trust him to protect us?

I don't know how long I've been daydreaming, but all of a sudden I realize he's stopped writing and is just looking at me. When he sees he has my attention again he begins to speak in a low voice, "Yes, Ms. Parker, I am sure your brother will be very motivated to be helpful. He cried like a small child when I called him."

His no doubt carefully chosen words are like a knife straight through my heart. He may not have shown a tendency toward violence so far, but I realize this is a very dangerous man. This is the first time we've made prolonged eye contact, and I can see there is fire raging behind his eyes.

Chapter 7: Amal

Mrs. Anderson arranged for tuition, room and board, and I started attending Dakar Institute, the premiere school in the country. Exclusive, expensive.

All the embassy kids went there, and the kids of whatever miscellaneous foreigner had dragged them to our little hellhole, and the children of corrupt local businessmen. And then there were the kids of missionaries intent on saving the heathen. It made for quite the volatile mix.

There were very few charity cases. You'd think with the fees they charged they could afford a little more charity, but since everybody was taking a little off the top there wasn't much left for us bottom feeders.

I attended the school for five and a half years. I suffered through learning English, and later tackled German. I flourished under the American curriculum and fell in love with all things American. Although truthfully it was much more than love — closer to obsession.

I guess it was to be expected. After everything that happened during my years with the *marabout*, or maybe more accurately, after a few months of the crippling guilt I felt at leaving Oumar behind, the only path forward was to seal the past up tight.

I was ripe for an internal takeover, and I gave myself heart and soul to the Andersons and the land of milk and honey they came from.

John decided to befriend me after sitting back quietly and observing the bullies have their way with me for the first couple months. He said he'd wanted to see what I was made of, but eventually decided to step in because I was going to drown without help.

I began hanging out with him on afternoons and weekends. Mrs. Anderson treated me better than I imagine my own mother would have, even if I could remember her. She'd sold me for a bag of rice, after all.

They told me up front they were Christians, but not those pesky Jesus freaks. Of course I didn't know what that meant beyond what the *marabout* had ranted about, but I observed them as closely as possible, so as to mimic everything.

Mr. and Mrs. Anderson had a glass of wine most nights, and he smoked like a chimney, although "not in the house" as Mrs. Anderson always chided. And they had bacon every Sunday morning from the supply the embassy flew in monthly, almost like it was some sort of religious ritual.

Mr. Anderson used to watch American cop shows with John and me. Every week another innocent or two was murdered, and when I made a comment about being worried about their safety as they returned to such a dangerous place, they laughed. They took great pains to explain to me that America wasn't really that dangerous, that this was just what their culture viewed for entertainment. John said he'd never known anyone who'd been murdered, or even experienced any kind of violent crime.

It seemed every couple of months the plot of one of our shows would revolve around someone being kidnapped, and each time Mr. A would make a rude comment and tell us what the hapless criminals were doing wrong. He never talked about what his job was at the embassy, but he seemed to know quite a bit about the subject.

Almost everything the *marabout* had told us about the Christians was true of them in behavior — the alcohol, the smoking, the pork, the pornographic movies they viewed together as a family that made me blush, and his father's harder pornography that John found and shared with me. And yet, even with all that, they were the most decent people I'd met up to that point in life. It was incredibly confusing.

I had Americanized myself as much as was humanly possible by the time our senior year rolled around. I played basketball and refused to join the soccer team even though I'd played every day of my life up to that point — I wouldn't even call it football like the rest of the world. I shunned everything connected to my heritage.

John and I planned to go to college together and Mrs. Anderson was working with us on our applications, and then they'd flown home to Tennessee for Christmas like they did every year. I didn't even know anything was amiss, because they never answered my emails when they were in the States.

I had their car keys in my pocket so I could pick them up at the airport, and was working over the hundredth edit of my application essay at the kitchen counter when the headmaster called me. The embassy had just called him. John and Mrs. Anderson had been killed in a car accident in America. Mr. Anderson would not be returning to Senegal.

And just like that, I was kicked out of school. The future I'd dreamed of and hoped for and worked toward evaporated like a mist. The culture I'd adopted as my own deserted me three yards from the finish line — even my internal metaphors were American.

In the office of the headmaster I begged; I wept. I was only one semester away from graduating, which would have been enough to get scholarships in the States. But that was it.

Budget. The almighty budget. I was out on the street that afternoon with nothing but two grocery bags of school uniforms and useless college application paperwork stuck in a Dakar Institute backpack. Gorgeous glossy brochures that the schools had mailed clear over to Senegal. Full-color, beautifully printed. Dreams. Hopes. A future.

In one instant I lost a brother, a father figure, and the closest thing to a mother that I could remember. I also lost the future I'd never dreamed was possible before they'd introduced me to it and taught me to hope. I wandered, and I don't remember anything from those first weeks on the street.

After six months of trying to make it on my own and looking at those brochures every night, I took them out into the street, looked over them one more time, then wept as I burned them one by one.

My hatred of Americans was born that night.

I never cried again, and the next morning went and offered my services to the gang that had been trying to recruit me. It was my only option for survival.

Within a few months I was told I was moving to a new area, and when I walked in I was thunderstruck to see Oumar standing there. I almost didn't recognize him at first; he had several scars on his face and a new nearly unrecognizable hardness in his eyes. But he recognized me, and ran to me, calling me his brother returned from the dead.

That was eight years ago. I've been working at Oumar's side ever since. As he rose, I rose. He moved into the kidnapping section, and I came with him. I rely on his charisma and brutality, he relies on my intellect and experience outside the norm.

As much as he pretends that everything is the same as it was, I can tell he feels ambivalent about me. We never talk about it, but I know he harbors anger toward me for leaving him. Any time I'm called upon to talk about my past with the Americans, a certain look comes over his face and he leaves the room. And sometimes he says things that seem designed to cause maximum damage to my psyche. But in the next moment he hugs me and makes a joke about our childhood. Sometimes I think I catch a glimpse of my old friend in there somewhere, but mostly he is Oumar in name only.

Of course I haven't mentioned it to him, but now that I've finally been given charge of a job, I've allowed myself to hope again. If I can bring this off, and maybe a couple more jobs, maybe I'll be able to get away.

Get on a boat, slip up to Spain. I've been working on Spanish in my free time, telling Oumar it'll help with the next Spaniards we catch. If I can get into Spain I can start making my way up into Europe. I'll never go to America — that dream died when I burned those brochures. I hate America. But I can make a better life in Europe.

I've put a lot of thought into this. Every time I watched a kidnapping go wrong, I'd think, "If I was in charge this would be different."

Well, it's my turn now. And things are deteriorating faster than I anticipated. I had to threaten one of the men at the point of my gun last night not to enter the girls' hut and rape them. He was alone, but I could see several men were hovering nearby, ready to follow if he could just break the ice.

Luckily he'd had too much to drink, "liquid courage" John used to call it, and he was easy to knock to the ground so I could assert my authority again. I don't know what will happen the next time.

………..

I look up from my notes and catch her staring at my sat phone. I can almost see the wheels turning in her head. The other one will be easy enough to control, but this one I'll need to keep my eye on. She's the one who needs to understand the rules.

I'm embarrassed by my earlier outburst against America. It doesn't go with the calm, professional image I'm trying to portray.

But neither does weakness, and I need her to understand I mean business. I clear my throat and her eyes flash back to me, a slight flush rising in her cheeks.

"Let me be clear, Ms. Parker, I will not hesitate to kill you. As far as I can tell, Ms. Wade is a goldmine, so she is the asset I will be pursuing with vigor. You, in comparison, are a do-gooder with no appreciable monetary value. Some of your family may scrape up enough money to make it worthwhile to keep you fed and alive, but…," I sigh regretfully and stare at her for a moment to let it sink in. "Well, to be honest, that will be a decision made further up in the organization."

She blinks, and I allow myself a small smile, trying to project the cold eyes I've seen in Oumar. I've practiced this in the mirror and I wonder if it's working.

"You know that it is only at my word that the men stay away from you. Might I suggest you try to be a little more cooperative in the future? If you give me the respect due me, I will make sure you are respected. Do we understand each other?"

She hesitates for a minute, swallows, and then starts speaking.

"I believe we do, Amal. I am only here because of a favor I was doing for my brother. My work in Egypt is very important to me, the girls I take care of are counting on me to return to them. I will do my best to help us come to a reasonable arrangement. I know you have pressures on you as well."

Her voice is low at first, but there is no tremble as I'd hoped. She seems as calm as if we were chatting at her request. It's maddening. The earlier rage I'd barely swallowed comes roaring back so quickly I have trouble breathing normally.

"I believe you know what I'm talking about Ms. Parker. I am the line keeping those men out of your hut. Do not cross me, or I will let them loose. It's no bother to me if you are damaged, so long as you remain living."

She blinks again, and I see the color rush up into her face. It gives me a quiet satisfaction.

"That will be all Ms. Parker. If you respect the rules as I have set them down, I believe you will have a pleasant and hopefully brief stay with us."

I call out for the guard and he comes in to escort her away. Her calmness leaves me chilled, and I'm glad our first meeting is over.

Chapter 8: Matt

I'm not sure what wakes me, but I luxuriate in the comfort of my bed for a good forty-five seconds before I remember. I fumble for my phone to see the time, and then I start to cry.

One week ago was the phone call. One week that my sister and best friend have been in hell, and I just slept a full twelve hours in an extremely comfortable bed, in my safe, quiet, and even trendy apartment in the Pearl.

It doesn't matter that the twelve hours only comes after a week of almost zero sleep torn apart by nightmares as I waited for a phone call that never came; that I fell onto my bed last night in a near coma. It still feels like I'm betraying them, being here in comfort and safety, when I can only imagine the torments they're going through.

It's a little before 6:00 a.m., but I lean over and text Ken. He said anytime.

....

Fifteen minutes later I've showered, taken the elevator down, and walked the block to Sisters. Ken is already there, two cups set on the table in front of him. As on previous occasions, his back is to the wall and he's facing the door.

I sit, and he slides a cup toward me and takes a sip from his own. He doesn't say anything. This is the third time I've called him, and I find his steadiness a balm.

It's odd I suppose, part of me thinks I should hate him for all that he's told me. He says it's his personality to be frank, that he will talk to me as he'd hope to be talked to if he were unfortunate enough to have this experience. Which I appreciate, mostly, except when I have to put my head on the table because he's just said something that makes my eyes water and my consciousness swim.

"Did you sleep?" he asks.

"Twelve hours," I say, trying to keep the uneven emotions out of my voice. Because even as I say it, I'm overwhelmed by both guilt and shame, and yet also relief at giving my body what it needed.

"Ahh, so this is a guilt call." I look up, surprised, but I guess I shouldn't be. He seems to be a professional in every facet of this process.

I look down at the table and remain silent.

"So you're feeling like you betrayed them. Like you should be suffering in solidarity instead of sipping a five-buck coffee after sleeping twelve hours on your cushy mattress."

I look down at the coffee in my hands and feel another stab of guilt — I hadn't even thought about the five-dollar coffee, I was too consumed with the comfy bed.

But that's another thing I like about Ken, he tells it like it is and doesn't immediately try to fix it with platitudes. "Yep, that about sums it up."

"Has it occurred to you that you won't be able to think clearly when Amal calls if you haven't been sleeping? That you need to have all your wits about you at all times, just in case he calls? That you won't do them any good if you're not taking as good of care of yourself as you can?"

In fact, no, I hadn't thought of that.

He abruptly changes the subject, "What did you decide to do about work?"

Ahh, my dear employers, to whom I'd given more than a decade of loyal, creative service. Winston had waited exactly one full day before calling me in, telling me that they were going to need to know if I could continue on Harry's account. Harry was flying in two days later, and if I wasn't up to appropriately compartmentalizing they would need the next day to bring my replacement up to speed.

Image management waits for no man, I guess. There goes my partnership. For a minute I was engulfed in rage, thinking of Lin or Javier, the two colleagues always nipping at my heels, and the most likely replacements — and then the rage abruptly melted away and I was left thinking about the futility of my job. They gave me a night to think it over, expecting an answer in the morning. I hadn't even gone in, I'd just cc'd Winston in my email to HR, asking for compassionate family leave.

And that was that. I didn't hear from anyone but my designated HR rep, with twenty-one pages of federal paperwork I had to fill out and a carefully-worded note about the tentative status of my future employment should I not return following the forty-five days to which I was entitled.

I hadn't yet filled out the paperwork. I couldn't think straight.

"I think you should go back to work, Matt, even if it's only a part-time thing. You need to have something else to put your mind on. It's been a week of nightmares and shock, but this will probably drag on for months, and you can't sit around moping in your underwear."

Another prescient comment. I hadn't told him, but that's almost precisely what I'd been doing this week — when I wasn't meeting with him or the partners.

"Why are you here exactly, Ken? Shouldn't you be in Senegal?"

"We have very qualified guys in Senegal. And I can easily manage the team from here. My main job is to be here with the client's negotiating contact, advising you through the process."

I snort, "Holding my hand you mean?"

He smiles, "You could put it that way, I guess. I choose to think of it as short term, intensive, unrequested friendship."

"Excuse me for saying so," and I wave in the general direction of his formidable figure, "but you don't seem like the hand-holding sort."

"Well," he sighs, "that's a bit of a longer story. I might tell you sometime, but suffice it to say that I asked for a temporary reassignment about six months ago. I was in the field for almost seven years, and it was time for a break."

"What about Javier? I haven't seen him since that first day in the conference room."

"Javier's the leader of the boots on the ground. Normally the company prefers we keep things a bit more detached, but Javier prefers meeting the client's contact before he goes in. He is a very effective operator, so the company overlooks the quirk."

I stare into the small fire in the corner for a while. We both sip our coffee. One thing I like about Ken, he doesn't feel the need to fill every moment with chatter. Becca's that way. When we were growing up she and I could sit for hours, each doing our own thing, just happy to be together. It was always a nice counterpoint to the extreme amount of people-pleasing and glad-handing that went on when we were with our parents.

The bell above the door rings and I look over to see a young professional come barreling in, no doubt late for work. He's followed by two hippies and a grandmother in yoga pants and a bright tangerine shirt. It's only 6:30 a.m., and Sisters is hopping. This would be about the time I'd come in, if my world hadn't flipped over.

"I'm serious about the work thing, Matt," Ken interrupts my thoughts. "I know it seems soon, but I've seen people go absolutely crackers sitting around waiting. You have to have something to put your mind to, especially as a man. You don't have a family, you don't have a wife or kids to focus on, so you need to go back to work."

"Um," I respond sarcastically, "thanks man."

He smiles, "I told you I tell it like it is, and statistically this is going to be harder on you because you have no one to share your pain. You need to ask Winston for a mommy-track account — I have no doubt they'd give it to you. Or get a job at McDonalds, or start volunteering at a shelter. You have to do something. Otherwise you will start to fragment, and that won't do Becca or Kate any good. You are the negotiating contact and we need you to try to stay as emotionally and mentally tough as you can."

....

He's right. When I return they give me the Bobby account, an aging actress who hasn't had a misstep since her granddaughter was born a couple years ago. Strictly mommy-track.

They've given Harry's account to Lin, like I suspected, and my assistant Judith chooses to stay with her. I pick up one-fourth of the services of Sandy, an older receptionist who's been around the company forever.

I think the partners might have gotten rid of me if they didn't have a longstanding policy of keeping loose cannons close by. It's easier to keep me on payroll and in the building on a semi-regular basis, but I can tell they don't have much interest in the work product I'm putting out.

I fall into a rhythm. I go to work. I go home. I eat haphazardly. I cry. I sit and stare at pictures. I rage. I wait for Amal to call and threaten. I meet Ken for coffee. I survive because I must.

The second time Amal calls I'm sitting at Sisters again with Ken, and quickly give him one of the earbuds. Amal mentions a number so high Ken rolls his eyes, but my hands are so slick with sweat I drop the phone and we lose the connection.

Ken says it was probably for the best, but I don't sleep well for days, wondering if Amal took my mistake out on the girls.

The next time he calls I'm alone, and he threatens things so vile, I'm opening the liquor cabinet before we get off the phone. I go on a four-day epic bender only ended by Ken breaking down my door and throwing me in the shower. By the time I get out and come to the kitchen, I see he's gone through the whole house and thrown out all my booze. Not that there was much left; I'd drunk through everything I could find.

I go sober but take up smoking, something I'd worked hard to give up after college. At first I only smoke on the balcony, but a few days later I realize I don't care if my apartment stinks.

I call Ken and rage at him about how raising money without alerting anyone is a joke. If I could utilize any of the resources I know of from work, I could have this out on every social media platform by noon. It's so frustrating. I could do a crowdfunding campaign and have it funded by the end of the day. I could get an advance on a book deal for her. I could even sell the story to Hollywood for enough to get her out.

But none of those industries are known for their discretion. And Ken keeps reminding me that any and all media attention would endanger the girls by raising their profile, and therefore their purchase price and/or chance of being killed. Then there's the small matter of Harry being exposed for the creep he is and that I wouldn't be allowed to receive calls if Winston had me thrown in jail for breaking my NDA.

Not a single word whispers its way into the news, or even on to gossip websites — the Stump doing its job. These days only image management seems to be able to keep secret the things people want kept secret. Sometimes, with our extensive background checks, our famous Non-Disclosure Agreements, and draconian security measures, I think I would have been better off joining the CIA.

But how else do you keep a lid on that time the Emmy-winner got arrested trying to break into a Krispy Kreme at 3:00 in the morning, out of his mind on no fewer than six different prescription medications? Oh, you never heard of that one? Yeah, I worked on that account for a while.

Or how about the international movie star who survived twenty scandal-free years before we were not able to act quickly enough to buy off one of the child costars he enjoyed playing inappropriate games with? Winston called us all in and gave us a lecture on that one — one of our biggest failures, he'd called it.

Later that day when the star called Winston to cancel his contract with us, telling him he needed the money for his defense, it was Winston who personally phoned the head of accounting and had the monthly hush money checks cut off. Within a few weeks twenty six different former child costars had come forward with accusations.

That might have been the weekend Kate and I broke our long-standing alcohol consumption record, and had to call in sick both Monday and Tuesday before we could stand to walk back through the doors.

We've certainly had fewer leaks than the Agency, as long as I've worked here, but then, we pay much better. And in our fame-obsessed culture, there's a certain cachet to saying you work at the Stump. People will buy you drinks, just to hear your veiled and entirely pre-planned misinformation about a certain celebrity you saw in the hall earlier that day. I used to be able to get a sure two or three drinks bought for me any time I went out, in exchange for information I was ordered to leak.

I know it's disgusting, what we do, but that's why I try so hard not to stop long enough to think of the ethics. If I pull back just far enough away from the morality of it, it's an interesting puzzle, a fascinating science experiment, and I love the game. Loved the game.

Chapter 9: Kate

"This is not what I imagined."

"What," Becca asks as she lies sprawled out on her mat, "the excellent cuisine or the spacious accommodations?"

It's not *that* funny, but when she uses the chicken bone she's picking her teeth with to indicate our penthouse, as we call it, I laugh out loud. And we're probably both a little drunk, this is only the second time we've been given meat since we got here.

I'm busily chewing at my toothbrush stick. Becca taught me how to use it after I complained about fuzzy teeth. It's been remarkably helpful. She'd never used one before, but she knew what they were for and asked Amal to round us up a couple. He must have regretted the ripeness of our breath as much as we did because he promptly produced two.

It doesn't result in the same minty-fresh feeling I grew up with, but it manages to do the job pretty well when all you're worried about is getting out the bits of sand that came with the rice. Plus you have to chew on it a couple hours a day so it gives us something to do.

That is, it did, until Becca started assigning jobs. First they were sort of silly and mundane, but when I began to see how a little bit of routine helped the day go by without wanting to lose my mind, I joined in wholeheartedly.

Now we sweep our little floor twice a day and fold our mats after each of our naps. There's not been another attempt at breaking in, and even though this has calmed both of us regarding our fears of being physically attacked, neither of us sleeps too well when it's dark.

After maybe two weeks, it seemed Amal was convinced that we meant to follow his rules, and he sent all but five men away. The men take turns on duty, which mainly consists of sitting across from the door of our hut with their gun beside them, while the others spend their time smoking or sleeping or scratching something. The woman appears to do nothing but work.

We keep careful record of the days by scratching on one of the poles stretched across the roof, re-scratching the correct number each time we're moved.

We make an attempt at personal hygiene, though that is, I'm afraid, a bit of a lost cause. Amal has given us a poor excuse for soap a couple times, but it can't begin to keep pace since water availability is so limited. Every so often a man appears on a horse cart, carrying the plastic inner-tube of a huge truck tire. I asked Becca what it was the first time it showed up, and she explained it's how they haul water in the desert.

Sure enough, the man poured water from the tire into whatever containers our men were able to produce. Since we never know when the next water delivery man will show up, water is severely limited. Some days we joke about how thirsty we are, describing in detail exactly what we'd be drinking if we had the chance. Other days we don't talk about it at all; the choking, clawing pain in our throats keeping us mostly silent.

However, it's nice to discover that, along with everything else, the nose can adjust. I know perfectly well that we reek, but I've gotten so used to it it doesn't bother me much.

We both had long hair that got worse and worse as time went on. We discussed the feasibility of dreadlocks for a while, as kind of a joke, but the morning we both woke up scratching our heads, we asked Amal for scissors. He refused, but did allow the woman to chop our hair as short as possible, under supervision. She used the same dull knife she uses to prepare our food every day.

I didn't even cry, for which I was unaccountably proud of myself, and we made a vow to warn each other away if we were ever about to come into proximity with a mirror.

We have contests about who can hold a drop of water in their mouths the longest before swallowing it. Actually, we have all kinds of contests. Becca thought of the first couple, but my family's competitive juices have stirred in me and I've invented many new diversions. Race the ants. Competitive air guitar. Pictionary in the dust.

We've also got a pretty rigid physical fitness routine. Becca says there's no point in letting ourselves go while we wait and watch for our escape opportunity. Creative too, how we've figured out how to use the stuff we've been given. We do chin lifts with the roof supports, although we almost brought the roof down in one place when the support snapped when Becca grabbed on. We were doubled over laughing when Amal came storming in to lecture us, and the menacing grins of the guards with him shut us up right quick.

We wear local clothing, basically a big colorful sheet draped over the clothes we came in, provided by Amal almost immediately. It took awhile to get used to, but now I can arrange it as quickly as Becca. Although we don't have to wear it all the time, even when we do, the headscarf doesn't bother me so much anymore.

At a distance we don't look American, which I imagine was the point of Amal's charity — but even up close there's not much difference now that we're allowed outside as long as we stay near our hut, and have browned up under the hot sun.

At least being outside offers a change of scenery, if not a fractionally cooler temperature when the wind kicks up. We heed Older Sister's unspoken advice, following the shade as it moves around the hut until it disappears. When we can't stand the full sun anymore we move inside again and leave the door open.

I've wracked my brain and can't remember any Hollywood picture that accurately portrayed the kidnap scenario I'm living through. For one thing, I imagine no one would watch, as there are vast swaths of time that are unrelentingly dull.

Although, if you cut away from the hours of boredom and low-level stress and just show the times the men shoot off their guns or scream at us from outside the hut, or the times they bust into the room unexpectedly to move us, I guess it'd turn into a pretty exciting picture.

One thing I've decided Hollywood does get right is when their stars proclaim their undying love about fifteen minutes into the action. It's unbelievable how intensely bonding this kind of stress and vulnerability is.

Honestly, I don't know what I'd do without Becca. She is keeping me sane in this place. Her and her schedules. The Routine. She said schedules make the world a saner place. In here I've got cause to agree with her, but if we'd met in any another environment I would have given her my "schedules make me feel like I'm in prison" speech. Alex always loved hearing that one.

I'm not mad at her anymore, and rarely get aggravated even though we're in such tight circumstances, together 24x7. That's never

73

happened to me before — I used to get stir-crazy if I was stuck with only Alex over a long weekend at home.

She has a weird penchant for pop music that matches my own, and we've laughed ourselves sick trying to remember obscure lyrics from the eighties.

I can't believe we're laughing in here. The first couple days I was so paralyzed, I didn't think I was going to make it. But there was Becca — strong Becca, kind Becca, caring, fearless Becca. I know there's no way I would have come out of that living coma so quickly without her.

One afternoon a couple weeks in, I was sitting staring at an ant colony in the corner of the hut, when I realized she hadn't spoken since breakfast. I was about to ask what was wrong, when I finally put it together that her mind-numbing lectures had declined in direct proportion to the return of my sanity. It made me grateful to her in yet another way, to see how much of her behavior was directed toward returning me to a semi-even keel mentally.

But that realization also made me feel small, remembering some of my initial thoughts about her and her quaint little beliefs and closed little worldview. I was a snob, holding back my snobbishness only because I needed her.

Most of the time I'm fine now, but I know good and well that's only because of the little bubble Becca has created for me. The Almighty Routine, the interesting stories, the way she is always thinking up something new to engage my mind.

And especially how she's managed to talk Amal into letting her represent me. He only called for me twice, and each time it took days for me to recover equilibrium. Any time he shows up, even now, the paralysis of fear comes over me and I'm nearly mute. He has stopped even trying to ask me direct questions — he just asks Becca to ask me when he wants some information from me. Mostly he ignores me.

Inside our bubble I'm pretty stable, but every time something changes I start to crumble again. This past week Amal started calling in Becca to teach him Spanish, and for the first few days I was in a full panic by the time she returned.

Whenever the routine is shaken or the guns go off, I realize just how tentative is my mental health. The slightest thing can set me off.

The gratefulness has stacked up so high I don't even find it annoying anymore that she falls asleep in ten seconds or insists on sucking the chicken bone for the rest of the day whenever we've been lucky enough to get one. Or that she continues to thank her friend in the sky for whatever piece of food crosses our path, no matter how disgusting.

That doesn't mean I'm exactly Ms. Cheerful; I just no longer get any satisfaction out of taking it out on her.

I don't understand how we can be in the same exact circumstances and have such different reactions. Now that I'm over the trauma of the first weeks, I know it's not just because she's somehow superhumanly stronger than me. There's something else. I find myself pondering the question at odd times.

She did tell me a couple days ago that she cried every time I fell asleep the first few days. I told her that was no big admission — if I was here alone I'd be in a ball against the wall, *still* crying!

I'm managing, that's the best that can be said — and it's a lot in comparison to the first weeks. But every time I look at her I realize the difference is greater than that. I'm managing under very precise circumstances, but she is truly calm.

We do laugh a lot now, which I never would have imagined at the beginning. She prods me for stories of my life to help me remember what I want to live for. And she has a thousand different stories about her time as a do-gooder, trotting around the armpits of the world helping the desperate and depraved.

She doesn't call it that, but that's how I think of the work she describes. She has me rolling in the straw sometimes, laughing so hard. It's astonishing how she can weave a story that takes me out of our reality. Astonishing, also, how quickly you can get used to almost any set of circumstances. Because except for a few minutes of terror each day, I've pretty much gotten used to this being my life for now.

We've named the main characters in our drama. Scarface, the leader of the pack always trying to undermine Amal's authority. He sends shivers down my spine every time he looks at me.

Then there's Thug One and Two. We named them the Thugs because they follow Scar's orders without fail, but they're easily distinguishable because one of them wears an old University of Michigan t-shirt and the other wears one with *I'm Lovin' It* written in big red letters across the back.

The loner of the group is Muhammed, the only one who prays five times a day. Becca named him that, and I objected on principal thinking it was a touch racist, until she pointed out that every third man in the region is named Muhammed. He vies with Scarface for meanest.

I named the tall one Julian because he reminded me of a guy in junior high who hit puberty first and shot up three inches taller than all the other guys. He wears a soccer jersey with Messi's name on the back. Julian's not bad. We can generally trust him.

There are maybe six or eight other guys who have rotated in and out, in dirty shorts and, more often than not, t-shirts with some American connection. The arrival of anyone new is a great event because we can wile away a whole afternoon observing them and coming up with an appropriate name. Shy Joe, Fat Sam, Dreads, Louis of the Lips, Jay-Z.

There's a teenage boy who came early on and never left. We christened him MJ after he told us he loved Michael Jackson. He told us eventually his name was Tariq, but he liked our nickname for him and started going by it.

We like him. He seems out of place here, displaying teenage characteristics recognizable the world over. He wants desperately to fit in, but the men kick him around, belittle and tease him. Because it's considered the worst job, he often escorts us to the bathroom we're now allowed to visit during the day. The dreaded bucket only makes its appearance at night.

MJ seems to be caught in between, smitten with us but wanting to follow in the other men's footsteps. He's actually fairly sweet. If Muhammed is taking a nap, MJ will try to speak to us sometimes. The only English words he knows besides the vile move-now speeches seem to be Mickey Mouse, Iron Man, Pop Tarts and okey-dokey. He repeats those four over and over, holding his thumb up and smiling. He's the only one who seems willing to teach us anything in Wolof, the language most of them speak, and we practice endlessly any words we manage to garner.

The days are starting to blur. At first everything was scary, but now I'm seeing that a lot of the violence appears to be staged. Most of the men are just going through the motions and yelling the same things, but their hearts don't seem to be in it. It's almost like they've memorized a script, and one morning when I'm thinking about this I realize it's true. Only Amal speaks English well, the others know some swear words and a few other choice selections, but that's it. They really have memorized a script! The things they yell at us, the vile threats and imprecations, all of it is just part of the game.

After the first couple weeks and the departure of the most violent guards, their anger seems to deflate considerably.

When I relate my discovery to Becca she's as thrilled as she always is when it appears I'm using my brain. I don't think either of us want to return to the first weeks when she had to pull me so carefully out of near catatonia.

Even the seemingly chaotic begins to take on a pattern — every third or fourth night they come yelling into the hut and tie and blindfold us, then throw us in the back of a car, a truck, even a couple times the bed of a cart pulled by some sort of four-footed creature I couldn't identify in the dark.

Whether it's a car or a cart or a boat, the roads are so ridiculous that I ache the next day and we entertain ourselves counting new bruises.

Sometimes we travel all night, sometimes it's just a couple of hours. Twice we've crossed a river. I have no idea where we are. Under the best of circumstances, my sense of direction has been described as not being able to find my way out of a paper bag. I am the optimal test case for which GPS was invented, and under normal circumstances, never leave home without it. Becca thinks we might have crossed into Mali, but we could also be in Senegal or back in Mauritania from week to week.

Neither of us was overweight before, but now we're looking a little cavernous. But something Becca pointed out early on and I finally, grudgingly, saw to be true — they're not feasting on three squares and day either, nor are they sleeping on air mattresses. Amal has his own hut, but most of the men sleep in the open.

And once we commenced our campaign to be kind to the woman who prepares our rice, we noticed our portions gradually increasing. The men seem to get a little more than we do, but not by much. We have one root kind of vegetable usually with the rice, and maybe once every eight or ten days a scrawny chicken will be sacrificed.

The vegetables we get are sort of pitiful. The day I flew out of Portland I went through and pitched most of the stuff out of my refrigerator. Normally I would have at least tried to find someone to give it to, but I was in such a hurry I threw away two big grocery bags of vegetables that were about a hundred percent better looking than anything I've seen in weeks.

One day the woman we'd named Older Sister came right into our hut with tea-making materials and began the fairly complicated procedure of making us tea. Her baby was strapped to her back, and we tried to make her smile, but mostly she just laid there unresponsive.

Becca said she thought it was a very large honor and quite a step forward in our relationship. We knew we couldn't talk to her, Becca had tried her Arabic on everyone in camp and received nothing but blank stares. When we finished with our third cup of tea she quietly told us her name was Fatima, before gliding out the door into the darkness.

I dreamt of a fruit salad last night, and woke up wondering if Fatima finds this as difficult as I do. After all, she's lived like this her whole life. It's only me and what I'm used to that is making this so difficult. I mean, obviously, notwithstanding the gunmen keeping me from escaping.

I find myself wondering about their lives. Is it true what Becca says, that the majority of the world lives closer to this style than they do to the two-bedroom apartment I share with no one? And that a step down, no less, from the apartment I shared with Alex, befitting my newly single and lowered socioeconomic status.

Sometimes Becca tells me stories about her life in Egypt. It makes me think I haven't known the world at all. My initial forays this past year are just scratching the barest of surfaces. I wonder if I've been asleep up until now.

Good grief. When I find myself feeling just a little bit guilty, I wonder if this is Stockholm Syndrome setting in. I bet Fatima doesn't even know what Stockholm Syndrome is — I only know because of Hollywood, and neither she nor the men seem to be spending excessive amounts of time mindlessly entertaining themselves.

Other than Fatima who never stops working, mostly the men sit around and stare at the dust at their feet, seeming bored and slightly downtrodden.

Chapter 10: Becca

We're playing our after-dinner game, which we created with two rocks, carefully etched, and much negotiation over rules.

I roll a story from me. This is getting harder as the weeks pass, trying to come up with something I haven't already told her that also fits into the category of morale-boosting. If it's a story she's heard before I lose ten points.

Kate is making herself as comfortable as possible, which is not as difficult as it was at the beginning. Neither of us complain about the scratchy, dirty blankets anymore, just thankful to have something to pull up tight around us when the sun goes down. Neither are we bothered by the straw floor after spending a few nights in the open, lying on the spiky plants that grow everywhere, which we now know the straw protects us from.

Suddenly I remember a story I'm surprised I haven't told before. "Okay. Imagine the scene, I'm new to the country, I'm trying to make a good impression. But I'm you're average, grade-A, American prude. I haven't been naked in front of anyone since those humiliating days of high school locker rooms, so I'm not prepared for the fact that we walk in the door of the *hamam* — do you know what a *hamam* is?"

Kate shakes her head no.

"It's basically group bathing in places that don't have indoor plumbing in each house. It's a great idea, actually, although I'm not a huge fan for reasons that should become clear.

"So we walk in the door and immediately everyone begins to strip right there. No towels. No changing rooms. No swimsuits. Down to your underwear. That was step one, very hard to do but I didn't see a choice without offending my host.

"Next I walk around the corner meekly following my nearly-nude colleague and enter a cement and brick-blocked steam room. It's big and steamy, but unfortunately not so steamy that I can't see every woman in the room turn to look at the white girl making her debut."

I pause for a moment to expertly wield the fly swatter. "One less," we both say at the same time and laugh. The flies aren't too bad since mostly they congregate around things even more disgusting and smelly than us, but we always try have the swatter within easy reach.

"The humiliation is pretty extreme, I've got to admit, but thankfully they point to a small side stall where I can go in and sit on the cement next to my coworker. Granted, it's not much better sitting right next to a coworker I only met a few hours earlier, pretending it's not that big of a deal to be nearly naked. But it's better than being in the center of the room. At least I can sort of hide and hum to myself until it's over.

"That is until my host comes over and says she has paid a local woman to give me the 'full treatment' since it's my first time. She signals me to come out and I have a very bad feeling in my stomach.

"I will not bore you with extreme details, but I was washed, waxed, buffed, flopped like a fish, massaged, smacked, and laughed at, repeatedly, until I was in a state of complete and utter submission.

"I was still traumatized a few hours later, trying to fall into the bliss of unconsciousness, when my coworker, who was sleeping on the next couch over, asked me how I liked my first experience.

"No matter my humiliation, I didn't want to disrespect either her, or our host, or the culture in general, so I was still formulating my reply when she said her mother raised her in the knowledge that you didn't get that naked in front of anyone until your wedding night!"

Kate bursts out laughing, and I feel a little smug as the story surges me ahead on our sand-scratched game board. Thinking about morale, we made it a rule that you get double points any time you make the other person laugh.

"Your turn." I toss the dice over to Kate.

She rolls a question for me. Swell.

She's quiet for a while, and I wonder what she'll come up with. She has had some wacky ones in the past that earned her loads of points, so I try to prepare myself not to laugh.

"Aren't you ever…" she stops as her voice cracks a little. I look up, but she won't make eye contact.

"Aren't you *ever* afraid?"

Oh Lord, why can't I get through to her?

I sigh, and think for a while. One good thing about this game is neither of us are ever in a hurry to finish it. Our rhythm here is so different from the real world, and all its hustle and bustle. The more we can stretch out any conversation, the quicker the hours of the day pass.

"I'm not unafraid," I begin quietly.

She looks up at me, skeptical. It's not surprising — she seems to have developed this image of me as some sort of superhero. I've told her all kinds of stories where I'm closer to the villain or the idiot sidekick, but nothing seems to break through. I don't know how to get her to see the truth that any good she sees in me is not even me.

"You've been living beside me all this time, you have to see that I'm often afraid! But I think you're asking something deeper than that — do you want to know why I'm not incapacitated by fear maybe as often as you are?"

I don't know if I've stepped over the line, she's still so fragile sometimes. After a moment she nods.

"Well for one thing, I've lived outside America and its relative safety half my life, and in some circumstances that were less than ideal safety wise. I've envisioned this scenario so many times, there's the tiniest sense of relief that it's finally here and I don't have to worry or anticipate anymore, or wonder if it's ever going to happen."

I pause again. That's not what I want to say. How can I make this more clear? I start again.

"When I first moved to Cairo I was enchanted by everything. The people, the chaos, the sights and sounds and smells. The invigorating work of trying to rescue girls from horrifying situations. The newness of the language and the challenge of trying to figure out how to communicate. All of it was wonderful.

"Then, I don't know, maybe six months later things started to change. There was just so much chaos, so much noise all the time, the language was destroying me intellectually, and the horror stories I heard at work every day were destroying me emotionally.

"You can't walk as a woman alone on the streets of Cairo without being verbally and sometimes physically assaulted — and what was at first just annoying, soon became more like daily arrows aimed at my emotional well-being. I started having trouble sleeping."

I pause, remembering the scene vividly. I'd been used to busy streets growing up in Guatemala, but I'd not had any trouble as long as I travelled during the day with other women. In Cairo it's like a battlefield just to go anywhere, and you certainly don't walk alone unless it's absolutely necessary.

"Night after night I'd lie awake, into the wee hours, and I started thinking about being robbed, or kidnapped, or raped. I thought about it so much I was almost able to visualize the events happening. It started affecting my daylight hours, my work, my language process, my friendships — it was like the joy bubble I'd been floating around in started sinking, bleeding out from a hundred small tears."

I pause as Kate takes off her sandal and smacks a spider crawling her way — she who used to scream whenever she saw one. She smiles and waves her sandal at me grandly to continue.

"One night an American newswoman was attacked while trying to do a broadcast in Tahrir Square. I was sitting inside my very safe apartment, doors locked, all by myself, and as I read the news describing what had happened to her I had an absolute panic attack. I was frozen in terror — I couldn't even finish the article. It was a palpable thing, a wet sheet across my nose and mouth, suffocating me. A heavy steel plate pushing down on my chest. All the hours thinking and wondering and worrying, they all congealed into that instant, and I thought I would die from the fear. I could see myself never leaving my room again because of it.

"I'd been sitting on my bed with my computer on my lap, and I remember I just shut it mid-article and got up onto my knees and told God point blank, 'You are going to have to take this terror away because I'm not going to be able to set foot outside my own door feeling the way I feel now.'

"And He did! Like He always does, sooner or later. In that moment when I needed Him to save me, He did. He lifted something so heavy it was crushing me, as if it were nothing. And it's been like that time and time and time again in my life."

I don't know if I'm getting through or not; she's just staring into space. But I don't feel like I can stop now.

"I can see the way you look at me — you think I'm doing such a good job being a hostage. You think I'm awesome in a crisis. You think it's because I'm such a good person.

"It's not because I'm a good person, Kate! I don't know how to explain it any clearer. I'm coping better than you are because I have experience with terror threatening my sanity. I have experience being a prisoner. This is not my first time being denied basic freedoms, or being threatened with bodily harm. It's not the first time I'm living in circumstances I wouldn't have chosen of my own free will.

"I've been in prisons constructed by my father, by well-meaning but well-off-the-mark Christians, by pimps running six-year-old girls in Cairo. And I've been in prisons constructed of fear, of anger, and of bitterness."

Suddenly my throat closes, choking off the flow of words. I'm overwhelmed as the memories roll over me. We sit in silence, or rather, in desert silence — which includes quite a variety of sound. Kate doesn't seem to be in any hurry, waiting for me to continue when I can. I begin again, slowly.

"I'm familiar with prison cells because I've been battling from inside of them most of my life. Amal, the other guys — they're new jailers, but this prison has a lot of similarities to ones I've known in the past in this bent and broken world. So I can see that Amal's not the enemy; none of them are. They're each losing their own personal battles against the enemy, engaged in the same war we all are.

"The real enemy is fear. And despair. Anger. Bitterness. All the things that rob us of peace, that rob us of joy. That make us forget who we are and what we believe. There are so many circumstances we can't control. People who hurt each other for no reason. Accidents. Earthquakes. Wars. Lovers who decide they no longer love. Cancer. Babies who die.

"All kinds of circumstances we wouldn't have chosen, and rarely are they under our control. I was thrown into a prison so early on I don't remember when it started, and I spent years railing against my father the jailer, screaming at God for putting me there. Until I quieted down enough to see that God was right inside there with me. That He transcends circumstances and prisons.

"It doesn't matter what we're facing, because He is there. Every time we change prison cells, He's there. He's there when we get brief stays of execution and dance around in our freedom, and He's there when we're locked up again by some fresh horror.

"No circumstance changes who He is. And no circumstance changes who I am — a child of God, valued, loved, cherished, cared for, forgiven over and over and over again.

"And because I have experienced that to be true, even though my heart spikes every time the guns go off, even though I look with fear on some of the guards, I know down deep that the rules of my life haven't changed. The foundation stones I walk on are the same, no matter what path He sets me on.

"God loves me. He saved me. He's always with me. He's good, and He always wins. And He expects me to do my job no matter what.

She nods, but I can see she doesn't get it. I feel a little desperate, realizing I might as well be speaking Arabic to her. If God doesn't choose to open her ears, it's gibberish. It's so unbelievably frustrating, hearing but not understanding, seeing but not comprehending.

I can't help but continue, if only for my benefit, just to reaffirm what I know to be true.

"He told me to love Him, and to love my neighbor, so that's what I'm going to try to do here, just as I've tried to do it in Cairo, and as I tried to do it in every other stage of my life.

"And I fail all the stinking time. It's infuriating, that regardless of how many times He's proven Himself, I still fall flat on my face in failure. After so many times He's turned ugly circumstances into a thing of beauty, still I doubt. But each time I fall He picks me up, and I try again — maybe I run for a mile, maybe I stumble within two steps, but I'll keep trying.

"So here in this set of circumstances He's moved me into, you're my new neighbor, and it's certainly not hard to love you. But Amal is my neighbor too. And it was absolutely impossible to love him at first. After a little while I didn't fear him as much, especially when he sent the worst guys away. And then we started meeting, and in between Spanish verbs I hear bits and pieces of his story that unthaw my heart toward him. Each day I try to remember the forgiveness God has given me, and after looking at the torment in his eyes, one day last week I realized I didn't hate him anymore.

"I don't love him yet, but every day I can see the battle that is raging inside of him, and I feel nothing but compassion. I want him to know the freedom I have known, even inside these walls. He does not hold me. He is not the master of my fate.

"God is in control, and He is good. I remind myself every morning of the things I know to be true. God is the one Who numbered my days before I was born, so I'm going to die on my appointed day whether it's here or walking across the street to get coffee when I'm home visiting Matt.

"I know we don't see eye to eye on this, but I'm trying to answer your question to the best of my ability. I'm not unafraid, but I'm entirely certain that the world works on a different set of foundational principals than the obvious ones, and it changes the way I see things."

Abruptly I run out of energy. Though I can see she's trying, my words are utterly foreign to her. She has the same expression on her face as when she's trying to understand something Fatima is saying in Wolof — she tries and tries, and then her eyes glaze over and she gives up.

I love her. I don't know what I'd do if I was here alone, but watching her reminds me over and over of my gratitude. She is the living and breathing evidence of the difference the knowledge of God makes, and that only He can reveal it.

"Kate, I don't mean to be callous to your fear. I'm just telling you, I believe that God was not surprised when Amal chose to kidnap us. I believe He allowed this for a reason. He chose this particular set of circumstances, this particular place, and this particular time, for you and me and Amal and the others to come together — and I'm very keen on discovering what that reason is. I think obeying Him in this situation, seeking and following His will, is just as important if not more so than doing that in my normal life."

"Yeah well," she sighs and smiles tightly, "I wish he'd have left me out of it." And she picks up the dice and puts them away.

....

Last night we didn't play our game. I think we were both tired from the previous night's openness. But tonight she picks up the dice as per usual. She rolls an eighties dance party, and we dance and laugh as we try to sing our way through "Thriller."

Then I roll a story from her. She thinks for a while, and I wonder what kind of mood she's in.

"I never set out to be some kind of crusader." Kate rolls her eyes as she says it, like it amuses her as well.

"I went into image management, for heaven's sake! I didn't care about much except making a good living, buying a home, joining a gym, having a couple kids eventually."

She pauses, looking thoughtfully at a piece of straw she's pulled from the wall.

"Matt and I were lucky, we both got jobs right out of college at the Stump. Working long, long hours, barely home. And then I met Alex at the gym and we eventually moved in together. We enjoyed our lives and were each moving up the ladder and starting to see some real perks from the hours we put in. I thought we were probably going to get married, but we were so busy and relatively happy with the status quo that we didn't talk about it.

"One night about two years ago I was walking home and got mugged. It was the scariest thing that had ever happened to me at that point, although now I'd just laugh in the mugger's face."

I snort and she rolls her eyes at the unladylike noise.

"Anyway, going through the process of trying to catch the guy and spending some time in the parts of Portland I normally steered clear of, I found out about the human trafficking problem in our city. I was appalled, and horrified, and sort of traumatized, actually."

Matt never told me why Kate stopped working with him. He never told me much about Kate period, and apparently vice versa — I've been surprised at how little we know about each other when she's known Matt so long.

"I went through a period where I would go into sort of these speechless moments of rage, feeling totally impotent like I had been blind my whole life. I read extensively, yelling quotes at Alex. Poor Alex, just trying to make partner.

"Finally I came across an organization in town that was doing something. And doing something helped me. Helped with the rage, the impotence. Just doing a small part. I started spending my off hours there, started putting in fewer hours at work so I could have more off hours. Matt tried to cover for me, but eventually my bosses started noticing. So did Alex.

"About six months after the mugging, Alex and I had it out. I came home and said I wanted to quit the Stump and start working full time at the center. A job had come open and they offered it to me — the salary was an embarrassment, but I knew the second they offered it that I wanted it. I wanted a different life."

She's silent for a long time, playing with that same piece of straw until it disintegrates in her hands. She looks down in surprise and sweeps the pieces off her lap.

"Alex flipped. Absolutely flipped. And after a long and painful series of fights over the next couple weeks I moved out. I never regretted my decision, but I wonder sometimes how Alex feels now. I've worked at the center almost a year, and I love it — but Alex and I were together almost eight years, so it's hard to believe sometimes that things ended up this way. I still wonder every now and then, if only Alex had been able to understand, to move a little in my direction, if we'd still be together."

Her hands are quiet in her lap and I wonder what it cost her to share this with me. She hasn't before been so vulnerable and I want to comfort her somehow.

"Have you thought about giving him a call when we get out of here?" I ask, tentatively.

"Who?" she looks up, confused.

I look at her with my own confusion. *Um, hello?* "Alex?"

She gets the funniest look on her face, laughs, and says, "Ohhhh. No. No, Alex isn't a…"

CRASH!

The door comes open so fast and hard it smashes into the wall and breaks the dinner plates we'd carefully stacked behind the door. Usually we hear them coming, but tonight we'd been too concentrated on our conversation.

"On your feet! We're moving!" Scarface yells, and seeing his furious face wipes my mind of all thought except following orders.

Chapter 11: Amal

"I know all about your country. It is a vast wasteland where people care only for themselves and their stomachs. Fat people. Rich people. People who will fight over a discounted pair of shoes when they already have fifty pairs in their closet. People who continue to choose the cheapest stores, even though it has been proven time and time again that the cheapest stores are only cheap because they employ despicable methods in their third-world factories.

"How many third-world workers have to die before you will wake up and decide to pay ten cents more for a t-shirt you'll only wear once before you lose it in the back of your overstuffed closet? Your Christian America is barren of real feeling."

Once again, we've started a small discussion to practice the Spanish I'm learning, and I've gotten so riled up that I've switched to English and started yelling.

What is it about Becca that makes me so angry? Or rather, what is it about her that so easily pricks the boil of fury that inhabits my insides and sets me spewing the fiery bile of bitterness?

I found a small Spanish Bible when I was going through her things, and told her I'd look on it positively if she would teach me Spanish.

"Nothing else to do around here," she'd said, "we might as well learn."

She's a good teacher. Patient, kind. I'm impressed in spite of myself. And I'm making a lot of progress since there's not much else for me to do around here except study. I find village life not to my liking at all — in Dakar there is always something to do, always some trouble to get into.

Studying keeps the boredom at bay, and also somewhat silences my demons. The sooner I learn Spanish, the easier my transition to life in Spain will be once I'm able to escape.

I think it must be her kindness that stirs my anger. She didn't start out that way. It was easier to get through our sessions when she was irritable and shied away from me in fear whenever something startled her. But as with everything, familiarity breeds contempt, and soon she was treating me I suppose as she would any other student.

The first time we laughed together at a mistake I'd made, I looked up and saw she was as startled as I was.

I don't like how it makes me feel, that she is so kind when she is here because of me. I don't like the days when I study with her, and then as soon as she leaves, call her brother and threaten him about what I plan to do to her if he doesn't come up with a higher number.

I can tell the men think I'm crazy, spending all this time with her and never touching her, but I am desperate for knowledge, desperate for anything that will help me get away from here. That desperation keeps me calling for her, but it also adds to my anger somehow.

"Amal, you're right," she answers quietly, startling me. I'd almost forgotten she was there. As happens so often now, any time I blow up at her, it seems I have less energy in reserve.

"I agree with you for the most part. The way my country fattens itself to the utter disregard of the rest of the world is a tragedy. But not everyone is that way. I know many people who actively think about the rest of the world, who work for the good of their fellow man and not just their own selves and family.

"But you are wrong in calling America Christian. A Christian is someone who loves Allah and obeys Him, and everything you just described does not mesh with what is written in the Bible. Our country has wandered far from its roots."

Her response reminds me of something else that irritates me and I respond with as much disdain as I can muster, "Why do you keep using the Muslim word for God? I know you Christians call him God not Allah; I am not an uneducated man you can trick with wordplay!"

She actually has the nerve to smile. "Did you know Christians used the word Allah for God before Muslims did? You should look it up."

And there it is, right there! Her calm voice, her utter certainty. It is infuriating. I have had a certain set opinion of Americans and Christians, everyone knows they are basically the same thing, for so many years — yet she does not fit into any of the familiar categories.

I don't know what to do with her, I only know that she causes things to resurrect within me that I'd rather stay dead.

"We're done for the day," I say curtly, and then roar for the guard, "Moustafa!"

She jumps a little at the volume of my voice, then stands and looks down at me. I can see her staring, no doubt waiting for a more civil goodbye, but I refuse to look up. Instead, I carefully arrange my notes and wait for Moustafa. The moment he arrives and escorts her roughly out the door, I lean forward and put my head in my hands.

....

I can't help myself, every night when the sun goes down I slip out of the village, then come back around to the far side of their hut. The men have gotten so lazy they've only once raised an alarm, and I was able to yell at them about allowing me to relieve myself in peace.

They play their game after dinner, and I tell myself that it's just research — the better I understand them and Americans in general, the better I will be at my job. But I know it's more than that. Their words, especially Becca's, resonate within me in a way I have given up trying to understand.

Most of the time they tell stories that are silly or stupid, or illustrate the vast differences in our lives, and I end up storming away in disgust before I forget myself and start yelling at them. But it's the other stories, the ones where they share something real, that keep drawing me back.

I tell myself tonight will be the last time. I need to put more time into studying if I want to perfect my Spanish. The negotiations are going better than expected, and this afternoon when I called in to report my progress Oumar told me we were getting close.

I crouch forward, as quietly as I can, and sit as close to the hut as possible. Becca is talking softly.

....

"You know Americans are the only ones I know who seem surprised whenever suffering comes around. Everywhere else in the world people expect bad things to happen. They understand it's a broken world we're living in. Americans not only don't expect it, they're outraged by it. They assume that if something bad happens then you've done something to deserve it, there's got to be some big underlying reason why.

"I don't hear the same questions from people who have experienced suffering on a scale difficult for us to even imagine, difficult to believe even when they're standing in front of you showing you the scars.

"I've seen mothers holding their children, dead in their arms, because they couldn't scrape together one lousy dollar for a medicine that would cure the kid. I've seen girls stacked up by age, four to twelve, waiting to be picked by the men who have flown in to a country that caters to their perversion. I've seen women sell their oldest child to pay for food for the rest of their children. I've seen refugees pour across borders with the tattered remnants of their family or their village, rendered homeless, widowed, and orphaned, by wars outside of their control or interest."

I'm surprised at some of the things Becca says. She tends to get on a soapbox and can't stop herself. The funny thing is, when it comes to Americans, so many of her soapboxes are similar to mine. I feel a little sorry for Kate sometimes, having to listen to Becca when she gets in a preaching mood. I want to say amen, preach it sistah, like I always see in black churches in the movies.

"It is a broken world we live in. Just because we are *privileged* to be in the one percent of the world where you don't even have to suffer through a mild headache if you don't want to, doesn't mean we're living in the reality the rest of the world lives with every day.

"Of course we have a degree of pain and suffering in the United States. Absolutely we do. I'm just saying we seem to be always blindsided by it, and immediately we rail at God and ask Him why, why, why did this happen to me? *I'm such a good person.*"

I almost laugh at the valley girl accent she adopted for that last line. I wonder if Becca and I might have been friends if we had met under more auspicious circumstances.

"Why do bad things happen to good people? I'm not saying it's not valid, I'm just saying that westerners in general and Americans very specifically are the only people I've come across who have such a high degree of perceived control over their lives that that question can even occur to them."

....

She stops talking, and it appears they've decided to go to sleep. I'm glad, because I'm heart sick. I try to slip away from where I've been crouched outside their hut as quietly as possible, not wanting to hear any more.

I've got to stop doing this. One of these days one of the men will catch me and report it to Oumar. More importantly, it's affecting my ability to do my job. She's messing with my head. All these new ideas, all this old emotion coming to the surface, all these layers of guilt I don't need to be dealing with to do my job effectively.

Last week I yelled at Matt, accusing him of preferring to save Kate and let Becca rot. He was so mad he yelled right back at me, so I threatened to throw Becca to my men if she wasn't worth anything to him.

I could hear him choking back his fury, trying to come up with an answer that would satisfy me, and I was so overcome by a wave of nausea at the thought of Muhammed laying his hands on Becca that I abruptly hung up.

I'm doing just what Oumar taught me, just what I planned out so carefully and methodically. To the letter. And it's going just as planned, it couldn't really be working out any better.

Oumar said that Diadji is very pleased with the way things are going and is thinking about who of his men I can train to use the same strategy. I should be happy. I'm that much closer to my goals. But instead I am sick.

I'm sick of the pity I see in Becca's eyes, the fear I see in Kate's. I'm sick of threatening the men every day to keep them in line. I am sick to death of this life, this "work."

....

Fatima's daughter dies in the night. I am awakened by her keening, and when I go outside to see what's going on, I see that the men are just standing around looking at her as she rocks the baby in her arms and wails. They watch for a few moments, and then return to their fire and game as if to say, another day in Senegal, another dead child.

I don't even know the baby's name, or who the father is, only that she was assigned to my group to cook and clean and provide comfort to the men. I've never asked her a single question, nor acknowledged her existence except when something is wrong with the food.

I see movement, and look up to see Becca striding toward Fatima with a look on her face that dares me to stop her. Tariq is on guard and stands up, unsure what to do. He looks at me and I wave him off. Let her expend her energy if she wants to.

I don't call Becca in for several days. I think she spends most of her time with Fatima, but I don't pay too much attention. I tell the men I don't care if the girls spend most of the day outside, just as long as they don't bother me.

Instead, I sit quietly on my cot, trying to visualize the future I've been working toward. Trying to harden my resolve for this final push. If I can just hold it together long enough, they'll both go home and I'll be free.

I'm certain Becca is an anomaly, and that the next group we kidnap won't offer me these same challenges. I don't need too many more jobs before I should be able to escape.

I've just about decided it's time to start studying again when one of the men yells from outside. I stand up and go to the door, and when I open it I'm taken by complete surprise. Kate is standing there, a frantic look in her eyes that, for once, doesn't have to do with me.

"Something is wrong," she says in a rush. "Becca woke up this morning with a fever and chills. She said it was probably just the water again, but she got worse as the day went on. We were just getting ready to ask to go to the bathroom, but when she stood up she passed out. She's still out cold, and I don't know what to do."

Chapter 12: Matt

"Caroline, I love you. I love you! I want to marry you. How many more ways can I say it?"

She's crying so hard she can't immediately speak. "I know you love me, Matt. But you love me more than you love God. Actually I'm not even sure you love God anymore. And I can't commit myself to someone who doesn't love God more than me. Marriage is too hard, it wouldn't work."

I grab at her arm but she spins away, heading toward the hallway to escape. I can't believe this is happening. I'm paralyzed for a few seconds, then run after her.

She's made it to the kitchen, and as I come around the corner I hear her telling her parents through sobs, "It's off, I called it off." Her mother looks as stunned as I feel, standing there holding a mop that drips dirty water all over the floor. Her brother, at the table, yells "Praise God" so loudly I want to go over and do him bodily harm.

But I don't have time for that, my world is imploding and I need to focus. I go to her and kneel, grab her hand. "Caroline, I will never love anyone like I love you. I want to marry you, have children with you, provide for us and grow old together. I have waited for you, kept myself pure for you. I don't see where my love for God factors in. I love Him all right, I just love you more. I don't see how that's wrong!"

I'm crying so hard I'm not even sure the last words are intelligible. She stares at me with agony in her eyes and I know her heart is breaking as much as mine, but she's stopped crying and I see the resolve that made me first notice her in the lunch line. She's made up her mind. I'm ruined.

I drop my forehead to the linoleum tile, and wake to the familiar wet pillow and clogged nose. I can still feel the cold of that yellow-checked kitchen tile on my forehead; still smell the hated lemon Pine-Sol from the mop.

"Dammit!" I yell to the wall, then throw a pillow across the room with as much force as I can muster. It hits a piece of miscellaneously trendy and expensive art and sends it crashing to the ground.

It's always the same, I wake feeling like it was yesterday that I was that sad sack, crying on the floor in front of my fiancé and her family, the morning of the wedding that wasn't.

But I'm not him anymore. I go into the mantra automatically, pulling myself back to the present. *He was just a naive boy. Confused. Embittered. I have moved on.*

It's just the emotions of the current situation. The dream always resurfaces when I'm in the middle of high stress. I reach across to the nightstand and pull out a bottle of sleeping pills prescribed for just such occasions. I'll start taking them again regularly until we get this resolved.

....

My mommy-track account is taken away from me when, unaccountably, Bobby has a public misstep and I can't marshal a decent strategy quickly enough. I'm assigned to the float pool, helping other accounts on an as-needed basis. I didn't even know we had a float pool.

I go to my smaller office on a much lower floor, and sit and stare out the window. Veronica somehow knows if I'm at work and makes sure I eat a good lunch, but other than that I can't be bothered. I go home and stare at the TV, never sure by the end of the evening what I've been looking at.

Ken is worried about me, who wouldn't be? He says everything I'm feeling is normal, which makes me feel better about myself, albeit briefly. He says my number one job is to keep it together, which I find harder and harder to do.

He's living in temporary executive housing a few blocks away, and makes me join a gym with him. We meet twice a week to play basketball, and usually he creams me. He has other cases he's helping out on, but continues to remind me I'm priority number one. I can't help but admire the business model.

We spend a horrible three days cleaning out Kate's apartment and moving all her stuff to a storage unit. Ken stays with me those nights, no doubt to make sure I don't hit the bottle the second he leaves my sight. Prescient on his part, as that had been my plan exactly.

I ask him again and again why I can't go to the press, the State Department, or even storm the gates of the White House if necessary. To his credit, he responds patiently every time. He brings me classified reports from his office and shows me step-by-step where things have gone wrong in the past. He shows me pictures of happy reunions with people who followed the advice of the professionals. He reassures me over and over that we're on the right track, following the most successful guidelines built up over the years. We're doing the very best we can, he says, it just takes a long time.

Amal calls fairly frequently, but not in any kind of scheduled manner, each time starting off professional, talking about how well the girls are doing. Then he ends with a parting threat, and each time it gets worse. I don't know how much more I can stand.

I no longer call Aunt Bertie, but wait for her to call me. She waits until mom is sleeping, and then I fill her in on any news. We talk a couple times a week. She always tells me she's praying for me. I bite back the rude comment I want to make and thank her. Usually.

Amal informs me that Becca's suffering from malaria, and I google until I can bear it no longer. Without proper medicine, there's a fair chance she could die. A million people die every year from malaria. How did I not know this? And why haven't we solved this already?

I rant in brief intervals, abruptly angry, then just as abruptly too exhausted to continue. Again, Ken says this is normal. I find I no longer care.

....

After Caroline called off the wedding, I drifted for a couple months, before moving to Portland and enrolling at Reed College. Dad had gone to Bible college in Portland and used to rail about Reed students — the annual nude run across campus, the lack of grades, purveyors of the terrible disease of liberalism that infected everyone it touched. It seemed poetic somehow that I now joined them.

A highly competitive school, I think they only let me in for the novelty of having a former Bible college student enrolled.

Unfortunately my two years of religion credits were practically useless toward my new communication degree. I had to start almost from scratch, but I didn't mind. I had a lot of things to work out.

I didn't speak to mom once that entire year, but Becca and I talked almost every night. She was in her senior year of high school and having a hard time. For a while we weren't sure she was going to graduate, but she finally scraped together enough extra credit to barely pass a couple of classes.

She didn't want me to come, and I wasn't too keen on seeing mom, so the morning after graduation Becca hopped a Greyhound bus and came my way.

We spent that summer living right off campus. I'd found a pretty cheap apartment, and it became ground central for some pretty epic parties. Back in those days I drank to have fun, but Becca went at it much more seriously. She drank methodically, scientifically, figuring out the best and quickest ways to get blotto with the fewest consequences the next morning.

I started to worry about her. I was able to keep my summer job in the midst of all our parties, but as the summer went on, every time I came home she was either drunk or stoned with a variety of new loser friends. We started to fight, something we hadn't done since early childhood, and I'd just about decided to ask her to go back to mom when I came home from work one afternoon in late July to find her facedown on the living room floor, out cold.

I thought she'd just gotten herself too drunk, but thankfully when I bent down to pick her up I saw the medicine bottle sticking out from under the skirt of the couch. She'd taken the whole thing.

The ambulance arrived faster than I thought it would, the paramedics working quickly, and at the ER her stomach was pumped with efficiency.

I was in a daze. Once I knew she'd be all right, I was so abruptly furious that she'd done this to me that I couldn't breathe. When the doctor came out and told me it'd be a few hours before I could see her, I stalked home and roughly threw all her stuff into her two duffel bags. I walked down to the bus station and bought her a one-way ticket to Alabama leaving the next afternoon.

Then I hefted her duffels, and with the ticket in my wallet went back to the hospital. She was just coming to when I came into the room, and when I saw the expression on her face when she saw her bags in my hands, all the fight went out of me.

I dropped the bags, went to the bed and crawled in beside her. We cried together until we both fell asleep.

The next morning I took her home and made pancakes and strong coffee for me, and oatmeal and tea for her still-tender stomach, and we had a long talk.

We decided not to tell Aunt Bertie, knowing that if we told her, she'd feel obligated to tell mom, and that would be like releasing the hounds of hell. She was worried they'd come get her and force her into some sort of Christian rehab/boot camp.

She was so angry with God she couldn't see straight, and the prospect of re-inserting herself inside the Christian bubble terrified her. I told her she could stay with me as long as she wanted, and tried to explain how my professors had helped me with my own anger — showing me how easy it was to set God aside once you realized how irrelevant he really was to our lives.

We made a pact that morning — neither of us would return to God unless we were convinced on our own, without the influence or pressure of anyone else, that he had any kind of relevance in our lives.

I found her a counselor at the school who was willing to see her at a discounted rate, and she started going twice a week. She got a job, and I felt like maybe she was making progress, but every month or so she'd drink herself into a stupor and I'd wonder if she was trying in a more passive way to end her life.

After six months of little to no progress as far as I could tell, the counselor suggested she visit Guatemala, the birthplace of most of Becca's demons. When she asked me what I thought, it took everything in me not to scream, "NEVER in a million years!" But she was desperate, so I agreed against all my own feelings and instincts.

We went over Christmas break the next year, staying with our old Tia Maria who wouldn't hear of us staying in a motel once we let her know we were coming. She and Tio Arturo picked us up at the airport, and feeling their arms wrap tightly around us brought back so many of the good memories of my childhood.

We arrived late Saturday night, so we were able to claim jet lag that first Sunday, but after a week of wandering around the old haunts and dusting off our Spanish, Tia Maria insisted that we accompany her to church. Neither of us felt like we could resist her, it was just like when she'd bullied us around as children, but once we found out she no longer attended the same church our father had started we didn't mind as much.

I can close my eyes and picture it like it was yesterday. The hard wooden pews with close-packed bodies, the interminable prayers, the way Tia Maria abandoned herself to the music in the very same way she'd taught us to worship dance when she cleaned the house. Teenage girls in the front corner waving brightly-colored flags in time to the music, drums thumping so loud and close that you can feel it in your chest, and inevitably someone fainting from either the Spirit or the heat, depending on whom you asked.

Tia Maria tried to pull me up but I held fast. She managed to get Becca to her feet, but I noticed Becca didn't sing. When the pastor began preaching, I felt Becca stiffen beside me. She started cracking jokes that weren't funny in a loud, panicky voice, until Tia Maria leaned over and glared, and we both quieted down for a while.

I don't even remember what the pastor was talking about. I was thinking about one of my classes, biding my time, trying not to let any childhood memories sneak in. Suddenly I realized Becca had started crying. I put my arm around her, unsure of what more I should do, and then she bent over and held her stomach like she was in pain. She began moaning and I really started to worry, and then she stood up abruptly.

I thought she was going to make a break for the door, but she staggered toward the front of the church instead. Tia Maria got up and helped support her when she nearly fell down several times, but then she seemed to get her legs under her and started running.

She never once looked back after leaving me there in the last row. Alone. Never more alone.

Chapter 13: Kate

We're now playing the anti-morale game. Something has opened up inside Becca and she can't seem to close it off again, even if she wants to. She's been talking about her father all morning, after a night of little sleep. I tell her to rest and she quiets for a few minutes, but then the stories start again, each one worse than the last.

"It usually happened on Sunday mornings, I'm not sure why. It used to trip me out, how he could do what he did to me, then walk into the church all energetic and full of passion. He would just bounce when he was onstage, preaching in his perfect Spanish with the accent everyone said was like heaven to listen to from a gringo. People rushed the stage sometimes, so eager to meet the Lord at one of his services. He preached for ten years and traveled all around the country.

"I was afraid all the time. Terrified that my mother would find out and kick me out of the house like he told me she would. Paralyzed by the fear that what he said would come true — that the whole church would turn their back on me, that my family wouldn't accept me, that I would never be able to go home if I told anyone. He told me he and mom would leave me in Guatemala and go back to the United States if I told."

Becca sounds so detached, staring off into a distance far greater than the wall four feet away. I wonder if she knows she's crying?

"But toward the end Sunday wasn't enough I guess, and one Saturday mom came home early from prayer meeting and caught him, and the world came crashing down on us. She'd had no idea and started yelling. He went ballistic and hit her. Matt had been at a youth meeting and came in a couple minutes later. He tried to step in front of mom and dad hit him so hard he knocked him across the room and broke Matt's collarbone."

I went to Amal for help two days ago. He took one look at Becca and said it was most likely malaria, and that I shouldn't worry because only about twenty-five percent of his people die from it.

My fist clenched and I paused for one sweet instant, wondering what the consequences would be of punching him, then I took a breath and left without waiting for permission.

I thought for sure she'd die that first long night. I held her and kept wiping the sweat off of her with a rag Fatima brought. She replenished our water bowl over and over through the night, until sometime near morning we ran out of water altogether.

I heard Muhammed yelling when he got up. There was no water to clean himself before his morning prayers. I watched through the open door as he hit Fatima so hard she flew several feet before hitting the ground. She didn't make a sound.

That morning Amal sent MJ off on foot for medicine since we didn't even have a donkey cart. Somehow he found quinine, and Amal told me it would help, but every time I give it to her she vomits.

"I don't know what got into him that night. He was usually so controlled, even when he punished Matt with the belt, all the while explaining it was for his own good. But he went wild, swinging at anything that moved. He tore the house apart when we were all on the ground, then ran out the door.

"Our housekeeper and gardener lived in an apartment at the back of our property and heard the racket, and when they came in — you should have heard them. They wouldn't call the police. The joke in Guatemala is it's better to make a deal with the thief than call the police. But they called the elders, who all came right over."

I try to shush her, wiping her down with warm, dirty water, unable to do anything else. Fatima sits just outside our door, gently humming as she prepares rice.

"Mom went into another room with them while Tia Maria took Matt and me to her apartment and cleaned our wounds. I guess I was in shock because I don't really remember the next part.

"We flew to the States and moved in with my mom's folks. It was awful. You should have seen the looks we got. In school. In church. Even the gas station. It was a very small town, very religious.

"My mom tried I guess, but I would hear her crying — weeping really — every night. It was mostly Aunt Bertie who looked after us from then on."

She's shivering so hard her teeth are chattering, and I try to hush her, but she seems determined to finish the story. I pull her up on my lap and rewrap the blankets around her.

"One time we were in the grocery store and a church member came up and told mom she shouldn't have said anything, that the Lord was doing such mighty things through my father that she should have kept quiet. Maybe sent me to live with my grandparents. Maybe been a more satisfying wife for him. Anything but ruin such a wonderful ministry. 'You should forget what lies behind and press forward,' she said.

"I don't know how we made it through. High school is a blur. I drank a lot and smoked weed. Matt put me in counseling when I tried to kill myself after graduation."

She says it so matter of factly, her voice low but fairly steady, that I think at first I must have misheard. She wields one blow after another, slamming down stories she'd not told me in all these weeks. Stories of pain that hit me like physical blows, now that I care for her so deeply.

I'd known they had a difficult childhood, but I had no idea just how bad it'd been. Her father was a monster, and I feel ashamed for thinking she was only so certain about God because she'd never faced something truly challenging.

"My counselor thought we should go back to Guatemala. I was terrified, but Matt thought it was a good idea and said he'd go with me. We went and I met God again. He'd been there patiently waiting for me to come home — and it was like I could breathe again for the first time in years.

"When we got back to Portland my counselor told me I'd taken a step backward, and if I was going to avoid my problems by taking a destructive, delusional turn, she couldn't treat me anymore. So I found a different counselor and enrolled at Portland State. I took one step at a time. But I lost Matt in Guatemala. It was never the same.

"I think he might have pulled through eventually, but his fiancé was the final straw. I was mad at God too, don't get me wrong. Plenty mad. I spent years with a ball of bitterness and anger that grew and grew — we made that stupid pact that he won't ever let me forget — but my anger ball kept growing until it exploded, whereas Matt's just settled good and solid in his gut. He's still nursing that tight little ball of hate."

It's weird hearing her talk about my best friend this way — kind and jolly, life-of-the-party Matt. But I think she's right, sometimes he gets a look in his eyes and I know it's time to disappear for a while. There are topics I've learned never to broach with him. It's weird, too, hearing her talk about herself, describing a person I've never met. She's not that person anymore.

"I wish he'd let it grow just a bit more and explode, then he could move forward. But he was always more controlled than I was. I've always been wild, emotional, over-dramatic, prone to excess. But I think it's my excess that saved me. I couldn't just be mad at God, I had to show Him how mad I was by flaunting it in His face. Thank God for His mercy, He put boundaries around me even in my rebellion."

She stops and it's so quiet I don't even hear the usual animal sounds outside. All of a sudden she seems to remember I'm there. She turns her gaze from looking out the open door and stares right at me with a fierce intensity in her fever-glazed eyes.

"I'm sure Kate, I'm one hundred percent sure of God's goodness and His care for me. He cared for me when my father was abusing me. He cared for me when I was questioning His goodness. He cared for me when I rebelled. And He cared for me when I came home running.

"There is nothing that would shake my faith in God's goodness. So if that's the case, if you can understand that, then maybe you can understand why this isn't much different. I know for a fact that He allowed this to happen. Maybe He even caused it to happen. My choice is to continue to follow the God whom I know, the God who has proven Himself to me time and time and time again — or decide maybe this one time, in this one moment, He was asleep at the wheel and didn't see this coming. "

....

She fell asleep for a while, but the fever has returned with a vengeance. I don't know what to do. I wonder if she know's she's dying? Is that why she won't stop talking? Is she trying to make some kind of last confession?

I wonder, too, if Amal knows she's dying but hasn't bothered to fill me in. We moved as usual the second day she was sick, but instead of coming to our normal empty village, the men set up several tents right smack in the middle of the desert. We've not moved since.

"It's too painful to be aware of how the world really is and keep going, to see children who've been drugged by their mothers, lifelessly laid out on the ground as their mothers hold their hands out. You walk past that every day with the tiniest bit of heart and you go mad.

"Lots of my NGO friends don't know God, they're just kind, good-hearted people trying to make the world a better place. So they don't always cope well — they have unsafe sex as frequently as possible. They gamble. They take drugs and drink to excess. I've lost more than one friend who's gone into unnecessary risk because they had a death wish."

Out of nowhere Becca starts choking, and I get her turned just in time to spew a small stream into the bowl Fatima holds steady. I don't know how she got here so quickly, last time I looked she was at her post sitting in front of the open door. She sits outside day and night, only moving when Muhammed sees her and flies at her, yelling and kicking. But inevitably when he moves away or falls asleep she creeps back.

Becca starts again, her voice scratching out in a barely audible whisper. "Just last month I watched a dear friend do it. He couldn't take it. The pain was too much. Several of us tried to get him to go home, take a break, see a counselor, at least pop up to Cyprus to the beach for a week. Anything to get away and get some rest, some perspective.

"It killed him. Sure, it was a gang who did the deed, but he provoked the situation. He didn't need to go there, certainly not at night and most certainly not alone. He went into that alley supposedly looking for a little girl he'd heard about, but he was really looking for an end to the pain."

She starts crying and I can do nothing. Nothing.

. . . .

Fever. Chills. Headache. Sweats. Fatigue. Nausea and vomiting.

Everything listed in tiny print on the side of the box of pills, she has it all. After several days of tragic and horrifying monologues she seems under some kind of compulsion to relate, she stops talking altogether. I think she's worn herself out and I wonder if now she's just waiting to die.

The medicine doesn't seem to be doing anything, and the fever rages a full eight days before it starts to abate.

By then, I've gone through several of the more violent stages of grief — all of it directed at this God of hers. At some point in the week He transforms from a hypothetical to a living force, because I start yelling at Him directly.

We've lived side by side all these months and I've watched her be nothing but faithful to Him. She's been kind and compassionate, doing whatever's necessary to keep me going. She's even following His dumb assignment to try to love our "neighbors."

I'm pretty much always grumpy, and certainly selfish, and I don't care most of the time for the "plight" of our guards because — I feel like I need to remind her — *they're trying to kill us!* But she's even got me feeling slightly sorry for Fatima and some of the others.

Not the mean ones of course, but I feel bad for MJ. She says these guys are more trapped than we are — caught in the cycle of poverty and violence and lack of options and hopelessness, and sometimes I get her point and sometimes I want to say *who cares!*

I don't think she's going to die from this anymore, but she is suffering and I can't stand it. There's no reason for this. No reason at all. On top of where we are, our "set of circumstances" as she calls it, it's excessive.

………．

Becca's fever finally breaks, but it's amazing to me how long it takes her to recover. It was a week before her head unclouded enough to notice I was giving her half my food, and two weeks before she could walk to the bathroom on her own.

I discovered that she's not quite the superhero I thought she was. She is, in fact, quite a horrible patient when she's not delirious. She's rude and impatient, and snippy when she has to be the one on the receiving end.

She hates that she needs my help, and though she never snapped at me once in the first months of our time together, she snapped just this morning when I reminded her to take it easy as she was trying a few light exercises. It was actually pretty cute, and I had to turn around and choke back my laughter so as not to aggravate her more.

It's funny, the more normal humanity she shows and the less in awe of her I am, the closer I feel to her. And somehow in the middle of her illness, Amal and I have made some kind of peace. My heart doesn't race when he knocks at the door to check on her progress.

It has made me feel better somehow, being the strong one for a change, instead of the dead weight she's stuck lugging around.

And still, even in this stage I admire her. Yes, she's more irritable, but she still looks for ways to help and kind words to say to Fatima. Even in her weakness and evident frustration, she pitches in with whatever she can without much complaint.

It's hard to look at her and reconcile the angry, suicidal young woman from her fever stories. It's hard to imagine with the life she lives in Cairo that she still has any level of optimism about the world. Her stories keep recycling through my head, as my brain tries to make some kind of sense of it all.

....

The stomach rumble shakes me from my reverie. I caught another bug a few days ago and need the bathroom with greater frequency. I would love to wait for Becca, but I'm not going to make it and I shudder at the thought of having to sleep with the smell all night if I use the bucket.

I look toward Amal's hut, hoping against hope that the door will open signaling the end of Spanish class. But no, since they were only able to start up again a few days ago, they're taking it more seriously than before.

Thankfully MJ is on duty right now. I call quietly to him with my request in Wolof, and he automatically corrects my pronunciation with a smile as he often does.

We head to the edge of the village, where the bathroom is normally located. This will be the first time I've used it — we only moved here this morning after staying in our tent camp for nearly a month while Becca was at her worst.

Generally the bathroom is a four-cornered thatch fence about neck high, with a small opening in one of the sides that you step through. You look for which corner of dirt in the five-foot square space seems to be wet, and do your business there. Kick a little dirt on it, pour a little water on your hands from the kettle hanging near the opening and you're good to go.

When I think of my pristine bathroom at home, cleaned twice weekly by a sweet Chinese woman before I experienced downward mobility, it can make a tear come to my eye.

As I come back around the corner of the bathroom fence I hear a thump and turn to see MJ crumpling to the ground. Someone looms over me in the light of the full moon, and the last thing I see is his gun coming toward my head.

Chapter 14: Becca

Everything has changed. I don't know exactly what happened while I was sick, but both Kate and Amal treat me differently now.

Kate no longer looks at me with that annoying hero-worship glaze over her eyes — which should make me happy, but instead makes me kind of irritable.

Amal doesn't rave at me as he used to for all the evils of my countrymen. He's calmer. Not as angry. But there is a different kind of fire behind his eyes that I can't quite get access to.

It's frustrating in the extreme. Here I thought I was making great progress with both of them, and then I get slammed with stupid malaria and can't lift my head for a month. I'm tired all the time, and irritable because I can't pull my own weight. And no matter how many different ways I dream up to plant little seeds, neither of them will even pretend to understand what I'm trying to say.

So much for my big chance to bloom where I'm planted — I seem to be withering, and taking them with me.

I'm frustrated that my level of Wolof hasn't risen to the level that I can share with Fatima or MJ, who seem like they'd be the most receptive.

And I'm frustrated with myself, on nearly all levels. Toward the end of my fevers, I had one blinding moment of self-realization when I recognized my efforts to evangelize the whole camp for what they were — a way to control my fear about the situation I'm in. If I could spiritualize this whole thing, it didn't need to be so scary.

It's depressing is what it is. I know good and well I wouldn't feel like such a failure on all fronts if my pride weren't so heavily invested in my efforts. My infernal pride, that can grow in the toughest, driest soil.

As evidence I hold up to condemn myself, I remember that right around about the two-week mark I started being able to go more than twelve seconds at a time without having a shiver of fear go through me, but those twelve seconds free of mortal fear were enough, and my pride started growing.

If Kate or Amal would finally open their eyes — but no, that's not what I actually believe. *If only You would open their eyes!*

No matter how much progress I make toward peace and joy and love and patience and self-control and all that rot, still there is so, so far to go.

....

"Ouch," Kate yells. I look up from where I'm sitting in the dirt next to Fatima and see that Kate has burned herself and is doing a little dance, and shaking her hand for all it's worth. Fatima and I look at each other and burst out laughing.

"Oh good," she yells, "I'm glad you can get some enjoyment out of my pain."

But she says it with a smile, as so often accompanies her words these days. She's changed, and there's something about her smiles that makes me uncomfortable in a way I don't want to think about.

At least Fatima seems the same, but that just might be because we don't yet understand each other completely. I find she's the only one I'm truly comfortable around in my recovery. She and I can sit on the ground for hours, not saying much, just working on our projects. Every so often she'll teach me a new word or phrase.

She taught me how to weave last week, but this morning she's showing me how to string little red dried seeds into a necklace. I've noticed she and the other women wear them, but I'm not sure what the seeds are, or even how to ask.

Even Muhammed seems to have chilled out since my illness. I wonder if he no longer sees me as a threat, or more likely, no longer finds me any kind of attractive in my sallow state.

But an hour ago I discovered that, as so many other things in life, it turned out not to be about me at all. A new guard arrived and Muhammed yelled curses at us and then cheerfully set out on foot. Fatima told me he's leaving us for a new job, so we shouldn't see him again.

I take an instant dislike to the new guard. We've never seen him before, which raises all my red flags, and then as I watch him, my hackles rise even more.

Every time I look over, his eyes are fixed on Kate. It gives me the creeps. I don't like the idea because I know it will worry her, but I decide to tell her to keep her eye out for him.

Fatima clucks and I look down to see I've hopelessly tangled the strings we were working with. Swell. Another thing I stink at.

....

I've been sitting with Amal for three hours, just waiting for him to give up and let me go. I'm so tired my eyes are starting to fog, and I'm pretty sure I just nodded off for a few seconds. Normally he's more observant than this and would have already sent me back, but he's so excited about learning the subjunctive tense that he doesn't notice. And of course I don't want to tell him. I've got to work up my stamina somehow.

I adjust myself on my seat, and he looks up, a half-smile on his face. And I am absolutely astonished by the flash of hate that shoots through me. How can he be smiling at me? He's kidnapped me! He's threatened to have me gang-raped! He calls my brother nearly every week and makes him cry! This is a wretched, horrible little excuse for a man, and I can't believe I ever felt any pity or compassion for him.

His smile wavers and fades, and he quickly looks down at his page. I hope he saw what I was feeling in my eyes. I hope he knows that I know what he is. A murderer. A kidnapper. A liar. A thief. How could I have thought for a second that Amal was becoming somewhat of an ally? I am amazed at my naiveté.

My eyes wander as I try to get control of my breathing, and I see that he's left his knife uncharacteristically near. I think I could easily get to it if I tried. I wonder if I could keep him quiet? I'm sure the new guard would kill Kate or me without a second thought, but I'm not sure about the others. They might hesitate a moment, just long enough.

Could I hold the knife on Amal long enough for Kate and me to get away? Where would we go? Perhaps it's better to escape at night when we'd have longer to walk before they knew we were gone. But if I take the knife I can cut us out of the hut. And defend us from whatever awaits us in the desert. I wonder if I could convince Fatima to come with us and guide us? Or maybe MJ? Perhaps he might be convinced to guide us through the desert? He's not bad, just under some bad influences.

I realize I've been wasting time trying to love these neighbors, what I should have been doing is looking for ways to escape. But I've gotten comfortable, complacent, worried more about their unredeemable souls than about returning to my girls in Cairo. They're the ones who need me, the ones who are open to listening to what I have to say.

I wonder if I can get the knife without Amal noticing? An old and familiar rage is smoldering in the pit of my stomach, making my legs jumpy. I haven't had this much adrenaline in a while, certainly not this much energy. It might be enough to carry us out of here before I collapse.

But do I really want to just sneak out? If I don't take care of Amal, he'll just go on kidnapping. How could I let the authorities know where he's camped?

I wish I could have taken Muhammed out of commission. He's truly evil. And the new guard — there was something about his eyes.

And thinking of him, suddenly, I'm struck by a need to check on Kate. Right. Now. It's an imperative. I never had a chance to tell her about the new guard, and Kate's got another round of Delhi Belly.

The rage drains right out of me, replaced by cold hard fear. I have got to get out of here and check on her.

"Amal," I manage to get out, around the lump in my throat.

He looks up more warily than the last time, and I know he saw something of what I was feeling in my eyes. He doesn't say anything, just waiting.

"I'm exhausted, do you mind if we call it a night?"

Suddenly his eyes change and his face contorts into an expression that looks a lot like guilt. He jumps up and I think he's about to apologize, then he sits down hard with a look of irritation.

"Yes that's fine," he says. "I suppose you are still too weak for a full session. We'll pick this up tomorrow."

I stand, waiting for him to accompany me as always, but he appears to be already reabsorbed by his studies. He makes a vague motion with his hand that I interpret as the command to go.

....

When I step out into the fresh air, I notice that the guard isn't at his post. Since Amal didn't escort me to the door, I realize that I could make a break for it right now if I wanted to. But can I get Kate and get out before the guard returns?

I walk quickly to our hut, spurred by some vague need. When I open the door, I see that Kate is not inside. The fear that latched onto me earlier flames into all-out panic. I turn and look wildly about. The moon is full, so I can see more than normal, and certainly my night vision has gotten better living without electricity, but still I don't see her in any corner of the village and I don't know where to look.

I can feel the fear rising, obscuring my ability to think clearly, when I hear something from the direction of the bathroom. I yell for Amal and start running.

I get around the other side of the bathroom fence and an image burns into me — Kate's terrified and bloodied face lit by moonlight, struggling futilely under the weight of a large figure, who seems to be grappling with his pants.

Before I even know what I'm doing I've let out a shriek and flown at him. With the force of my rage, if not actual body weight, I manage to knock him off of her and we go tumbling.

I hit as hard as I can, yelling like a mad woman. Maybe MJ will hear and come to our rescue; I doubt Fatima could stand against his size but she might try to help.

I can just barely hear Kate crying over the blood roaring in my ears, and it unaccountably doubles the rage inside of me. I swing at him with a force I didn't know I had, and feel a satisfying crunch.

But still it is not enough. He is twice as big, and has me pinned in less than a minute. He brings his gun up with a look in his eyes that says he's going to knock my head clean off. My left arm is pinned painfully under his knee, but I manage to throw up my right. The gun comes down, I hear a crack and an ocean of pain crests over me. And then nothing.

Chapter 15: Amal

It is such a relief to focus again on intellectual pursuits. Studying Spanish with Becca quiets the voices that threaten me on every side when I'm not studying — the worry about whether I can control the men, or whether my grand experiment will fail. Fear for my future, and despair at what kind of future is possible for a man like me. Attacks of conscience that paralyze me.

I feel guilt for the horrible things I tell her brother. He cried when I told him about the malaria — he hasn't cried in months. I get harsher and harsher with him in order to resolve this. He is not coming to the number Diadji wants as fast as I want him to; it is as simple as that.

Diadji is happy, he thinks the process is going perfectly, and is already scheming about franchising our ideas. I just want it to be over. I know Matt could get the money if he really wanted to — I had one of my men go into town and look up the company he works for after hearing Kate mention it during one of my eavesdropping sessions.

I am both furious at him, and guilt-ridden for what I'm doing to him, which makes it difficult in the extreme when we talk. I wonder if he thinks I'm bipolar.

I snuck to their tent every night of Becca's fever, and heard her telling stories that chilled my bones. And now I find myself in a position I never expected — I am ashamed. Ashamed of my countrymen, of Oumar and Diadji, of the decision to kidnap and imprison innocent women as a money-making opportunity. I am ashamed to have any part of it.

I know from my research what her illness did — it humanized them — as if they weren't well on their way to that state beforehand. And now there is no going back.

All of these conflicting thoughts are silenced as I study. I can focus on that one, good part of my brain, and forget all the others. I can dream about a life in Spain — never again will I give my soul to a country as I did America, but I can easily imagine a life much better than the one I lead now.

I am completely absorbed when Becca moves and I look up, smiling. Her eyes nail me to my chair — she's looking at me as if I were the devil himself, crawled up out of hell to commune with her.

It is so far from the expression she usually gives me that I feel sick.

I can't concentrate on the problems in front of me, the text wavers in and out. My mind is racing, trying to remember what I could have done to cause this change, before it grinds to a halt when I realize the truth.

So. Finally, she's decided to treat me as I deserve. I guess it is to be expected. I imagine it will make our dealings easier, since her kindness only added fuel to my guilt. But I feel bereft, losing something I didn't realize I valued.

"Amal," she says stonily. I gather my courage and look up, expecting the worst.

"I'm exhausted. Do you mind if we call it a night?"

And there it is again, the shower of guilt. I shouldn't have kept her here this long — she's still in recovery. I leap to my feet, starting to mumble "I'm sorry" before I clamp my tongue down over the words. I am in charge, not her. I will not be made to feel this way. I sit back down, pretend to focus on my work, and wave her away.

When the door closes I lay my head on my desk. What am I going to do?

Maybe a minute goes by, and then I hear Becca scream. I'm through the door and to their hut in seconds, but neither of them are there. I look around, confused, and see not a single guard on duty. The others are asleep, unmoved by a woman's cry. I storm over and kick them, then hear screaming coming from the bathroom.

I grab one of the guns and run. When I come skidding around the corner I see Kate on the ground crying, and Solaiman on top of Becca.

His gun is coming down with lethal speed, and my heart stops. But she's put her arm up to block the blow, and an instant later I hear the sickening sound of bone crunching. I aim the butt of my gun at Solaiman's head and bring it down with as much force as I have in me.

He crumples to the side, and I kick his legs off of Becca. She's screaming, and when I bend down I can see why. Bone gleams brightly in the light of the moon, and when I move closer she tries to back away. The movement causes the bottom half of her arm to fall off her chest and dangle loosely. She screams even louder for a long, agonizing moment, and then passes out.

I look over at Kate, who's just picking herself up off the ground, eyes wide and focused on Becca. She's got blood streaming down her forehead. There's another body crumpled a few feet away in the shadows. I think it's Tariq, but can't be sure.

What am I going to do? My mind freezes, and I feel the beginning of panic rumbling in my gut. I don't know how long I stand there unmoving, but suddenly I realize Kate is standing right in front of me, yelling. She shouts my name and it is as if she's slapped me, enough to get my brain working.

First things first, we need to get her to my hut. I've got a few medical supplies in there. Nothing for this magnitude of injury, but at least we can lay her out on my cot. I think I've still got some of the bottle of whiskey Oumar gave me at the start of the job.

"Fatima," I roar, and when she responds I realize she's already at my side. I order her to boil some water and she scurries off. Just as she rounds the corner Abdoul stumbles toward me. I yell for him, and with his help, start to grab Becca.

Her arm comes loose and starts to swing sickeningly, but then Kate is there, holding it firm. The three of us manage to get her into my hut and onto my cot, then I send Abdoul out to check on Tariq.

I'm left in the small hut with Kate and I pause again, wondering where to start. The arm is bleeding, but not profusely, thankfully. But I honestly have no idea what to do. My eyes cast about, looking for something to help, and land on my sat phone. I decide it's worth the chance of calling, although I'm not supposed to use it for anything but emergencies. But if this isn't one, I don't know what is.

I don't know if I wake Oumar, but I can tell from his tone that I'm certainly disturbing him. I briefly explain what's happened, that the new man he sent out has attacked and severely injured one of the women. He sounds worried and asks which one, and I briefly consider lying as I realize it makes a difference to him. But I know he would find out easily enough.

"It's Becca."

He laughs, "Amal, you had me worried. You have told me we will be lucky to recoup the cost of her housing, I'm certainly not going to waste money or take the risk of sending a doctor out there."

I am seething, but keep a tight reign on my voice. "What should I do with Solaiman?"

"Shoot him for all I care. You're in charge of security on your own project. I'll send you out somebody new in the morning. Thanks for the update. I'll expect a full report tomorrow."

He hangs up before I have a chance to think of another reason, any reason, to convince him to send a doctor. I have no idea what to do. I can try to set it as I saw once in a health video in school. Or I can cut off her arm. I'm almost positive those are my two options. I might not have a choice anyway — I have no antibiotics, nothing sterile to wrap the arm with.

I look at Kate, her pale face staring at Becca with intensity. I don't think I have the stomach for cutting the arm off just yet. Perhaps if I try to set it and stop the bleeding, I can send one of the men to a local village tomorrow and ask for help. It breaks some of our protocols, but I can't do any less.

Becca is starting to come around, moaning, and Kate's eyes whip up to mine. What am I going to do?

I don't have a choice. I dig under my bed and come up with the whiskey bottle. I hand it to Kate. "Try to get her to drink as much of this as possible."

It takes a moment for her to move, but then Kate seems to understand. I turn to pick up the sat phone again with my other hand, and realize I never set it down. I dial a doctor friend in Dakar, put him on speaker phone, and he explains to me step by step what I must do.

It is one of the most horrifying experiences of my life. Kate only gets a few sips down Becca's throat before she passes out again, but she comes around when I set her arm. She screams in a way I will never forget, and then knocks out cold. She's still not bleeding much, which my friend confirms is a good thing.

Kate follows my orders without question. She gets the water Fatima has boiled over the fire and we apply as sterile a dressing as we can manage.

I'll send someone at first light to try to find the medicine my friend recommended to help with the infection that will no doubt come. Over her objections, I use the last of the alcohol to clean

Kate's head wound. It's not large, but it's fairly deep. Then we sit down side by side against the wall of the hut and wait for morning.

Chapter 16: Matt

The wait is slowly driving me insane. Or rather, trying to live a normal life as I wait, trying to not let my imagination get the better of me. I regret every one of the movies I watched over the years that filled in images I can't help but re-see in my nightmares.

Amal and I usually talk about once a week, although he went three weeks without calling one time. That nearly killed me. When he finally called I yelled at him, and he apologized politely. He said he'd had to order parts from Germany to fix his phone. Ken is with me sometimes, but doesn't ever speak. We tried to have him take over negotiations, but Amal wouldn't hear of it. He said we had a rapport, and why mess with that? So I call Ken after each conversation with Amal, and we meet and debrief.

The negotiations seem to be taking forever, but Ken assures me that this is very normal, and all part of the delicate process. You can't accept the first offer, nor even the fiftieth. You have to follow the established protocol or they'll start sending body parts. You have to come to agreement on a number that benefits you both. A number the market can bear, so everyone wins and no one gets too greedy.

How he and Amal talk about this like a business, with profit margins and expense ratios, makes me want to strangle them both sometimes.

It's also hard to reach these agreements in ninety second or less phone calls, which is all Amal will ever stay on the line, and which we can never trace. Another reason, Ken says, that we can count on his professionalism. He won't get mad one day and kill the girls.

Of course, I'm also completely conflicted about how fast I want these negotiations to go — the closer we get to a number for Kate, the closer we are to a number for Becca that I haven't yet been able to raise. Kate's number is strictly a matter of negotiation between the two sides of this industry, and I'm fairly confident that no one will get killed until her deal is done — but what happens if we make her deal and I don't have the money for Becca? What happens to her then?

Ken also speaks with what seems to me an inappropriate amount of respect about Amal's abilities in that the operatives on the ground haven't been able to pick up hide nor hair of his group. He informs me that half the time, before the negotiations reach their end, his colleagues are able to buy someone off with the amount of money they spread around like water. Or they hear a rumor that leads them to where the hostages are being held. They, of course, try to steer clear of local military since "rescues" led by locals end up killing the hostages half the time.

But with Amal's group, there is only silence.

So what in the world am I supposed to do with the rest of my time?

....

"Hey Aunt Bertie, I've got good news and bad news. What do you want first?"

I don't even bother with small talk, I don't have it in me.

"How about we start with the good," her strong voice answers.

"We're getting awfully close to making the deal for Kate. My friend laid it out as plain as he could for me today. He wishes we had more time for Becca, but morally and ethically he's bound to get Kate out as soon as possible. He thinks from the way things are going it'll only be a couple weeks more."

"That's wonderful news Matt!"

I bite my tongue at the retort just dying to come out. It takes a moment to swallow it, then I continue. "They've come in at just around five million dollars and he thinks, unofficially, that we'll be able to get Becca for half that. Her profile is much smaller, and more importantly, she has no K&R policy. Amal thinks his bosses will be very happy with the deal they've made for Kate and give us a deal for Becca.

"The bottom line is, the second Kate is out of that camp, not only do we lose our best chance of keeping Becca safe, but our chances of recovering her at all go down considerably. So far I've been able to beg, borrow and steal a million and a half, but that's it.

If there's anything else you can do to get some money together, now's the time I need you to make it happen."

"I know you don't want to hear this Matt…" Her voice is so hesitant that I know exactly where she's going, "but we could call your father."

Even under these circumstances, where she might just be right if you can just manage to remove all emotion from the equation, by mentioning him she may as well have punched me in the gut. It takes me a moment to recover my breath, and twice as long to speak.

"If you want to call him, I won't stop you. Becca's life is worth it, but I can't be involved. I just can't."

My phone beeps and I look down to see Amal is calling. "I've gotta go Aunt Bertie," and dump the call.

. . . .

I hear Ken's key in the door, then his slow, steady stride down the hall. He made me give him a copy after the last binge, and he rarely bothers knocking.

"Becca's got a compound fracture." I say dully, reporting the contents of Amal's call, and the reason I texted him to come over.

"He actually sounded like he felt bad about it. He said they didn't have a doctor available, but he spoke to one over the phone and Kate helped him set the bone. He urged me in the strongest terms to work on her payment because he's not sure how long they'll be able to stave off infection. He said they'll cut her arm off if an infection starts, and hope that is enough. He didn't even end with his usual threats, he just hung up."

I repeat the words without emotion, devoid of the sense of horror I'd felt when Amal's voice was on the other end of the line. There is none of the nausea that caused me to bend over and lose my breakfast right in the middle of the kitchen the moment he hung up.

Ken sits down heavily beside me on the couch and hands me a cup of coffee. Small. Black. I hate the taste, but I need the caffeine, and he's picked up on the fact that I can no longer order the bells and whistles coffees I used to take for granted.

We sit in silence and sip our coffees. I forget sometimes that this must be old hat for Ken, something he's heard a version of over and over again. How can you continue to be so close to this kind of thing and not lose your humanity? It's different than hearing about it on

123

the news. Different, even, than watching a realistic movie or even a youtube beheading video.

Knowing it's real, that it's happening in the real, honest-to-God world. Knowing the person. Knowing it's Becca who's alive and in pain, that she just went through a medical "procedure" that I wouldn't wish on my worst enemy; that she might not survive even so — it is more than I can bear.

I suddenly realize that Ken is quietly speaking, and he must have been going on for a while before I keyed into it.

"...Nigeria last April. I've worked six cases in Nigeria, all businessmen, successfully recovered. But this time our client was the daughter of an embassy official, accidentally rounded up with a bunch of girls taken to be war wives. She was just 11, and when we found her, she was barely alive. We did everything we could in the hour it took to get her to a hospital, but..." he stops abruptly, and he's silent a long time. I play with the cigarette pack that is never far from my hands.

"It's the reason I asked for the home assignment for a while. They didn't want to let me — I'm very good at what I do — but the company shrink agreed that it was time to give me a break. This side is just one degree easier to handle."

He's silent again for a while. I don't mind. Neither of us has anywhere to be.

"My wife and I are separated because I couldn't bear it. I couldn't make it work — spending months at a time seeing the absolute worst of humanity, then coming home and listening to my wife talk about renovating the kitchen.

"She tried, she really did. I don't want to make out like it's all her fault. But she had no idea what I was going through, and I didn't like talking about it, even the little bits that weren't classified. So she lived her life like most average Americans. I came home every couple months, and observing her average American life made me sick. I'm not sure we'll be able to make it work. I think our life experiences have veered too far away from each other at this point.

"The last time I saw my daughter she was arguing how she was eleven-years-old and deserved to have a new iPhone like all her friends. She said I was making her life not worth living, that I was a monster.

"I'd just come home from the Nigerian case — and all I could see was that little girl's face, the same age as my daughter. I said things I can never take back."

I'm surprised to find my fingers trembling just a bit as I try to dial the number Bertie gave me. I misdial twice, before finally getting it right. As the phone rings I rehearse what I plan to say, hoping against hope he has a machine.

The news about Becca's arm and Ken's story have pushed me over the edge and given me the courage to call.

By the third ring I have to switch hands because the phone is slick with sweat. On the fifth ring I'm beginning to wonder if I wrote the number down correctly, and then he's there.

"Hello?" Hearing his voice has what I imagine might be the same effect as an apparition suddenly rising from my kitchen floor. I start to tremble, bile rises up my throat, and I nearly drop the phone.

I can't believe I still recognize it — it's been twenty years since I heard it last, but I spent the first fifteen years of my life mesmerized by that voice. I thought he was akin to God himself, and tried to form my speech patterns after his. The smooth voice the Guatemalans called "el voz del Espiritu" — the voice of the Spirit.

"Hello?" he says again and I realize I've forgotten to speak.

"Hello Dad."

Silence. Thirty seconds pass, but I'm determined not to be the one to break first.

"Matthew?"

I bite my tongue, cutting off my automatic correction. Then I decide I don't care and say it anyway, "Matt. Nobody calls me Matthew anymore."

Silence.

"Well if this isn't a day I never thought would come. Must be frozen over somewhere warm and toasty."

He remembered. That's what I'd yelled at him across the courtroom — when hell freezes.

"Trust me, I wouldn't be calling if there was any other choice."

Another pause.

"How are you son?"

Is it just my imagination, or did his voice crack at "son?" No matter, I've got work to do and it won't get done if I don't get started.

"How I am is not why I'm calling. Aunt Bertie said she called you to let you know what's going on with Becca. I'm calling to tell you the criminals holding her are demanding three million in ransom. I've worked every angle I can, and have only come up with half that. I'm calling because her life is at stake, no more no less. I think you know I wouldn't have called unless it was that serious."

The silence stretches and I can almost see him contemplating, taking it in without breaking a sweat. He used to pride himself on not overreacting to difficult news — he once told me it was a sign of a serious lack of faith to react to news, no matter how dire, in any but a calm and rational manner. One of the many things I had to relearn as an adult.

"I'm not sure if your mother has told you what my life is like, but I often have trouble making rent. It's just a room in a house I share with five other men, but it's still difficult when you have trouble keeping a job. Not many people want to hire a registered sex offender."

It surprises me how easily that title rolls off his tongue. Then I realize it's not an admission on his part, just what he's been labeled. As far as I know, he still doesn't admit to actual wrong doing, only to being misunderstood.

I realize he's still been oozing forward in the same smooth voice of my childhood, spinning webs of half truths and outright lies.

"…so I don't see how I can help you. I can barely keep myself fed. Although, now that I think about it, I do have a couple things going that might turn into something next week. If you give me your number I'll give you a call. I'm sure I can help if my plans work out as I expect they will."

"That's about what I was expecting."

He doesn't say anything, and I find I want to hang up now and go take a shower, but I have one more duty.

"Please don't forget what Bertie said about the media — if this gets out it will harm Becca's chance of surviving."

"I remember. I haven't told anyone. Not that I've got a big list of friends to chat with."

More silence. "Listen son, if something happens to Rebecca — God forbid — but if something happens, I was wondering if you'd be interested in getting together sometime? Catching up? I've got a couple things you might be interested in. I just need a little capital to get me going, and it sounds like you've got a good amount together."

I hang up the phone and deflate. All that effort, all the stress and the tiny sliver of hope I'd allowed myself to have, and he is the same old swindler.

He was my last chance, and he's found a fresh, new way to betray me.

Chapter 17: Kate

I'm just rewrapping Becca's arm as gently as possible, trying to think of something positive to say about the angry red streaks just starting to creep out of the wound, when Amal comes to the open door and knocks, as much as one can on a stick-and-grass doorframe.

"May I enter ladies?" He has the oddest sense of humor.

We sit side by side, unsure of what is coming, but sure it's something momentous. Things have been very strange in the camp the last few days. And just now we heard the Land Rover return, this time without Oumar.

"Ms. Wade, I am pleased to inform you that our business transaction has been completed. Mr. Sullivan has come through as you said he would, and we are going to take you to the transfer point this evening. By tomorrow you may no doubt be returned to the vulgar soil of your beloved America. May I suggest you never return to ours and that you reiterate to Mr. Sullivan what I have already tried to convey, that time is running short for his sister. I will give you five minutes to say your goodbyes."

He turns and exits, shutting the door behind him.

Neither of us speak. I'm in shock. I had begun to think this day would never come. But more than that, I never dreamed I'd be leaving on my own. I can't believe this is happening.

As usual, Becca seems to have it a bit more together. She squeezes my hand and leans over and wipes the tear rolling down my cheek. I hadn't realized I'd started crying.

I know I should be over the moon, but a surprising sadness overwhelms me and I close my eyes and let the tears come. She surrounds me in an awkward hug. I know I should say something as I feel time slipping away, but what can I say?

You saved me? Thank you? I love you? How trite.

I lay my forehead against hers for a minute, saying nothing, but eventually I lift my head so I can see her eyes. I see such affection there, feel the kindness in her touch and remember all the times she's cared for me so selflessly in these past months. Even now she holds me with her good arm, the sling we rigged up just barely protecting the barbarous fix we engineered only a week ago. All for defending me again.

How can I leave her here alone? Part of me would rather stay and take my chances; at least we'd be together.

And for just an instant I don't care about anything else as I allow myself to feel for the first time how much I love her, how much I can't stand the thought of leaving her here alone. It's just her and me in this silent moment, and I lean forward and kiss her with all the love in my heart.

Her gasp and immediate separation breaks me from the fog, the look of surprise in her eyes like a knife through my gut.

How could I have forgotten myself so completely?

The door bursts open again before I have a chance to think of a way to fix things. Scarface reaches in and grabs my arm, and suddenly I'm filled with panic thinking I'll never see her again, never be able to explain what she means to me.

I thought surely she had guessed, though I'd never said anything. But seeing the look in her eyes, I realize it came as a complete shock. And it's obvious she doesn't feel the same.

But as Scar hustles me along, I realize it doesn't matter if she will never reciprocate, I love her deeply.

"I love you" I whisper as I pass through the door. Her widened eyes watch me the whole way, and I'll never forget the horrified look in them.

. . . .

US Bank Tower
Portland, Oregon

I immediately develop a strong dislike for Dr. *please call me Beverly* Kolms, mainly because her office smells like money. Well, to be fair, the whole building smells like money. And the elevator ride all the way up to the 41st floor, complete with a man paid to stand there all day in a silly uniform and push the buttons for you. An elevator not much smaller than the huts I recently called home.

Everything about this place pushes my own buttons and I'm fairly vibrating with fury by the time *Beverly* comes out of her office and walks up to me with a friendly smile and handshake.

Now that we're inside her office I can't decide what unnerves me more. The silence? The feel of the soft and supple leather chair I'm sitting in? The unbelievable view of the Morrison and Hawthorne bridges out the panoramic windows? The pleasingly faint scent of vanilla?

Or maybe it's the locally-sourced, ethically-produced, organic scone that the secretary brought in, sitting untouched on the table in front of me beside the also untouched large, triple shot, soy, no foam, hazelnut cappuccino Matt ordered for me at Sisters before we walked over here. The barista asked me what I wanted, and when I didn't reply Matt rattled off my old favorite. I'd carried it here, but hadn't taken a single drink.

Matt's supposed to pick me up again in two hours to walk me to my daily medical check-up, everything so neatly and efficiently arranged here in the Pearl.

The doctors at the American base in Germany only kept me for six days. The time blurred — medical tests interspersed with interviews from State Department Todd who had all kinds of questions about the Fist of Allah. Usually those interviews ended when I fell asleep, but at least twice he touched on a topic that started me yelling about why they weren't rescuing Becca and I had to be sedated.

Since all my medical issues were relatively minor, and since they knew I'd be more comfortable recuperating with loved ones, the doctors had signed off on sending me on to Portland with a sack full of broad-spectrum antibiotics, de-wormers, anti-anxiety meds, multi-vitamins and the like. I was to check in every day at a clinic near Matt's apartment for a couple weeks to monitor my progress.

As usual, I got off easier than Becca. I'd described her issues to one of the more sympathetic doctors, and he'd informed me she might need surgery on her nose, but most definitely a couple surgeries on her arm — and even with that she might not get back her full range of motion. That on top of chronic, lifelong malaria which can flare up in moments of high stress.

That's of course assuming she gets out, which is an open question. The K&R company arranged for a private plane, which I

131

would have enjoyed in another lifetime, and I flew home in style with Matt's friend Ken and State Department Todd taking turns questioning me.

Through it all, Matt just held my hand and cried.

At one point I exploded and Ken conceded to explain to me Becca's position, which is all kinds of not good. The official debrief is supposed to happen sometime this week, but I could tell Ken and Todd were conspiring to record any tidbit that fell from my mouth.

So this is my life now. Eight days ago I was in a hut in North Africa, with no immediate hope for the future. Today I am in a soft leather chair in a peaceful office sitting in silence while an hourly rate ticks by that is probably higher than the cost of all the food they gave us in six months of captivity.

It's unbearable.

I wonder how much longer I have to sit here. I used to be able to measure quarter hours for billing purposes down to the second in my head, but that kind of time watching ceased to have meaning months ago, and I find I can no longer accurately judge its passing. I want to check the clock on the wall I see out of the corner of my eye, but I don't want her to see me doing it.

I'm literally starting to sweat just sitting here. How long has it been? All *Beverly* did was introduce herself and then we both sat down. I steal a sideways peek at her and see she's looking out the windows as well.

I guess it's a pretty good gig if you can get it. Matt said the Stump arranged for me to visit two hours each morning for a month, then we'll go to three times a week for the second month, and twice a week for the third. Then I should be cured, is, I believe, the implication.

I wonder if the K&R company has an actuarial table for my type of case — how long does it take to put a broken kidnap victim back together? Five hundred hours of intensive therapy with the region's premiere trauma and PTSD counselor.

But there's gotta be an asterisk on the table for broken kidnap victims who leave behind a loved one to continue suffering and maybe die whilst they eat locally-sourced, ethically-produced, organic scones and sleep on Tempur-Pedic mattresses. That's gotta add at least 100 hours to the therapeutic prescription.

All of a sudden I'm so angry I can't sit for one second more. I bolt out of the chair and start pacing. I don't care what Beverly says, I don't care about getting better, I just want the images to stop.

The guard's face as his gun comes at my head. That hellish night in Amal's hut trying to set Becca's arm. Waking up to the abject terror of a viper sliding across my leg. Unspeakable thirst. Vomiting blood while Becca holds my hair back. Oumar and Scarface and the other faces of evil incarnate. Washing out the same dirty rag every morning to use when I had my period, until I stopped having it altogether. Trying to hold Becca still when her malarial fevers caused her to shake so much her teeth rattled. The first time I realized I ate rat. Trying to get sand out of my teeth. Waking to the sound of gunfire. The way your body shakes in the back of a donkey cart. The moment you realize you have lice. The tomb-like feel of the blindfold. The dead face of Fatima's baby girl.

When I come to I'm on the floor, rocking back and forth, and I don't recognize the sound coming out of my mouth. Beverly is on the floor next to me rubbing my back, and I recognize a thawing in the way I feel about her when I see the wrinkles already appearing in her fine linen pantsuit.

She's put a box of Kleenex in front of me. Lotion Kleenex. Are you kidding me? A picture of an old newspaper we were so pleased to find and use flits across my mind and I feel sick. Is there nowhere I can look that doesn't remind me? I don't want to touch lotion Kleenex, so I scrub my face with my sleeves.

"I don't know what I'm supposed to say here."

"Kate, I want you to know that I have walked with a lot of people coming out of similar situations, and I can tell you there is no right way to do this. You aren't *supposed* to say anything. You *can* talk about anything you'd like to talk about in here. Whenever you want to. At whatever pace. There's no pressure here Kate. You're safe in this space."

Safe. Yeah right. I stare at the Kleenex box.

"Whenever you feel comfortable you can begin," she continues, "but there's no rush."

You want me to feel comfortable? Maybe you should set up your couch in a grass hut in the middle of the desert, and bring in special, locally-sourced bugs to bite my legs while we drink brown water. I look again at the scone, and feel as intense a loathing as I've ever felt for an inanimate object.

I know she's right, I have to talk to someone. And I realized this morning that it can't be Matt. I answered a very casual question on the way here about what we normally ate for breakfast, and the blood drained from his face.

I knew instantly that he was closed off from me, that anything I tell him now will be like a sword through his heart, knowing his sister is still enduring whatever I might describe. There is, in fact, nothing about the experience that I can say to him now. And the pain of that realization almost started me crying right then. I was able to hold it together and tell him I needed the restroom, where I cried for ten minutes before getting it together enough to come out again.

I want to talk to Matt. He's my best friend and Becca's brother, which is now of equal importance. But I can't talk to him. It wouldn't be fair. Just one more thing Amal took from me.

So if it can't be him, maybe Beverly can help instead. I know it's what Becca would want. She'd want me to get better. She'd tell me to be brave.

So for Becca, and to be honest, because I'm not sure but I'm not on the verge of going stark raving crackers, I decide to talk. I slowly reach out and grab a lotion Kleenex, and blow my nose long and hard. I wonder if Beverly realizes what a painfully deliberate step this is for me.

I stand up and go to sit in my soft chair, and watch as Beverly performs a delicate maneuver to return to her chair with fewer wrinkles. She picks up her notepad again and looks at me. She must see that I'm willing to talk, but don't know where to begin, because she's ready with a question.

"Why don't you start by telling me why you're not touching your coffee or scone?"

The question startles me. It makes me immediately suspicious, but I don't see how it could do any harm. And I do need to start somewhere.

"I had some dry toast for breakfast. My stomach is still adjusting."

There, I think, that was truthful. Easy.

"So you're not eating this because it will upset your stomach?"

So. Not so easy.

And all at once I decide to go for it. It's what Becca would do. If she was able to be brave with that guard's gun coming down at her arm, surely I can face this hellacious gaping wound in my stomach that no one seems to see but me. Dr. Beverly is one of the best, according to Matt's friend Ken.

"Matt ordered my favorite drink — large, triple-shot, soy, no foam, hazelnut cappuccino. I watched them make it. Clean water. Fresh milk. Sterilized equipment. Clean hands. Gentle music. Air conditioning. Spotless bathrooms. A ceiling high enough that you don't have to stoop. And a line nearly out the door of people staring at their phones, impatiently waiting to pay five dollars for a fancy alternative to a five-cent packet of Nescafe.

"You know what was missing? The dysenteric water you had to walk five kilometers to retrieve. The sand. The bugs you strain out if you've got the energy. The dust that clogs your lungs. The dirty bucket in the corner to relieve yourself. The man with a gun standing over you. Or the sound of Fatima getting her morning beating, without raising her voice because that's just what she expects out of life. Watching her child hang listlessly on her back, and thinking that her life will be exactly the same as her mother's, until she just up and dies!"

My voice raises louder and louder, and I find myself out of my chair again, stalking around the room. I am seized by an intense desire to huck that ergonomically correct chair straight through those perfectly clean plate-glass windows, and I am shrieking.

"I'm not drinking my favorite coffee, even though I actually dreamed about it multiple times over the last six months, because this morning Becca is going to be lucky if she's eating sandy rice with a glass of dysenteric water as a chaser!"

Chapter 18: Becca

"I love you."

Kate's words still echo in the air, just as I can still feel the echo of her soft, tentative lips on mine. I know I should do something. Anything. To keep myself busy, to distract myself. All the things I did for Kate to keep her spirits up.

I should read my Bible. Amal let me start bringing it with me from our lessons months ago. But there it sits in the corner, daily gathering more dust. I find it's a lot easier to leave it lying there, now that I no longer have someone watching my every move. Now that I no longer feel like I'm on some great secret assignment, now that I've failed utterly.

It's been eight days and I've sat here cross-legged on the floor through all of them. Silent. Stunned.

What did I do wrong? How could this have happened? How could I not see that this is what was happening? Again?

I am listless. I am hopeless. I am everything I bossed Kate out of and lectured against us becoming. I lose what little weight I have left to lose. I sleep all day, shiver all night. I don't even wash my face or clean my teeth.

All my ambitious thoughts of being what God wanted me to be in this place — all my hopes of showing Kate a better way, of pointing the way for Amal or Fatima or MJ out of the darkness — lie in the dust at my feet.

And as my spiritual ambitions fade, the old fears find new room to grow. I startle at every sound, and imagine the men plotting against me. I see with renewed focus the lust and hatred mixed in their eyes every time I set foot outside. I even see malice in sweet MJ's eyes when he offers to take me to the bathroom.

Underneath it all I feel the pain in my arm, stronger every day. Fatima now comes in to change the bandages. I haven't looked, but I know the infection must be growing.

I have done nothing right.

How can this have happened?

Against my fervent wishes, my mind drifts to high school.

I'd still been heavily damaged, unable to relate in normal ways, feeling like everyone could see right through me. I was drawn to someone else on the fringe, and we became fast friends. Our damage seemed to mesh, as did our hobbies, and when she told me the night of graduation that she couldn't stand to go another day without telling me she loved me — at first I didn't understand — but then my world tilted.

I'm sure it wasn't sudden for her, but for me it came out of the clear blue sky. And it felt like betrayal at my very core, an abuse of something I held sacred. I hadn't realized I'd had any innocence left to lose after the childhood I'd survived, but I'd been wrong about that as so many other things.

The whole thing terrified me. I'd never felt that way about her, but there must have been something wrong with me for her to feel like that kind of a relationship was a possibility. I told her I didn't feel the same way, got on a bus to Matt's, and we never spoke again.

I know that unnamed terror lives under the water, far down, where I keep it silenced and buried. But as the days pass I find the question rising, echoing out of the deep. I am powerless to keep it down there after all this time.

I'm able to relate on a deep and meaningful level with women friends. I have great working friendships with married men, but I always choose unsuitable single men to place my affections upon.

Somewhere there is still a crack. Deep, deep down, I'm still broken.

....

I've felt something building all day. The men are jittery, for one. Normally at least one of them is asleep at all times, but they're all awake now and huddled around the fire. Amal looks worried. His eyes keep looking west, and soon I see a dust cloud. It's the Land Rover, if I'm not mistaken; the same one that took Kate away — was that only last week? Time is blurring now that I've done away with the routine.

138

Amal approaches and engages in conversation with the driver. It's very animated, and when he turns and looks toward where I'm propped up against the side of my hut, the look on his face absolutely chills me. He finally nods and opens the passenger door to remove two boxes of what look like beer, then walks over to Scarface and says something briefly. He grabs one bottle and walks my way. I move slightly closer to Fatima, who's cooking beside me.

"Becca I've got to go into town. Oumar sent the men some beer as a congratulations for a job well done with Kate, so I've brought you a bottle."

He leans down and hands it to me, before quickly straightening again. "I think it should work to clean your wound. I'll try to get some more supplies while I'm in town."

He's talking rapidly, and won't make eye contact, so I take it he knows exactly what he's doing, leaving me here alone with Scarface in charge.

Then I guess there's nothing to say. Cold washes over me, and I wrap my hand more tightly around the bottle. He strides back to the car without a backward glance, and then he's gone.

I'm alone. If he'd given me a bottle of something stronger I might have drunk myself into unconsciousness to avoid what's to come, but this one little bottle won't do me any good in that department. I slowly stand and start to pull the sling over my neck. When I head into my hut Fatima follows. Her terrified eyes confirm that I'm not being paranoid.

. . . .

The men spend the next couple hours getting progressively more drunk off the two boxes Amal unloaded. I don't know whether it's any good or not, but they certainly seem to be enjoying it. For my part, it burned like fire, and I must have finally passed out because I wake up in Fatima's lap, her hands stroking my hair as her tears drip silently onto my forehead.

Every once in a while someone fires off a weapon. There are a couple fights. Lots of yelling and laughing. MJ seems to be the butt of most of the jokes, as per usual. He drinks slower than the others, but he too is making his way through his share.

Fatime leaves and shuts the door, but I'm drawn again and again to the peephole, even though watching has given me a terrible pain in my stomach. For the first time since it happened, I'm completely distracted from the pain in my arm, and I start praying the same generic, muted *oh God's* of the first couple days.

I watch as Scar gets up, rifles through the boxes, and comes up empty. He yells at no one in particular, then throws his bottle at MJ, standing a few feet away. The bottle hits him in the head, and when MJ drops to the ground Scar laughs. Eventually he goes over and leans down to help MJ stand. Throwing an arm around his shoulder, Scar starts to lead him in my direction. I start to tremble.

Fatima is nowhere in sight. She must be hiding in her hut, trying to stay out of their way. Toothless gets up to follow, grabbing his gun as an afterthought, and weaves along behind them. I slide away from the door into the furthest corner, my whole body trembling. I can feel myself going into shock. I can't believe after all this time this is actually happening.

Oh God, oh Jesus, please don't leave me!

The door bangs open and Toothless comes staggering in and motions me to stand. I slowly get to my feet, but when he motions me over to the door, I find I can't feel my legs. Scar yells from outside, and Toothless strides forward and grabs my arm, then drags me out in front of the hut.

Toothless pushes me forward and I stumble. When I straighten up, Scar is standing so close I can smell him, and a quick glance at his eyes makes me think I'm going to vomit right here and now on his feet.

My brain forces my gaze to skip off of his, looking for some friendlier perch before going crazy, and I focus on MJ. I can't believe he's standing here willingly. I can't believe he's participating in this. He won't meet my eyes, but just looking at him I feel a stab of betrayal.

When Scar sees where I'm looking I can tell he knows what I'm thinking, because he gets a wicked gleam in his eye, grabs MJ and brings him forward. Presumably to go first.

I keep my eyes glued to MJ, repeating my mantra, trying to keep the terror under control. I think about making a run for my tooth cleaning stick, the only sharp object I have. I refuse to go quietly, but I'm certain this will only end one way. Maybe I can at least provoke them into making it end quicker.

I decide to count to three and make a run for it when Scar speaks. "You are alone now!" he growls, his eyes wide and threatening as never before. "We can do anything we want to you, and there is no one who will see. No one who will stop us."

I feel my mouth open of its own accord, and listen with amazement as I have no thought in my head to speak.

"I am not alone."

To my ears it doesn't even sound like my voice, and I'm still trying to figure out why I said it when Scar's eyes bug and he jumps backward, bringing his gun up. The other men look equally startled, bringing their guns up as well, and then they all start backing away and talking excitedly to each other.

They stand at a distance, nervously, for what seems like hours. I have no idea what's going on, but finally I decide to take advantage of whatever this is and start to back up into my hut. I close the door, and spend the rest of the night with my tooth stick clamped tightly in my good hand, rocking and repeating the strange words to myself.

Chapter 19: Amal

Nice Cream
Dakar

The sight of normal people eating ice cream is so bizarre after all these months in the desert that I just sit on the bench against the wall and try to absorb the scene. I used to come to this shop when I was a student. I wonder if Oumar knows that, if he's trying to remind me I now have nothing without the gang. He is good that way, digging the knife in while offering the seeming hand of friendship.

A large group of students comes piling in the door, crisp uniforms, laughing and joking, and I wonder for the millionth time what my life could have been. What I could have done differently to end up on another path than the dead end I'm now walking toward. I've wracked my brain and never come up with another viable solution.

I suppose I could have let myself starve, or jumped in the river, or stolen from a gang and let the end come quickly. That would have freed me from the misery of the last decade. I could have joined a different gang. Maybe tried to gain passage on one of the death boats that make their way for the Spanish coast with only a thirty percent success rate.

This is Becca's last shot, but it is also mine. I sense that's why Oumar made the unusual decision to summon me to Dakar. I wonder if he's set me up, arranged this elaborate scenario — talking up my plans before Diadji, only to have them fail so he had permission for the undeniable outcome. Has he been trying to arrange a reason to kill me?

Why else would he summon me? He's gone out to camp any number of times over the years when we were at further distances. And now we're the closest we've been in months, only a two-hour drive away from Dakar, and tomorrow we're packing up and heading out for the Mali border.

Or is this all just an elaborate power trip? I've seen first-hand how much he loves making those under his command jump through hoops. The most dangerous thing about Oumar is that you never know what he's really thinking.

The bell tinkles and my eyes are drawn up to see Oumar enter, crisp white shirt as usual, aviator sunglasses, buffed upper body from hours at the gym — something that causes all the girls to look his way.

He takes off his sunglasses and winks at them. If only they knew — another area he's in charge of is rounding up girls just like them and selling them off to men just like him in Thailand and India, and maybe even Egypt.

On the surface he appears to fit in here, with all these normal people living their normal lives. This is what I'm fighting for, the chance to live a more normal life. To waste a lazy afternoon in the ice cream shop. He speaks to his guard, then saunters over next to me.

"Amal."

"Oumar."

He is full of himself, giddy with success.

"Congratulations on your recent sale, it seems to have gone off without a hitch. Diadji wanted me to congratulate you on a job well done."

He leans over and hits me on the arm, a little too hard to be strictly friendly. "He would have come himself but he's got another meeting. But he's very pleased with your work on this little test run of yours. He'd like you to wrap things up as soon as possible and come in for some debriefing and planning. Overall you used fewer men, you evaded notice, and we didn't even hear rumors of you around town. Well done, very good job!"

I feel sick. He's talking about the success of our operation, like we just sold a life insurance policy instead of a human being. It's even worse realizing I'm the one who taught him to speak in these terms.

"Thank you Oumar. I appreciate your support of my ideas." I get it out, but only barely, around my clenched jaw.

"So let's wrap things up and get you back to town so we can celebrate and make plans for expansion."

I can't stop thinking about Becca. I know what I will return to, I could see it in the men's eyes when I left. No matter what I said, they were going to go after her the moment my car was out of sight.

I knew it. I knew I was her only protection, and still I left. But what choice did I have? Oumar summoned me. It was her or me. I chose me. Of course I chose me. I don't owe her anything.

Yet unaccountably, I feel shame. An emotion I'm all too familiar with, and one I can never seem to hide from for long.

For all my big talk, all my attempts at professionalism and keeping a certain detachment, I see I am nothing but a common thief, a petty criminal. And a murderer, don't forget that — I killed the guard who attacked Becca and didn't think twice.

I've looked down on Muhammed and Mustafa, and even Oumar, for their violence and their lack of conscience, but at least they are straightforward about who they are. Oumar tells anyone who asks that he is a thug.

I realize the problem lies in spending too much time with Becca. I let her get too close to me, let her spin her web and break down the walls I'd built up around my heart. I grew to respect her and what she does with her life. She has unsettled me on a number of fronts. I find myself swallowing down bile when I think of what is no doubt going on right now.

I'll have to refine my strategy for next time, because of course there will be a next time. For certain, now that I've gotten Diadji's approval. Yet even the thought that there will be a next time sends a wave of despair over me.

In the end I'm fighting to preserve her life, so if she gets knocked around a bit in the process, she should at least be grateful for that.

Oumar sent his driver to get me. There was no refusing that. It was her or me.

And I chose me. Of course I chose me.

. . . .

I stop at a pharmacy on the way out of town to get a first aid kit and at a liquor store for something to clean her wounds. I'm not sure how great her injuries will be, but I've seen before what the men can do when given the chance. At least I was able to finally pick up the heavy antibiotic my doctor friend recommended.

As the camp comes into view, I still haven't decided how to handle it when I discover for sure that the men have disobeyed me. I thought killing one of them would have earned me a little more respect, but I guess I should have known better.

To say I'm surprised when I see Becca squatted down next to Fatima helping her with the dishes is an understatement. The rest of the camp looks to be in an uproar. As expected, there are empty and broken bottles strewn all over the ground.

One guard is walking aimlessly to and fro, dragging his gun carelessly behind him. Another is seated by the fire, rocking and mumbling. Muhammed is still as stone where he sits, staring into the distance. Only Fatima seems unchanged, slowly taking one dish after another from Becca.

It's Muhammed I was most worried about, so I go to him for answers. Surprisingly, he won't meet my eyes. He begins very carefully, telling me they heard a noise last night and went to check on the prisoner.

Yeah right, I think. *Why don't you just be honest about it, you went to rape her. Just as I knew you would.*

But then his voice loses its cool, he raises wild eyes to mine, and starts speaking with great agitation.

"When we brought her outside her door, suddenly there were four huge men standing on both sides of her with swords as tall as a man. They were as big as I have ever seen. They looked like some kind of soldier, but there were no markings on their uniforms."

I notice his hands are trembling, and see the other men have started edging toward us. Mustafa tells me their eyes were blue as the sea. Tariq says the swords were so sharp they pierced even the air. They wore wide gleaming belts over white tunics. Dark complexions. Fierce expressions.

Muhammed breaks through the cacophony of men trying to explain, "I swear, they came out of nowhere, and they guarded her door all night. We weren't sure whether we should kill them, so we backed off and waited for your instructions."

....

By the time I've got the men calmed down and half-convinced they all consumed a bad batch of beer, I turn around and see that

Becca has returned to her hut. I ask someone to go get her so I can talk to her, but not one of them will do it.

I stomp off to her hut, unsure of what I will find and aggravated by the flutter in my stomach while all the men are watching. I'm almost positive they were just drunk, and Becca got off easier than I could have imagined, but my hand still shakes just a bit with doubt as I reach for the door handle.

When I duck down to enter, it takes my eyes the usual few moments to adjust to the darkness, and when I finally make out her form in the corner, I'm startled.

It's like I'm seeing her for the first time. In the car on the way back here I was remembering her as she was when we first pulled her over so many months ago. She was strong, beautiful, healthy, clean.

Now I look at her and feel a wave of shame wash over me unlike anything I've felt since those first days when I left Oumar behind to go with Mrs. Anderson.

She is beyond filthy. Her hair is matted. She's lost so much weight that her cheekbones protrude unhealthily and her nose tilts a little to the left. Her arms are covered in angry red insect bites and the ripped cloth sling holding her arm up is dingy. I don't even want to think about what the skin looks like underneath where I attempted to sew it back together.

I also don't want to think about the unseen injuries. Or how long it will take her to return to normal if she ever gets out of here.

When Kate was with us they were as clean as they could make themselves and their morale was something to admire. I can tell from her expression now that she has lost hope, and it hurts me more than I thought it would. I did this. I took that vibrant woman, out in the world doing good as she said and I now believe, and turned her into this shell.

She looks at me steadily, waiting for me to decide her fate, no doubt, and I find I do not have the energy to even question her. I turn without speaking, and quietly close the door behind me.

Chapter 20: Matt

Mill Ends Park
Portland, Oregon

Sitting here on a sunny day, coffees in hand, children playing in front of us — if I close my eyes and focus, I can almost believe Kate and I have met up for one of our famous Sun Breaks. Whenever the sun would make one of its brief Portland layovers, we'd dash out of the office and talk shop while topping up our Vitamin D.

I can almost believe it, until a car backfires and I look down and Kate is on the ground, her coffee splashed in a wide arc. I just stare, unsure what to do, but she stays down there so long that I finally kneel down and place my hand on her shoulder. I can feel her shuddering.

Last night I took her to her favorite restaurant for dinner. I thought we were having a decent time, considering all the conversational land mines we have to avoid, when suddenly she threw her burger down and shoved her plate away.

She's always been a drama queen, and I was about to make a crack about it being undercooked, but I got a glimpse at her face and quickly asked for the check.

Ken did his best to warn me, but I don't think anything could have prepared me for this. When he talked about it I thought I understood, but it's jarring to see it actually play out right in front of you in someone you love.

Post-Traumatic Stress Disorder. Severe trauma. Survivor's guilt. Ken gave me a fistful of glossy brochures his company had produced. I'd glanced through them initially, but now I study them every moment I'm not with Kate. I don't know what to do, but at least I find comfort in knowing I can put my hand on her back without causing harm.

At least I know the room where she's sleeping, if not the bed. I tucked her in the first night, nice and tight, in the extra plush guest bed in what has always been officially my guest room and unofficially her room, but when I went to check on her in the morning she was asleep on the hardwood floor, with a towel covering her.

She can't seem to bear it, being here safe while she knows what Becca is going through. I thought I had it bad, but now that I see her, I realize there's a higher level of suffering I'm not privy to.

I've asked her to talk to me about it, but she's tight-lipped since those first couple days when she dropped one bomb after another on me. I think she's trying to protect me, but it's keeping her in her own private hell all alone.

At the strangest times she'll break into a story — *Becca was so smart when this happened, Becca never faltered when that came up. I can't believe how strong she was. This one time I didn't think I'd make it, but Becca said such and so.*

It drives me crazy, it's like she's dredging up positive memories for the recently deceased person's relative. It sounds exactly like mourning to me, and I'm not ready to mourn.

....

"Are you not taking me seriously Matt?" Amal's familiar and angry voice rings through the speaker.

"Do you not believe that I am telling you the truth? Your sister is running out of time. The men have already attacked her once, I'm not sure I can keep them off of her again. Besides, I'm not sure how much longer she can survive the infection in her arm."

I have no response.

"My bosses will accept no fewer than three million. You paid five million for Kate Wade, a mere employee. How can you not be willing to pay the same for your own sister, your family, your blood?"

And I can't take it anymore, not one more time.

"I didn't pay that money, the insurance company did. There is no insurance company for my sister. I have called in every favor I can, sold everything I own and can borrow, and 1.5 million is it. I can't go any higher. Please, please! There's nothing more I can get."

"I'm sorry Matt, I can tell you with certainty that that is not going to be enough."

I hang up and put my head on the counter. I'm so tired of this. How much longer can it go on?

I blew through all my ideas for raising money in the first month — I sold all my artwork, cleared out my 401k, and cursed myself up one side and down the other that I'd never been much of a saver.

If I'd owned my apartment I could have sold it, but as I could never have afforded an apartment in the Pearl, and didn't want to live in exile out in Hillsboro where I could afford to buy, here I'd stayed. Throwing money away each month, assuming more could always be earned.

Aunt Bertie and Mom sent what they could, but it was minuscule in comparison to what Amal was looking for.

The money has been cooling its heels in my bank account, waiting for an infusion sufficient enough to end this thing. What Becca could use now is a smarter brother.

. . . .

I still have my head on the table when Kate wanders out in her pajamas. She runs her fingers through my hair on her way by.

"You know," she says as she measures out a spoonful of grounds, "Amal got us coffee sometimes."

I raise my head up and watch her, feeling at once utterly grateful to have her back, and completely hopeless about ever again seeing my sister do something as simple as make coffee for me. It makes me feel like I'm in danger of tearing in two.

"It was, in a word," she stops as she lifts the coffee bag to her nose and sniffs deeply, "foul."

She smiles, and sets the bag down.

"But your sister, she'd always ask me, 'and what are you having today Kate?' And I'd say, well today I'm feeling a little flirty, so I got a full caff caramel macchiato, heavy on the whip. But look, the barista spelled my name wrong!"

She's quiet, filling the kettle with water, then watching until it boils.

"This is a miracle, really. Do you know how much work Fatima had to do to make that foul coffee for us? And when this situation is resolved and we have Becca with us again and we're going on with our lives, Fatima will still be over there searching for firewood, walking five kilometers for dirty water, and boiling up nasty coffee for men who will kick her sooner than thank her."

151

She pours the hot water into the french press, then bends down and puts her face right up next to the glass.

"You remember how I got sick several times on the plane home?" She looks at me, and I nod. It was the only time I let her out of my sight.

"I was on my knees with my face in the toilet, and all I could think was it was the most beautiful thing I'd ever seen. It made me cry, how clean that toilet was."

....

We're lying on the couch later, staring out at the grey sky. Her appointment with Dr. Beverly isn't until the afternoon today, and she's continued this kind of dreamy, singsongy story-telling all morning.

"Becca told me something — not at first, but maybe two or three months in when we knew each other better. She said she prayed as we were tied up in the back of the car that first day, going only God knows where. I was nearly catatonic with fear at that point, but of course Becca would have the peace of mind to pray.

"She said — God, I subject myself to Your will. You have chosen to allow this to happen, I certainly know not why. It's not what I would have chosen in a million years, but I submit to it, Your will be done. In my life and in this experience, as Your will is done in heaven."

I close my eyes. Take a breath against the heavy weight on my chest. You'd think I'd have gotten used to breathing with it after all these months, but sometimes it's still too hard to lift.

"Her counselor got her started doing that," I say.

"Which one," she asks, "pre-Guatemala *clove smoker* or post-Guatemala sweater set?"

Becca is such a private person, I'm amazed at the depth at which she shared — Kate even made quote marks with her fingers as she said "clove smoker," just like Becca does.

I feel a powerful shot of jealousy pulse through me, having previously been the only person who knew many of these stories.

I close my eyes again and breathe in. "Sweater set."

Old Kate would have pestered me for more details. She was terrible with silence and had to fill every moment. It was annoying sometimes, but it's physically jarring trying to get used to so many aspects of New Kate at the same time.

Maybe because she doesn't ask, I continue.

"Becca struggles with control, always has. You can imagine why. So that's a way for her to remind herself who is really in control. Not our father, not the warlords, not even your guy Amal. If she reminds herself God is in control and has allowed whatever situation to happen for whatever reason in His grand scheme of things, then she feels it will be all right. I have to admit, it's gotten her through some pretty rough times."

. . . .

It's raining when we head out for Kate's appointment, and I watch in amazement as she kicks through puddles and does a little jig. Old Kate was more of a stickler about her appearance and taught me what little I know about fashion so that I could pay a little closer attention myself.

New Kate doesn't seem to notice that her hair is plastered to the side of her head. Now that I think about it, she didn't even look in the mirror before we left to see that her clothes didn't match.

I watch from the overhang of a building, waiting for a break in the downpour, but she yells at me to come join her and I think, *why not?*

"It rained one time," she says, with her eyes closed and her face raised to the sky. "Only for like an hour, but it was heavenly. I want to teach you the dance Becca taught me."

And we dance in the rain.

Chapter 21: Kate

US Bank Tower
Portland, Oregon

"It's so strange how Becca would talk. We could be talking about the most mundane thing and she'd drop God in there like it was nothing. I've never known anyone who talks like that. She talked about Him like He was a real person, like He was a friend in one of her many stories. She talked to Him like He was right there in the room when she prayed.

"I didn't mind exactly, especially when she prayed. It gave me kind of a peaceful feeling. It's not like I don't believe in God, I've just found Him kind of irrelevant up to now. My parents are Methodist, but they're the kind that joined a church instead of a country club."

I imitate my dad's gruff voice, "Cheaper, and more opportunities for getting clients."

Beverly smiles and writes something in her ever-present notebook. I've promised myself one of these days I'll swipe it and see how far along she thinks I'm coming in the recovery matrix.

"Mostly I've had kind of a low opinion of Christians growing up. Bigoted, intolerant, killjoys tied to the past — that's pretty much how I was raised. Christians are close-minded and only want to impose their rules on other people. They're outliers, weaklings, odd ducks, and they'll soon be as extinct as the dinosaurs.

"But Becca changed all that. If I'm honest, I'm not sure we would have been friends in any other situation — but as it was, I got to know who she really was, past the snobby labels I'd grown up with.

"I remember this horrible moment I had, after maybe a month — she was talking about some classic intellectual book or other, and I thought for the hundredth time, 'Wow I've never read that!' I

155

realized I'd been looking down on her to some extent, thinking she was some kind of Duck Dynasty and NASCAR enthusiast.

"She'd thought more deeply about a lot of things than I ever had, — she'd been forced to, I think, to some extent because of the different parts of the world and its horrors that she'd seen. All of a sudden I was ashamed of my prejudice. Even if we didn't agree on many fundamentals, I felt like she had a right to her worldview; she'd earned it in the trenches.

"One time we were laughing about what a gossip Fatima was, and she told me she loves gossips, like she loves adulterers and liars and thieves and murderers — because she'd been every one of them, and worse, so why wouldn't she love them? I'm certain she'd say the same about homosexuals, just as I'm certain she would add my *sin* onto the list.

"And still, the kind of God she talked about might be one worth getting to know. I'd certainly go to church with her if she ever comes back."

And then I laugh, and look a little shamefacedly at Dr. Beverly, "Who am I kidding, I'd probably do anything with her that she asked me to. It's tenth grade all over again and I've got a crush on Samantha Keene even though she's dating the senior quarterback."

Dr. Beverly looks up, sighs and smiles a little, "But it's not the same is it? It's not nearly the same?"

And this simple act of understanding makes me want to cry. Because no, it's not the same.

"I don't know what to do here. It's not really like tenth grade at all — it's so much more complicated than that. I admire Becca. I respect her and what she's doing with her life. I can't believe how much she has overcome, and how she's putting her past to use. She's amazing.

"If we had met under other circumstances, even with the God-thing, I'm not sure what would have happened. As it is, she was the lone guard watching over my sanity and I can't bear to be separated from her right now, knowing what she's still suffering. Maybe once she's okay I'll be able to talk this through with her and hear she doesn't feel the same way and move on — but now, now I feel like I'm going to go crazy."

I stop abruptly, cutting off the words fighting to come out. But Dr. Beverly seems to understand this and waits for me to force myself past the block.

It's misting outside, and from this height Portland is glorious. I can't get over how aesthetically pleasing everything is. We put so much effort into beauty and order — what a gift it is to live in this town.

I promised the Becca in my mind that I'd do my best to get well, so I grab the armrests of the beautiful leather chair that so easily conforms to my handprint.

"But even if she does come back," I continue, as if I never paused, "I'm screwed! She's genuine about her faith, which is something I respect, and I know she won't turn her back on. So even if she did have some sort of revelation, she'd be one of those masochistic Christian gays who stay celibate.

"My ex-girlfriend Alex had a cousin like that, and it drove her absolutely batty that she couldn't convince him it was a natural lifestyle. He fully admitted the probability that he was made that way, but he said the rules still applied. He said it'd be like having six generations of alcoholics ahead of you — you still had to stay away from the bottle even though you sorely wanted it.

"So either way, no matter what happens, I'm set up for heartbreak."

We sit in silence for a while, but it's not difficult. Another legacy I hope I won't lose from my unwilling time in the desert. The mist has turned into rain and the soft sound of it hitting the windows is immensely soothing. It also feels good to verbalize the thoughts that have been banging around inside my head. I doubt Beverly has any solutions, but I feel better having said it all.

Finally, she breaks the silence. "Do you realize you've talked about nothing but your love for Becca for the last two hours?"

I feel heat crawling up my neck and the tenth grade analogy comes back to mind. "Umm, no, I hadn't realized that."

I pause, wondering what she wants me to say. "You always ask me to talk about my time there. Becca is one of the central figures in my story. And besides," I say, getting angry, "I've spent hours and hours telling you all the horrible stuff. I just wanted to talk about something pleasant today."

She sets her pen down and looks at me with her usual dose of compassion — I wish I could figure out how she manages to radiate that.

"I realize that Kate, and I don't want you *not* to talk about her. I'm just wondering why you think you're focusing on the romantic love aspect of your relationship?"

"So you're saying I don't love her?" I challenge, instantly aggressive although I don't understand exactly why.

"Of course you love her. I'm not denying that or trying to talk you out of it. I'm just saying the situation is much, much more complicated as you just said. You have to unpack what has happened to you before you can see what part romantic love plays."

Her tone deflates my anger and I'm ashamed of my hot response.

"Kate, I want you to think about something for tomorrow. Is it possible you're focusing on the romantic love aspect of this because it's easier than facing some of the tougher parts of your recovery? Because talking about Becca brings you some happiness in the middle of an extremely difficult time in your life?"

"What happiness?" I huff, "She'd never love me back."

"That may be true," she smiles kindly, "but unrequited love is a kind of happiness on its own. Studies show that feelings of romantic love elevate serotonin, and other key chemicals related to positive feelings. It doesn't matter if it's unrequited, or if there's drama, it's a net raise to your emotional condition.

"And all I'm saying is, you have a lot of work ahead of you, sorting through and dealing with your experiences. You need to process everything that happened, and you also need to process the fact that you were yanked out and Becca's still living inside the nightmare. That you are relatively healthy and she is going to have some serious health issues to deal with, if she makes it out at all. You have a lot to work through.

"I'm just suggesting that it might be helpful if you could park the romantic love aspect for a little while and try to focus on some of the other issues. I think if we can do some more work on those areas, when you pull the topic out again you might have more clarity."

I watch the rain coming down outside in sheets, but still feel the dryness of dust and sand closing up my throat.

....

Walking home from another debrief with the FBI and State Department Todd, who flew in from New York especially for this get-together, I can hardly keep my anger under control.

They've made zero progress, even with me giving them every scrap of information I can unearth from my memory. It is mind boggling to me that they haven't been able to figure out where Amal's camp is, or who some of his associates are. How common can the

158

name Diadji be for heaven's sake? We overheard Amal one time talking about the name of the big boss.

But worst of all, a new fury burns because of a remark I overheard one of the nameless, grey-suited Feds make to Todd about running out of time now that the paying client was home. I looked over quickly at Matt to see if he'd heard, but he was, as he is so often, in another world.

This must be hell on earth for him, having me here while Becca is still out of reach. I wish I could think of some way to comfort him. I've tried to think through all the things Becca did to comfort me, but all the ones I've tried don't seem to work on Matt.

Becca made me feel better time and time again by regaling me with tales of Matt as a child, but every time I tell him a funny story about Becca in captivity, he seems to flinch away.

For the oddest second, I find myself wishing he believed in God. He doesn't have the steadiness I relied on so heavily in Becca, and I miss it.

We walk along under the mist, taking a meandering trip in the vague direction of home. Matt has gotten used to my odd turns, following my lead as to how long I want the journey to take.

These walks are our compromise with Dr. Beverly. She wanted me to take up yoga, saying studies had proven it to be extremely helpful for people suffering with PTSD, but Matt and I were kicked out after one session because we couldn't stop giggling.

So now we walk, which in Portland for most of the year means we walk in the rain. It used to bother me, but now I get a sense of well-being walking in it, especially lifting my face to it. I never want to be thirsty again.

"You don't curse anymore," he says, out of nowhere.

"What?" I ask.

"You don't curse anymore. I just realized it. We were in that meeting and you were so angry with Todd, and you said dadgummit instead of dropping an f-bomb."

I don't know what to say, so I don't say anything.

"Old Kate, she wasn't exactly a big potty mouth, but she did curse with regular frequency. It was endearing. I'm not sure I've ever heard New Kate swear."

This startles me. I'm daily aware of so many changes in myself, it's jarring to hear about ones I haven't even recognized as happening.

"Do you honestly have Old Kate and New Kate categories in your mind?"

159

"Are you kidding me?" He stops walking, looking at me incredulously. "I categorize all the time. I was friends with Old Kate for fifteen years. Sure, she changed and grew and matured and had her heart broken and took on new challenges and hobbies — but I was there for all of it so I could go with the flow.

"New Kate came to me abruptly one day, and she is very different. And if I want to stay best friends with her, I'm going to have to figure out how she ticks. But it's jarring. Like the fact that we're standing here, literally in front of your favorite store," he gestures to the window beside us on the sidewalk, "and not only didn't you suggest we stop in for five minutes, but you didn't even seem to notice."

He's smiling, but his words trigger a profound sense of loss.

"What else," I ask, subdued. I turn to stare at the shop window but don't notice anything except colors, blurring in and out of my watery vision.

"Hmm. New Kate sleeps on the floor, even though the bed she once called heaven on earth is ready and waiting beside her."

"True," I respond. "But that's only because the mattress is so soft it hurts my back." I don't bother to give the other reason, that I can't sleep on that soft bed until Becca is home or dead.

"New Kate doesn't eat the blueberry-cinnamon scones from Trader Joe's she used to beg me to run out and get so she could stay in her pajamas. I had to give them to Guillermo down the hall."

"Also true." But I give no further explanation, as I can't tell him it's a holdover from that first scone at Dr. Beverly's, and related to Becca's current breakfast options.

I turn from the window, ready to keep walking, but Matt doesn't follow. When I stop and look back at what's keeping him I see he has a serious expression on his face.

"And New Kate is much more secretive. Old Kate told me everything she was thinking, she shared all her hurts and sorrows and joy and victories. New Kate pauses, screens, and filters. I try to understand, but I don't like it."

I see the loss I feel mirrored and multiplied on his face. This kind, good man, who has known me so well over all these years, who has loved me through many a trial, and now is manfully trying to know me again, the me who has been fractured and broken and who even I don't understand or recognize sometimes.

I walk back to him and we hug in silence, and then I look up with a big smile, and curse with enthusiasm.

Chapter 22: Becca

Just as I decide to refuse to teach Amal, he stops sending for me. He must have recognized how worthless it was, me staring into space, forgetful of what I was saying from one minute to the next.

The last time he spoke to me he said there is nothing to be done but wait. Wait for Matt to pull together money that will not come. In a moment of humanity, perhaps, he told me his boss gave him a one-month deadline. I doubt Matt will be able to come up with the money at this late date, so I watch what is left of my life slowly spool out in front of me.

Since the aborted attack, something is different about Amal, and especially the other men. There is something in their eyes I can't figure out, but I can no longer work up the energy to care.

The men leave me alone for days. They don't come near the hut, and no longer give Fatima a hard time for spending most of the day near me. She sits with me quietly while I eat my rice one-handed, before taking my bowl away. All the while looking at me with a speculation I can't answer.

It finally becomes obvious to me that she's pregnant. I have no idea who the father is, but I've long suspected she's here for more than just cooking and cleaning. I speculate about the men, looking at them all with, if possible, even more disgust.

Every day she unwraps my arm and cleans it with the alcohol Amal brought from his trip, and I guess I'm making progress because I stop passing out every time. Then she gently rewraps my bandages and forces a couple pills down me, and they must be working because the fever has gone away. The ache never does, and I still can black out if I accidentally bump my arm.

I can't say exactly how I spend my time. Mostly I stare into space. Waiting. Always waiting. Now, when I have possibly the most freedom ever, I only leave the hut because Fatima comes in each morning and drags me outside. I sit and watch the men, the sky, the animals, the sand, the never-ending supply of small bugs that parade across my legs. I can't be bothered to move the fly swatter she places in my hand, so finally she gives up and swats them for me whenever she notices them congregating around my bloody bandages.

Amal seems to have arranged for some transfers, because the only men left are the ones who've displayed, if not kindness, then at least no outright hostility. Every time Fatima escorts me to the bathroom, it seems like they evaporate to the edge of the camp, unwilling to be anywhere within ten feet of me.

Only MJ displays any kind of guilt. He spends his days wandering the camp aimlessly, randomly changing direction and occasionally talking to himself. I've even seen him wipe angrily at his eyes a few times.

As the days wear on and my arm continues to throb, my frustration rises. I wish they would just get it over with already. Surely Scarface and the others will come back and finish the job, after all these months of threatening. Or Amal's boss will finally realize once and for all that Matt is not a millionaire and order the end.

This unending waiting for either outcome is torturous.

I have terrible nightmares. Wretched, horrible apparitions haunt me. I dream of Kate being attacked. I dream of my girls in Cairo, and the hellish conditions they've described to me. I dream of my failures, recycled in the worst possible ways. Each time I wake up screaming.

The darkness of night begins to leak into the day. I'm too afraid to sleep. I know what's coming if I do, so I only lie quietly, mumbling sometimes, trying to keep the voices from overtaking me.

My routine is forgotten. My hope has vanished. My assignment a bust. There is nothing but despair, and it continues to snowball.

. . . .

"You are as stubborn as your brother," Amal spits at me. He's called me in for a little chat after his last conversation with Matt and I can see that whatever brief truce we negotiated during our Spanish classes has now been called off.

"We wouldn't be in this situation if he was an honorable man. If he would just accomplish what is required of him."

The flashfire of hatred relights in a moment, and this time I don't want to keep a lid on it. "My *brother* is dishonorable? Are you joking? My *brother*?"

His eyes widen and I know I'm heading down an unwise path, but I can't seem to stop myself.

"What kind of an honorable man attacks a woman on her way to the bathroom? Your Koran speaks against the violation of women, and men are charged to protect the women in their care. Your Koran says you must stand in the way of a man going to attack the helpless."

I find I am suddenly shrieking, and there is no stopping me. All the months of stress and impotence are boiling over in this one explosive moment.

"You have kidnapped us. You have mistreated us. You have daily threatened us with rape and death. You let your guard come for Kate. You let him break my arm. You stood aside and did nothing! And then you left me alone with all your men like a common camp whore.

"And we followed your orders. We did exactly what you told us to do, everything you asked of us. We had an agreement and you broke it again and again."

I feel like I'm not even the one doing the yelling, somehow. Like I'm just watching, detached from this shouting, filthy, out-of-control wreck of a human being, and I want to advise myself to pipe down.

Can't you see he's about to lose it? Can't you see he's going to shoot you right now? Are you out of your mind?

And then I realize — wait, is that what you want? Are you trying to provoke him into killing you? To get this over with once and for all?

"My brother is honorably trying to deal with the evil situation you have put him in. You are the dishonorable man. You are the weak man. You should be ashamed!"

And I see that I have finally crossed the line, as something explodes behind his eyes and he reaches for his gun.

. . . .

I awake much later to discover my head in Fatima's lap. She's gently washing the area around my right eye, which I can't seem to get open. When she finishes, she starts reading quietly to me from a book she holds up very close to her face. I didn't even know she could read.

163

My head throbs in a nice counterpoint to my arm. He must have hit me hard, I don't even remember being brought back to my hut.

I don't understand what Fatima's reading. It seems to be in a different dialect, but something about it comforts me. It reminds me of my mother reading to me from the Psalms when I was a child, whenever I was afraid.

I study her face as she reads, wondering about her life. She has been with us from the beginning, and I've never seen her do anything but work. I've also never seen her complain about her lot, or raise her hand to any of the men who have mistreated her. The only time I saw her display any emotion at all, really, was when she cried the day her baby died, and her tears had dried up by the following day.

Is she really that resigned to her fate? Does she not dream of anything more? Did she have a husband at one point? What did God have planned for this life of hers before the enemy hijacked the plans?

I'm surprised when that question slips through. I've been avoiding God ever since Kate left. I suppose I'm a bit ticked — here I thought I was doing such a good job shining His light in the darkness, etc., etc., and all I managed to do is make her want to kiss me. I'm embarrassed about it, and ashamed about how I've handled her leaving. I just want to mope, and not have any mirrors held up to my face.

Fatima stops reading and I look up, automatically, to see why. I'm surprised to see a tear course down her face.

. . . .

The next day I awake again to Fatima reading to me, with the same feeling of calm. When she stops, there's another tear she doesn't seem to notice — but when she looks down and sees my eyes open, she gets up abruptly and leaves the hut.

I'm not sure what I've done to upset her, and I'm still trying to puzzle it out when she returns with a bucket of water and some soap. She lets me know in no uncertain terms what I'm to do with it.

. . . .

A new routine develops slowly. I sleep more. I meekly follow Fatima's orders for personal care and hygiene and start finishing my bowls of rice without prodding. The swelling in my eye goes down pretty quickly, and soon I'm able to open it. My arm is always painful and healing somewhat crooked, but at least the open wound has closed and the angry red streaks are gone.

Fatima's reading sessions somehow blow away the fog around my head and I start thinking clearly.

One afternoon as she reads I finally broach the question that's been haunting me since Kate left — am I gay? I try to think about it logically, removing the emotional weight and just thinking it through to the end instead of freezing up and throwing it back into the depths of the sea where I've kept it all these years.

If this broken world caused me to get screwed up in yet another way, would I honestly be that surprised? I guess not. So am I gay or not?

Exposed in the light, excised from the darkness where it's been hissing at me, I discover the answer pretty easily.

I realize that I don't notice anyone, male or female, in a sexual way, which probably has something to do with my father. But I feel a frisson of excitement when several memories in a row come to mind where a man did something that made my mouth go dry. I'm finally able to draw together two dots that have always been disconnected for me, and recognize the memories as attraction in its most raw form.

So that's not actually the problem. Funny how it took fifteen minutes of concentrated effort with a bright light to shelve something that's haunted me from the darkness for years.

. . . .

The next time Fatima picks up her book, I decide to read with her. I pick up my Spanish Bible and smack the dust off of it. She looks on approvingly, and then motions from her book to mine and says something I don't understand.

I return her smile, and we sit and read quietly.

165

Chapter 23: Amal

Becca and Fatima have taken to reading in the sun for hours at a time. I know what Becca's reading, she's only got one book, but I didn't even know Fatima could read. Every time I see them out there, peaceful and quiet, it makes me angrier.

I say something to the men, hoping one of them will break up their little book club, but they refuse to have anything to do with Becca these days, and as the two of them are almost always together, her immunity now extends to Fatima.

I moved us into our own tent camp again a couple days ago. I think it will be the last move and I'm glad. Other than staying put during Becca's illness, I've kept us to the prescribed schedule, fighting the men and their laziness all the way. After the first month we started doing our moves during the day, but it has still added a lot of work to the already exhausting prospect of keeping everything on track.

Oumar called last night to report that Diadji is not happy. My soaring success with Kate is quickly fading into the past, and my hopeless future weighed down on me again as I listened to his threats. Somehow it is worse now than it has ever been, maybe because in my mind I'd gotten so close to escape.

I try to comfort myself with the fact that Becca looks better, under Fatima's care, and I haven't had to cut her arm off yet as I'd worried I might have to. But I find I don't care as much about that as I used to — now I'm worried I'm going to be forced to kill her, and I know if that happens it will be the last death gasp of my humanity.

This has gone on long enough!

I throw my tent flap open and stride across to the women. I rip the book out of Fatima's hands and tell her to get back to work. The men look on, silent and useless. I shout at Becca to follow me, and return to my hut.

....

I've just figured out what the book is when Becca comes through the door, and I raise hate-filled eyes to her. She is the cause of all my problems, the reason I'm not on my way to Spain right now.

"Where did you get a Bible in Soninke?" I shout at her.

She takes a step back, no doubt startled by my anger, and has the gall to pretend to look surprised.

"That's a Bible?" she asks, feigning confusion.

"You know good and well it's a Bible. And in Fatima's mother tongue no less. Where did you get it?"

She takes a breath, probably trying to decide whether or not to tell me the truth. She comes from the door and sits down in front of me.

"Amal, I didn't know that was a Bible. Fatima started reading to me from it maybe two weeks ago. I found it soothing, but I didn't understand anything she said. You know I've hardly been able to pick up any Wolof. I didn't even recognize the language. I had no idea."

I almost believe her, but then she smiles — the first genuine smile I've seen since Kate left.

"I can't say I'm sad to hear it's a Bible. That's great news as far as I'm concerned."

Her evident happiness makes me so angry I throw the Bible as hard as I can across the room and it hits the wall with a thud. It falls in several chunks, the cheap binding unable to withstand the impact.

"You listen to me Becca, there is nothing to smile about in this situation. I just heard from my boss that I have one week to make the deal with your brother, and if we can't do it, both of us will experience a wrath I cannot adequately describe to you."

I'm breathing hard, but she looks as relaxed as if we were studying Spanish again, not talking about our looming deaths.

"Did you hear what I said? One week!"

She just looks at my desk. The silence stretches out, but I refuse to speak again until she answers me. Finally, she makes eye contact and starts speaking in a calm voice.

"I've been living under this death sentence for more than six months now Amal. You and the guards threaten my life every couple

168

of days. I'm truly sorry that your life is being threatened now as well, but this is not news to me."

She might as well have waved a red flag in front of me.

"And furthermore," she continues in that same calm voice that makes me want to reach across the desk and strangle her, "I don't believe that anything important has changed with this last phone call you just received. Allah chose the number of my days before I was born. If He has chosen next week as the day of my death, nothing you or I or your bosses or my brother can do will change that. If not, I can promise you if you tried to cut off my head right now, Allah would break your sword."

Something inside me explodes at this challenge to my absolute power over her, and I yell, "You think Allah can do anything for you here? I am the one in charge of your life. I am the one who chooses whether you live or die today. You are alone here!"

I am staring right into her eyes as I scream this, waiting for the flicker of fear that is sure to show up there. I am stunned when I see something like fire erupt from them instead.

"I am not alone."

Her voice seems to amplify somehow, as if it's not just her speaking. There is suddenly power here in this small tent with us, a power I do not understand, and it slams me right in the center of my chest.

"There is Someone who watches over me and sees what is done. You and I will stand in front of Allah one day, and He will be my reckoning."

She stands up and leaves the tent without my permission, and the power goes with her.

. . . .

"Oh, get off your high horse, Amal!" John's voice is sarcastic, but also contains affection. It took me awhile to identify the affection so as not to shrink from the tone, but now I can debate with him without leaving with my feelings hurt. Most of the time.

"If you would just read a history book, you'd see that Christianity began in the Middle East. The fact that Jesus lived is one of the most proven of historical events, and He lived within walking distance of Jerusalem His entire life."

We've been arguing over an assigned paper for one of our classes, debating the historical roots of the big three — Judaism, Christianity, and Islam. I made what, to me, was an unarguably factual assertion I'd heard my entire life about the western origins of Christianity and John blew up.

"I wish you guys would at least be honest about history. We can argue all you want about whose belief system is better or whether Jesus was lunatic, liar or Lord, but you can't argue with the historical record. Christianity only moved to the west after the fall of Constantinople. The Hagia Sophia was the center of our faith for over a thousand years until Sultan Mehmet's final siege! You can read about it in about a hundred different books in my dad's library."

I don't know how to respond, so I sit silently looking at my pen and the blank paper I've yet to fill.

As usual when John sees that I'm at a loss, he stops arguing, wraps his arm around me and changes the topic.

....

One of the men yelling at the door wakes me from my dream and I bolt upright. I lift my hand to my face at an unfamiliar sensation to find tears streaming down.

"I'll be out in a little while," I shout gruffly. I certainly can't let the men see me this way. Besides, I haven't dreamt about John in years and the remembered dream-feeling of his arm around me makes me bite my lip to keep from groaning in sorrow.

Oumar was my first brother, but John was a truer brother. He teased, rough-housed and bullied me in private, but he was my strongest defender at school and with our other friends.

We loved to debate and spent hours arguing about religion, history, culture, who was the best basketball player in the NBA and what was the best meal at the restaurant down the street from school where we often did homework.

It was from him I first heard the basic value system of Christianity explained — that the final weight of good deeds versus bad deeds didn't matter as in my faith, only whether or not you let Jesus pay for your bad deeds. It seemed too easy to me and we frequently returned to that argument.

And yet, as often as we disagreed, I had no doubt that he loved me. It was the first time in my life I knew that to be true. And the last.

170

If I'm going to die in a week, I guess there's no harm in remembering the few good times in my life. I lay my head back down on my cot and let them come.

Chapter 24: Matt

"You never told her I was gay?" Kate asks, incredulous.

"I didn't," I say, "I don't know why, it's not like she was liable to stop talking to you, or to me for being near you. But Becca did always try to avoid asking me questions that might highlight my moral failures. She probably thought we were living in sin until I said I'd moved out."

We sit staring at the water, occupying one of the many available benches. We've started walking the bridge loop every morning before her counseling session, and sometimes afterward, depending on how it goes. We keep saying we're going to start running it, but so far haven't gotten around to it. I feel better physically than I have in ages with all this fresh air and exercise.

I find I'm glad I discovered we have a float-pool at work, as no one seems to notice that I rarely show up these days, but neither is any harm done.

Sometimes Ken meets me while Kate's in counseling, and sometimes he joins us on our walk. He spent a week at company headquarters closing up Kate's account, then showed up at my doorstep saying he'd taken a leave of absence. He says he needs to work out some of his own stuff, which is convenient because he also wants to keep tabs on mine. He says it's a two-for-one deal, and I'm too grateful for his continued steadying presence to insist he go back to work. I know it's hypocritical, considering how happy I am he made me go back to work.

"I assumed she knew; it's not like it's something I hide," Kate breaks into my thoughts, then pauses again. I'm getting used to her new rhythm of speaking. It's soothing somehow, these long, drawn-out thoughts and stories, especially considering we're usually talking about things that make my stomach boil.

"I figured it out about halfway through — I was telling her about Alex and she asked a question about 'him.' I didn't know who she was talking about." She laughs.

"So did you tell her then?" I ask, the old anxiousness rising in my stomach.

It's not that I was ever truly worried that Becca would try to cast Kate into the lake of fire, it's just that they were both integral to my life and I took the coward's way out, keeping information about each of their lives compartmentalized from the other.

I didn't expect Becca to disappoint me, per se, it was just better not to give her the opportunity. Nor did I expect Kate to do anything but roll her eyes if I ever explained the full depth of Becca's faith, but I respected Becca's beliefs, even if I didn't agree with them, and I didn't want to hold her up to the opportunity for scorn, even at a distance.

"No. No, I didn't."

Another long pause as she watches a woman jog by decked out in exercise chic, a small Pomeranian huffing at her feet, working to keep up.

"I would have, but the guards came in right then telling us it was time to move, and by the time we got settled in our new camp I'd thought it through and decided I didn't want to tell her. I didn't want to rock the boat."

She's started crying again. I think I've seen her cry more in these weeks than in our entire friendship, and it hurts me each time. I pull out a tissue from the stash I now always keep handy, and pass it over.

She accepts it without a word, and blows her nose.

"She knows now," she says with something a little bit like a chuckle.

"What do you mean?" I ask, startled.

"I kissed her."

"You WHAT?"

"Yep!" She laughs, but it's kind of a miserable sound. "Amal gave us five minutes to say goodbye and I panicked. I forgot about all the very good reasons I'd thought of for not telling her. I forgot that I'd already worked it all out in my mind that this was nothing but a one-sided crush — all I could think about was how I might never see her again and I laid one on her. She had the most surprised look on her face — that's my last image of her."

Surprised is right. I try to imagine Becca's expression, and what must have been going through her mind, and I can't help it — I giggle.

Kate shoots me a disgusted look, and I try to smother it, but it bubbles up again and then I can't stop laughing, and soon she joins me.

....

Kate hasn't shown any interest in looking for a new apartment, but I don't mind that she's staying with me. I'm glad actually — it makes me feel less panicky to have her close by. It also helps to not have so many hours alone to stare at the wall and imagine the worst.

I took her to the storage unit where I put all her stuff one afternoon, but in fewer than five minutes she went into a rage and started throwing things. I dragged her out of there crying and we haven't returned.

We did go to Target eventually, so she could pick up a few pieces of clothing and some other essentials. I don't remember her ever shopping at Target; she used to be a Nordstrom Rack kind of gal. It went ok, other than some tense moments in the deodorant aisle. She mumbled something about dying for choice and seemed to pick one at random before darting out of the aisle.

She wasn't a huge shopper compared to some women I've dated, but as her income went from college student to young professional, she'd acquired the commensurate wardrobe.

She did tell me once she'd grown to love dressing up for work, and that the hardest thing to give up with the new job was having to show up in jeans.

But that's all filed under Old Kate. New Kate still spends a good part of every day in my hand-me-down sweatpants.

....

A week later we're at another bench, enjoying another of the infrequent sunny days we've been offered this year. Kate hasn't said a word since I picked her up. She started walking slowly toward the park, so I followed along.

"It's been a month," she says, so quietly that I only hear because I'm working hard at it.

I assume she means since we made the deal, but I've been trying to practice what Dr. Beverly told me — unless asked a direct question, just listen; if she stops, ask another leading question and shut up. It's the best way to get her to share what's all bottled up inside, and she desperately needs to share.

I've begun seeing Dr. Beverly once a week for my own crazy.

"It's been a month since Scarface dragged me out of there. It's been two weeks since you heard from Amal." Her voice cracks on his name, and I reach automatically into my tissue pocket.

"She's dead."

The words skewer me, and suddenly I'm in full panic. I'm wondering how she knows, who told her? Did Ken hear something and think the news would be better coming from Kate?

"How do you know that? Who told you?" I get out between gritted teeth, my voice a high-pitched squeak, my heart racing so fast it's hard to catch a breath.

She turns and gives me such a vicious look it pierces right into my soul. "No one told me, Matt, I just know."

My panic notches down a bit at this, and the vice over my heart loosens. "So you don't know for sure, you just think so." It probably comes out a little angrier than I intended, but that was just mean of her to say.

"I know!" she says angrily, and jumps up. The couple sitting on the next bench over looks our way.

"I know she's dead, Matt! She had red streaks going up her arm when I left her. I googled it. There's no way she's still alive. And it's your fault!"

Her voice has been rising, but she positively hollers the last line.

It's been good for me, having someone to focus on besides myself. Trying to care for her, get her the help she needs, get her to her appointments, make sure she has enough tissue and is eating enough. She's been my project, and I haven't had to think as much about Becca's actual condition.

Of course the fear and panic are always there, just hovering outside the borders of my vision, but taking care of Kate and having her so close have offered an anesthetic of sorts.

But with this, she's ripped out the morphine drip. I feel the old wound roar back, worse than before, and all my efforts to treat her with kid gloves while barely keeping my own panic under control go out the window.

"My fault!" I roar, and out of the corner of my eye I see the couple get up and walk away quickly. "What in the world did I have to do with it? I'm the one working my ass off trying to raise the money to pay her ransom. I'm the one who has to keep talking to Amal and hearing his horrible threats. I'm the one who has to listen to your stories about how you left her just this side of dead. I'm her brother! How is this my fault?"

We are toe-to-toe, both red-faced, and everyone in the area has cleared out.

"You should have left me there until you were sure to get us both! I can't believe you paid my ransom when you knew it would hurt her chances. You should have waited! I'd rather be back there with her and know she's okay than here with you wondering."

And then she chokes, like her throat closes up on her, and she bends over with huge heaving shudders. My anger evaporates instantly, and I reach for her just as she drops through my grasp. She sinks to the ground and rolls over into a ball, right there on the public sidewalk. Old Kate would have been mortified.

"It's my fault," she mumbles over and over. "I left her there just this side of dead. I left her there to die."

I grab her and drag her to the bench, and rock her as she weeps.

Chapter 25: Kate

I'm not sure how good Matt and I are for each other. I've got my own issues, but he's also trying to deal with his grief and anxiety, and we never seem to be at the same stage at the same time. When I'm in the mood to laugh, he wants to cry. When I've just started to weep, he walks in with a movie because he doesn't want to think about it anymore.

I think it's time to start looking for a place of my own. We walk on eggshells more and more, the ease of my first couple weeks home evaporated into the ether. But no matter how much we both try, at least once a day we start shrieking at each other and one of us will storm out. Inevitably we end up huddled together crying on the couch — drawn together like magnets, the only two who still wait for her.

Matt walks around like a dead man. Really ever since I got home, although I didn't see it at first with my own grief blinding me. But after a couple weeks I could see he was just going through the motions.

. . . .

"You think she's Ms. Patient, Ms. Kind? Come on, Kate! I am sick to death of all your stories painting Becca like a saint."

I don't even remember the story I was telling him three seconds ago, his interruption has caught me so off guard. I just stare at him, slack-jawed.

But he's just getting started. "Oh, I could tell you a story or five. I will tell you one thing Jesus has done for her — He's made her much more patient, much more kind. You say she never seemed to get

179

angry — well, I once saw her nearly kill a woman with her bare hands."

I roll my eyes, sure he's exaggerating, but he grabs my arms and shakes.

"I'm serious! One minute we were both irritated, late for a movie, driving around and around in circles trying to find a parking spot. She was snipping at me and I was snipping at her, until finally a spot opened up. We had to back up a little, but a woman came screeching in behind us and wouldn't move. Becca was out of the car before I could stop her, ready to kill the woman. She had her hand on the door handle when she saw a kid in the backseat with wide eyes staring at her in fear.

"She hustled back to the car and drove away, her whole body shaking. She said she'd never felt that kind of rage directed at another human being. That's also my sister. And she's no saint."

It's not that I don't believe him; it's just that that is not the woman I know, the woman I lived through the most dire of experiences with. I don't understand what he's so mad about, but I also don't understand how we could be talking about the same person.

I suddenly recognize the feeling — it's the same disconnect I experienced when I was trying to reconcile the stories she told me during her malarial fevers.

"Okay," I start again slowly, "you tell me that story, and then I tell you that under the most difficult and straining of circumstances — where we were hostages held at the point of a gun and daily threatened — she exhibited patience and kindness and love to me and, for the most part, to those same gun-wielding crazies.

"She used to talk to me about the kind of life they were probably living, the choices they'd had to make to survive. I'll tell you what, I couldn't have cared less, but she was serious about it. She treated them with kindness, especially Fatima and the younger men. The only anger I ever saw her display was when the men kicked Fatima around."

The fight seems to have gone out of him. He walks away from me and slouches down onto the couch, staring at his hands. But I want to understand. I walk over and sit beside him, speaking more quietly.

"So you're telling me that she was not that way, that she was filled with rage over what happened with your father and nearly killed some lady over a parking spot. And then she was a crazed alcoholic weed-smoker who tried to kill herself. And then you went to Guatemala and all of a sudden she turned into this — okay, not saint, but certainly rather saintly. What happened?"

He turns to look at me, and I could swear I see panic flit across his face, but that doesn't make any sense to me. I'm just trying to logically work this out — if she used to be one way and now is another, something sort of huge must have happened. I want to know what.

He takes a deep breath, seeming almost reluctant. "Well I can tell you what she'd say. I have her answer memorized."

He pauses again, but I don't mind waiting.

"She would tell you it doesn't matter if you're gay. It doesn't matter if you're straight. It doesn't matter if you're a thief. Or a liar. Or a murderer. Or a child molester. Or a gossiper. Or a sluggard. Or a democrat. Or a republican.

"She would say she used to identify as a suicidal, alcoholic, drug-using abuse victim who didn't deserve any better than she got. She would say that we all have false identities that we've accepted and internalized, but the only thing that really matters is understanding and accepting our true identity — that of a child of God. Everything else God will work out later, once we've seen and accepted this one clear truth."

He pauses for a minute, then continues in a sing-song voice, almost as if he's in a trance. "What you see in Becca is the change that believing in Jesus can bring. You believe that He is the Son of God, and that He came to earth to pay the penalty for sin so that your broken relationship with God can be restored. You repent of all your sins, turn to Him, and ask Him to be your Lord and Savior — and then He starts to change you from the inside out."

The sing-song voice is gone now, replaced by full sarcasm. "So basically, you start out as a dirty, rotten sinner. He drops a love bomb on you and forgives all your sins and suddenly you're white as snow and he starts his campaign to renew your mind so that you can one day be kind and patient and loving of your enemies. Bing. Bang. Boom."

I know he doesn't believe, that he's just playing along with my questions. But there is a great deal of sense to me in what he's saying. We've got example A on one side of the equation — suicidal abuse victim Becca, and on the other side — okay, not the saint I sometimes paint her as, but a completely, certifiably changed Becca.

It would have to be something radical to effect that kind of change, and suddenly it all clicks into place. I get it.

"Okay," I smile at him tentatively, "I guess that makes sense."

"Are you kidding me!" He explodes as he nearly comes out of his seat, "You think that makes sense!"

He is as agitated as I have ever seen him, and owing to the fact that we've been screaming at each other off and on for weeks, that's saying something. He storms off and the entire apartment rattles when he slams the door, but I stay put, pondering his words.

....

I've been talking on and off to God since Becca's malarial fevers, but I still feel a little foolish speaking out loud when there's no one else in the room. Matt still hasn't returned from his abrupt exit, and I want to get this done while he isn't around to either hear or mock me.

"Hello God. It's me, Kate." Silence.

"Umm, Parker," I add, in case there's any doubt.

Silence. I clear my throat, not sure what I was expecting. For a moment I waver, but then I decide to barrel ahead full speed.

"I think it makes a lot of sense that You must have been involved in changing Becca from what she was into what she is, and I feel a great need of being changed. I'm so angry all the time. I am selfish and unloving. I'm mean and spiteful. I don't have any patience whatsoever. I want to be a better person."

I pause there, unsure again. Something is coming up my throat, threatening to choke me. It drops me to my knees and I gasp for air.

"No, it's more than that. It's more than just that I want to be different, to be better. God, I want to have the certainty that Becca has. She was certain every day that You were there with us in that hellhole. She never wavered. And I crave that.

"I crave a world that makes sense, with order and solid foundations, instead of the rules always changing and the floor always moving and everybody living by *hey if it feels good do it* and hurting each other.

"I don't want to live my life for money or things or any of that other crap I've pursued so far that I can see means absolutely nothing. I want what Becca has. I want to know You. Please, how can I know You?"

I stop, spent, and try to catch my breath. My chest hurts, and I don't know what more to say. I wipe my nose on Matt's old t-shirt and wait.

A warmth descends on me, and a peace so strong I've never felt anything like it before. I feel like someone is in the room with me, and suddenly the question I really want to ask shoots right up from my gut, burning like acid all the way.

"Why did You let this happen to us?" I cry out. "Maybe to me, maybe it was some sort of punishment I deserved, but why did You let this happen to Becca? She's got to be one of your most faithful, loyal servants. Why did you let this happen to her?"

My face is smashed into the carpet, tears flowing freely, and I wait, although for what I'm not sure.

For you.

My head pops up and spins around toward the door. Did Matt come back? It didn't sound like his voice, but no one else is here.

No one else is here! Chills run up and down my spine as I realize I'm sure I just heard a whisper when there's no one else in the room.

I did it for you.

I must be losing it, because I could swear that one came from inside me, a gentle brush across my mind. I remember something Becca said about God speaking to her, that it was like a small quiet voice inside her head.

You wouldn't come to me, so I came to you. Through her. I allowed Becca to be put into that situation because I love you.

This whisper is accompanied by a wave of love so profound it's like nothing I've ever experienced. I give myself completely to the wave and ride it for I don't know how long.

When I come back to myself I find I'm still face down on the floor, tears long dried, with a terrible crick in my neck.

I have no idea what this means. Did I just become a Christian? Or at least, a follower of Jesus like Becca? It feels like it.

Am I still gay? pops immediately to mind. I don't know how to test this other than to drum up some lustful thoughts, and somehow I think that might not be the right way to go. But then I realize, somehow, the answer to that question is no longer so important to me.

Yes, something is definitely different. He did something with that wave. I feel like some kind of exchange was made.

He.

Just thinking about Him brings a feeling of peace. He. Him. God. The One who came to know me.

Chapter 26: Becca

Beans and eggs.

It's always the same. My mother in the kitchen below, preparing the special Sunday morning breakfast dad prefers before preaching. It takes extra time and she's always very busy trying to finish on time, but it turns out he prefers that as well.

Before the sound of her singing a hymn, before I hear the creak on the stairs that alerts me he is coming, the smell wafts up the stairs, crawls across the floor stretching its tendrils in my direction and bolts me upright.

Every time, it's the smell. I start to tremble and almost immediately break into a sweat, knowing the creak on the stairs will sound any minute.

Always the same stair, the third from the top. I know I have fifteen, maybe twenty seconds, then the peculiar squeak of the handle on my door. The swish as it brushes across the too-tall throw rug Tia Maria made me for my eighth birthday. Unicorns, because I loved them.

The gentle way he closes the door. And locks it.

I try to control my breathing, knowing as I always do at this point that this is just a dream. Not real.

Not real.

But it *was* real.

The realization of which is always the point at which I begin to hyperventilate. I feel his presence as he nears, the weight of the chain he brings along with him almost physical. In fact, in some versions of this dream I do see the chain, trailing heavy and serpent-like behind him.

I keep my eyes closed tightly, praying that this will be the time he merely kisses my forehead and tells me it's time to get up for church. But it's not to be.

He never says a word at the beginning, only at the end. It's those words I wait for, knowing only then that I can get up and try to make it to the bathroom before mom finishes cooking and calls up the stairs, wondering what's taking so long.

I tried to make sense of them at first, for decades really, but now I see that his words of explanation are as meaningless as his supposed faith. He is a sepulcher, he is a grave, and he is trying to inter me inside him.

He stills and I feel his stare above me, his black eyes burrowing through to my closed ones. In the day his eyes are a bright, brilliant green that people always comment on — *oh, aren't you lucky you inherited his eyes!*

But in the night they are an abyss that steals my breath and sucks me under.

I resist as long as I can, knowing what awaits — but I also know that he will not move, he will not finish, until I look him in the eye.

So finally I work up my nerve, hold my breath, and crack my eyes open.

The hell that yawns in front of me is so endless, the red flames burning where they have no right to so startling, that I scream myself awake. I come to as I smack my head hard into one of the tent stakes, having scuttled my way backwards off my mat.

I realize I'm still screaming only belatedly and clamp my mouth shut, but terror fills me and my skin is crawling. I'm afraid, terrified for my life to a level that Amal has never reached. Primal, soul-shaking terror.

In the corner there is a darkness, creeping, shifting. The full moon sends more of itself through the various rips in the fabric than normal, but it does no good. Formless, yet still somehow weighty, the darkness sucks the light out of the very air around it, creating a space that is darker still.

Even from the far corner I feel its heaviness upon my chest. The air itself is liquefied and I'm barely able to push it in and out of my gasping lungs. Desperation joins the fear and spikes my pulse even higher.

I know what this is, but knowledge and familiarity offer no assistance, they only intensify my feelings of helplessness. There is only one help against this.

"Jesus."

It comes out in the barest whisper, the effort required to squeeze the air up the long passage from my lungs and out through my mouth nearly suffocates me.

"Jesus," I whisper again, but this time it's perceptively louder.

Again.

"Jesus."

And again.

"Jesus!"

With each repetition the weight lessens, the shape diminishes, until finally I am alone.

But not really alone.

I feel its absence as keenly as I felt its presence. One minute there, the next non-existent.

"Jesus."

....

I awake battered of body and spirit, but clearer of mind, cleaner and lighter, than I've been since Kate left. It always happens that way, somehow I know the dream is coming and it builds and builds, me twisting and turning like the worm on the hook, waiting for the agony to be over.

The way Jesus evaporates the darkness is always the end of the cycle. I can never tell how long it will be until the cycle starts building again, but I'm relieved for the reprieve.

....

I'm slowly pushing my body through the old morning routine. I'm stiff, but know that I need to start fresh this morning if I'm to start at all.

New mercies, every morning.

Fatima walks in with my breakfast rice and sees me stretching. She gives me a big grin and thumbs up, and I feel instantly cheered.

I'm wondering how long it will take me to work up to a one-armed pull-up when I hear shouting. Crawling over to the door, I see a dust cloud in the distance, and a few moments later, Oumar's car comes into the open.

So that's it then.

187

....

"Don't do this!"

Amal is frantic. Part of my brain tries to figure out if he will be next, as the other is concerned with more practical matters regarding where this is heading.

Once a friend in Cairo showed me a youtube video of a beheading. She loved me and was worried about a trip I was making into an unstable area. If I'd known what she wanted to show me I'd have tried to get out of it, but she just shoved me in front of her computer and hit play.

After it was over, even as I wrestled with the unspeakable horror, I told her I'd be fine. And I'd meant it.

I would say the same now — I'm fine. If I ever believed in the life to come, it's at this exact moment. I look up and see a madman with a knife, and know that mere seconds and a few empty words from my captor are all that stand between me and eternity.

Will this hurt? For exactly how long will it hurt? Will I have time to scream? Will he finish with one swipe or have to work at it awhile like the video I saw?

My internal line of questioning is interrupted by Fatima — she who I've never heard raise her voice, even as she's being beaten, is yelling as she jumps between Oumar and me. She's shouting and hitting him and I want to tell her to stop, but I find I can't speak. Oumar lifts his arm but Amal yanks Fatima away and savagely knocks her to the ground. I'm sure he's saved her life. Meanwhile, Oumar continues toward me.

I start to picture it. I can almost feel the chains of gravity vibrating as they ready to free me to fly to Him, and suddenly I crave it with such force that my knees buckle.

One part of my brain notes that this seems to be the last straw for Amal. His eyes bug and I imagine he must think the whole falling to my knees thing is a fear swoon. I wish I had time to explain it to him, that I'm swooning at the thought that this whole ordeal is finally coming to a close, that I have made it to the end of my race, and I realize I didn't run in vain.

I hear Amal yelling, but I'm too busy watching as my life really does flash before my eyes — I thought that was just a Hollywood cliché, but what is passing through my mind's eye could quite reasonably be termed flashes.

Moments. Trials. Victories. Pain. Laughter. Joy. Injustice. I'm overwhelmed at the thought that it might all finally be over, and my real life is moments away from beginning. All the struggle, all the fear, all the worry that I wouldn't be able to stand until the end — all of it is moments from completion.

I can feel it pulling me — the Real, the True — and with everything in me I long to go. I feel tears streaming, but if I had to explain them I'd claim ecstasy. My bones begin to shiver and I feel the start of a body-wide tremble.

I reach toward where I can see Him, as if through a shifting mirage, holding out His arms to me.

Poor Amal, I wish I could explain to him that he's pleading against the most exquisite moment of my existence. I have never wanted *anything* like I want that knife to fall.

Inside this strange moment of ecstasy I've tuned out the soundtrack, but the sudden silence pulls my head up in time to see Amal turn away as Oumar lifts the knife and pivots toward me.

Chapter 27: Amal

THWACK!

I cannot stand to look. I have failed. This was my last chance to keep hold of my soul, and now it's gone. I'm lost.

The silence seems to go on and on. Then I hear Fatima crying. I hear the men murmuring. I hear my own breathing. And suddenly I hear hers. I recognize her breathing from the nights I've sat outside their hut, from the hours I've spent across the table from her studying. I lift my head as if drawn by a magnet and see hers still attached to her body.

There is blood streaming from the side of her head — he's chopped off her ear! I look up quickly to see if this was a mistake and see that he's laughing at me. But the laugh is accompanied by an expression that paralyzes me with fear. I have never seen evil as clearly as it shines through his eyes.

"I will be back Amal, and the next time you will have brought this to a satisfactory conclusion, or I will finish the job and retire you."

He leans down and picks up the small bloody mass of flesh and slaps it into my hand. It's still warm and I immediately have to swallow hard to keep my breakfast down.

"Send this to her family; they will come up with the money."

He signals to one of the men who quickly steps forward and drags Becca to her tent, then he walks to his car, kicking Fatima in the stomach on the way by.

Becca never said a word, yet I could hear her in my head, former words tormenting me as they lashed my soul over and over.

I am not alone. There is Someone who watches over me and sees what is done. And He will be my reckoning.

191

There is a hell, and I will be going there. There is no question about it now. I sent one of the men to the nearest town to send the ear to Matt, special delivery. It should arrive the day after tomorrow, and I will call him, and I will say that the next part to arrive will be a more vital one. I will give him one week. And then it will be over.

There is a line I have danced around for years, but now I have crossed it. No amount of good deeds will outweigh the evil I released into the world when I sent that box.

I wish I didn't believe in hell. I think life would be easier if this were the case, but it is not what I was raised to believe. I remember the long ago words of my faceless father, explaining to me the weight of our heart on the balance scales at death. Our good deeds and actions must outweigh our wrongdoings; how even Mohammed, peace be upon him, did not know if he'd done enough good to earn him a place in paradise.

The *marabout* always said it was better to die in jihad, as did the string of imams Oumar brought in to preach to us. That was the only way to be sure. Well this is not jihad, this is just business. And for the sake of business I will go to hell.

There is no other choice. Oumar has given me no other choice. I've made my choices and I must follow through. If only if I had chosen a different gang to join, or found a different way to keep from starving. If only the Andersons hadn't died, or died only six months later when I was already in America with my scholarship. If only the driver who killed them had made a different turn — had one more beer, or one fewer. If only I had died of starvation instead of being sold to the *marabout*. If only I had died at birth, like three of my brothers.

But this is the life I have been given. These are the decisions I have made. I have crossed the line, and there is no drawing back from it.

. . . .

I can never see my mother's face, but I sense her anguish as my faceless father brusquely rips me from her arms and hands me over to the *marabout*, muttering words I do not understand. I see her arms held out to me, slowly dropping as her body curls in on itself. I see the dust my feet kicks up as he drags me along the road. I feel the despair rise up within me, knowing in this dream state what I couldn't know at the time — the hell that is to come.

But for the first time in the countless instances I've dreamt of this last moment with my parents, there is a new person present. I can't see his face, but he radiates strength and peace. He watches silently and I wonder what his role is. Through the whole scene he stays beside me, and as I am dragged along, for the first time my eyes are drawn from their fixation with the dust at my feet up to his face.

I see you.

The dream fast-forwards to my bed at the *marabout's* house, the dirty corner in a concrete box of a room, crammed between Oumar and the wall. We are whispering as we did whenever we could get away with it, and my heart aches at the sweet glow in his eyes that I remember but no longer see. I know what's coming and I grab his arm. But the dream repeats as real life did, and the *marabout* comes for me. Oumar stands and offers himself, and the *marabout* drags him away. I don't see him again until he is no longer the Oumar I knew.

But again, the new man is here. He is standing against the wall in the corner watching the scene, watching with such concentration that he seems to be memorizing the details. I can feel his presence here, but my eyes are locked on Oumar as he is yanked away. The tears stream down my dirty face, leaving muddy trails in their wake. Finally I lift my eyes to him, shouting silent questions through my pain.

I see Oumar.

We move to the street where I used to wash windshields. He leaves me briefly and I feel panic start, but he turns and his eyes calm me. He reaches inside the car somehow, as if the laws of physics don't apply to him, and gently lifts Mrs. Anderson's chin, so her eyes move from focusing on John's face to seeing mine.

I made her see you.

In the next scene I look for him, and find him early on. I am sitting in the director's room as he tells me my life is over. The Andersons are dead. My scholarship has come to an abrupt end. My dreams lie in ashes at my feet. The tears come silently, but they come. I haven't wept with noise since I was a child, but I have allowed myself the luxury of giant hopes, and the pain wreaks havoc.

This time he comes forward and places his hand on my shoulder, the weight of it somehow heavier than anything I've ever felt, yet it doesn't crush me.

I see you.

The dream speeds up and I witness the downward spiral of life in the gang. Lies, thievery, murder, slavery. The reintroduction to Oumar. Despair, anger, pity, weariness.

Survival.

He is there in each memory, sometimes touching my shoulder, other times standing in the corner. Always near. Always watching with the same concentration, memorizing the details.

And finally we fast-forward to the scene I have imagined but only ever heard about, when the men came for Becca that night. I see her trembling and my heart aches, but then the soldiers appear and I realize my men's descriptions didn't do them justice. For one thing, they didn't mention the glowing.

But the man is not with me this time; he stands behind her with hands on both her shoulders, flanked by the soldiers. He is glowing brighter than they do, and even though my eyes burn to look at him, I know I won't stop looking even when his light makes me go blind.

I understand suddenly — they never would have been able to touch her. These soldiers make it clear they would have ripped the arms off my men before they were allowed to touch her. No wonder my men freaked out.

After all she'd done for me, all her kindnesses and treating me with a respect I didn't deserve in normal life, let alone as her captor — this is what I left her to face. I would never in a million years have guessed that these soldiers would show up to protect her, so the guilt is still mine.

When he raises his eyes to look at me I feel I'm about to disintegrate. The weight of his stare exposes all my sins and it feels like the very blood under my skin is boiling, my bones melting away.

All the various guilts and shames I've felt these last months is nothing compared to this weight.

I see you.

Suddenly I'm in a new space. It's dark, a dark I've never experienced. The darkness is weighty, it closes in on me and is hard to breathe in. It's also cold — but more than mere cold, there's an absence of warmth.

And then, just as I begin to panic, I see in the distance a light, advancing at a pace so rapid I can make out the man's features in a matter of seconds.

And then He is here. And I see Him. And I am undone.

I am Jesus, Son of the Living God.

His words come with a force that makes my marrow vibrate, and my bones no longer have the strength to hold me upright. I melt at His feet and await the sword of justice.

I have loved you with an everlasting love.

I feel Him draw closer. Though my eyes are closed it's as if the sun has shifted in orbit to come down and warm me here on earth. The heat radiating off of Him scorches, but in a way I've never felt before. He touches my back and it's an exquisite pain as a burn begins somewhere deep inside. I feel my flesh melting, searing away the offensive.

I don't know how long I burn, but eventually He pulls me to my feet and clasps me in a hug unlike any I have ever experienced. The closest would be the whispered memory of hugs from my mother, or the more solid ones from Mrs. Anderson, but they pale in comparison to this. His hug is healing, radiating, breathing life and air into my burnt corpse.

I have called you by name, and you are mine.

His life is pulsing through me now, binding me to Him like gravity. I cling to Him with renewed energy, holding on lest He cast me aside. But somehow I know He never will.

Gently he pushes me back so He can look in my eyes, and I see that we are no longer in the dark place. He points down and somehow I'm able to see through the hut into the place where Becca sleeps. My eyes are working better than normal, and I can see her clearly in the darkness — the bloody mess on the side of her head with the filthy bandage taped on haphazardly, the tear streaks through the dirt on her face, the awkward way she guards her crooked arm even in her sleep.

She is mine, and the time of her suffering is coming to a close.

He looks deeply into my eyes and I see a universe in His.

I will be with you, always.

He reaches up and I have time to notice a scar on His hand just before He touches my forehead and I wake with a start in my hut.

Chapter 28: Matt

"I did what you said."

Kate's voice still echoes in my ears as I pound along, running out my frustration. Our hypothetical conversation, when I tried to explain to her why Christianity was basically a prison sentence even though it had helped my sister, and what she got out of it was a step-by-step instruction manual. Un-freakin-believable.

Her eyes had that dreamy, cult-like haze covering them this morning. One more person drinking the Kool-Aid. I can't believe it.

Pursuing Kate was a calculated move on my part after I lost Becca in Guatemala. I took a good hard look at my relationship options, not wanting to invest in anyone that he might get his claws into. So I picked her. I knew God could never get to a lesbian. Too many walls to break through. Too much bad blood between them and the Christian community.

But I can see that I've lost her, just like that. She'd sipped her coffee with a new zen attitude, then had the nerve to ask if I knew of any churches in the area she could go to. I told her I needed a quick run and got out of there before I exploded.

I literally can't believe this is happening. Again. God swoops in again and steals someone I love. First my father, then my adoptive home and community, then my fiancé, then my sister, now the gay best friend. He has taken every single one. It's the final straw. The last buzzer. Game over.

I am so mad I'm actually seeing red — I didn't realize that was possible — and I have to stop. I lean over one of the railings and try to catch my breath. The red begins to recede and I feel a little calmer.

I start running again at a more reasonable pace, and suddenly feel a buzz of excitement from the possibility that this could just be a result of the trauma. She could, like so many others before her, come to her senses after a crazy weekend at a Billy Graham crusade and snap back to reality.

Lots of people make instantaneous conversion decisions, but then find the road too hard and/or annoying to walk. I've seen it time and time again. I cling to this hope fiercely.

But meanwhile, I've been a big brother for too long to let her get slaughtered by some nutjob. I'm at a standstill about what to do for Becca, but I can do this one thing for Kate.

Later, after a shower, I walk Kate to Dr. Beverly's and then do a little research. Within thirty seconds on my browser I have a listing for a couple dozen churches in the Portland area. It's a bit easier to narrow down when you know the buzzwords: "Evangelical, seeker, contemporary service."

....

Sisters Coffee Shop
Portland, Oregon

I'm drumming my fingers, sweat trickling down the back of my shirt. All my hackles are up, and he's not even here yet. Poor guy, he probably doesn't have any idea what he's walking into.

I know who he is the second he walks in the door. The tie, cross pin and ostentatiously huge Bible to let everyone know whose side he's on. I wave him over, "Lucas?"

"No," he says, "sorry."

Huh.

A few seconds later somebody taps me on the shoulder. It's the guy who was sitting in the corner when I walked in, whom I immediately dismissed because of the Dawkins' book in his hand and the generally wrinkled look of the beer t-shirt he was sporting.

"Sorry, I didn't realize it was you until you asked that guy if he was me." He extends his hand, "Lucas Woodley, nice to meet you."

I'm embarrassed by my pre-judgement, but I don't have time to feel that right now.

"Yeah, hey, I'm Matt." We shake hands and he sits down next to me.

Nothing for it but to start right in. "Look, the reason I called is I've got a friend who's gay and believed in Jesus yesterday, and I want to make sure I direct her to a church that won't traumatize her any further. I'd send her to the methodists with no qualms, but she's got it in her head she wants to be an evangelical."

He smirks at this, and looks like he'd like to say something, but then decides against it.

"I know if she continues, in no time at all she's going to run into the brick wall of her identity. She's been gay since childhood, now she believes Jesus loves her. She's going to hit that wall hard and I want to find her a church that knows how to handle the issue delicately. None of this 'pray away the gay' shit, no offense."

"None taken," he says with a smile. He doesn't look shocked, like it's not the first time he's heard someone cuss and denigrate his faith to his face. It almost makes me want to cuss a little more, but I remember the conversation with Aunt Bertie last week where she told me I could swear all I wanted but it wouldn't make her love me any less. Maybe it *is* a defense mechanism.

"Kate is very important to me, and she's made what feels to her like a genuine commitment to Jesus. For now, anyway. You know how these things go. I don't want you to mess her up any more than she's gonna be messed up when she gets to Romans and sees she's screwed."

He waits a while before responding, presumably to make sure I don't have any further barrels to unload.

"Well, I can tell you there are a number of people in our community who deal with same-sex attraction. Our position is that it is not our place to judge, but that a person who is seeking God, reading the Bible and listening to the Holy Spirit, will in time come to recognize any number of lies they've believed about who they really are.

"I'm happy to tell you that I was a corporate raider in another lifetime, married, with a pornography addiction that ruined my marriage. It had such a hold on me, I lost my job and marriage on the same day, when they found porn on my work computer. I believed that that was my identity, that I needed porn to function."

He smiles and shakes his head, as if even he can't believe it.

"At the lowest point of my life, when I was living in a rent-by-the-week rathole because my wife had kicked me out, one of the other losers staying at the hotel asked me to come to a service. I went because I had nothing better to do and thought it'd be a laugh — but I met Jesus that night and He showed me I had a different identity. It doesn't mean I don't still struggle. It's been ten years and images still come to my mind. I still get cravings for that thing that poisoned me, but it's not who I am anymore, it's just something I used to do."

He pauses, and I wonder how he'd like me to respond. At least he doesn't remind me of my dad. Dad would have never confessed to even the mildest of sins, especially not to a perfect stranger.

He must decide that I'm not going to comment, because he continues, "That kind of story is repeated all throughout our church. We've got former addicts of every flavor — drugs, money, alcohol, food, every form of sexual deviancy. We all know who we are, and who we were, and Who showed us the difference.

"You seem to know what the Bible says about homosexuality, but that is not what we focus on. We focus on identity in Christ, finding out who it was He created you to be, where you've believed lies about yourself, and what lies you've had to believe to survive."

He takes a sip of his coffee and grimaces, then reaches over and grabs another packet of sugar.

"My wife was abused horribly as a child. She believed for a majority of her life that if she didn't take care of herself, no one would. It took a long time for her to recognize that lie, and a long time to root it out, both the cancer and its tentacles. She's still working on it, actually."

It occurs to me that this is the longest conversation I've had with a real believer besides Becca or Aunt Bertie since the day of my aborted wedding. By design of course — first sign of Jesus Freak and I'm outta there.

That makes almost twenty years where all the conversations in my head feature my dad's voice as the voice of Christianity, and usually end in a screaming match and a bottle.

He seems to notice I'm no longer with him, because he's stopped talking. He doesn't seem to be in a hurry though. I don't know what to say, so I keep staring at the empty coffee cup in my hands.

His eyes are kind, nothing like my father's, when he says, "Matt, your friend is very welcome in our church, and I will promise you to take a special interest in her." He pauses for a moment, then smiles and says, "And you'd be welcome anytime as well."

Could have expected that, but it was said so casually and with no pressure attached, so I don't feel the need to make a smart ass comment like I normally would. "Thanks for the offer, but me and God have a long, sordid history. We know where things stand."

We shake hands and I walk out, my thoughts returning to the pact Becca and I made so long ago. If we'd known more people like

Lucas and fewer people like my father growing up, maybe then I wouldn't be so rigid about even being near Christians now. But the bottom line is the same — I'm never going back to him unless I'm convinced. Regardless of meeting people who follow him who are actually decent, he has to prove to me he's relevant to my here and now.

. . . .

I lie awake, staring at the ceiling, wishing for just one bottle of any type of alcohol to slow the pace of my thoughts and numb the pain. Ken is leaving next week. He says it's time to make things right with his family. He's thinking about finding a new job.

Kate and I shared a silent dinner, then she picked up her Bible and I told her I was tired so I wouldn't have to pretend not to watch her reading it.

Becca and I have worked so hard over the years to keep our relationship intact and close. Much harder than I worked with mom, but Becca's also more flexible than mom about the life I've chosen to live. But there has always been a big, fat figure standing between us sucking all the air out of the room.

He takes everything. Everyone.

And now He stands between Kate and me, and I can no longer breathe.

Chapter 29: Kate

Stumptown Global
Portland, Oregon

Veronica called this morning while I was making coffee. She issued a summons from Winston, so in we came. I'm not sure what it's about — maybe they just want to check on my progress back in the land of the living. Or maybe they want to see if Matt's ever going to come back, a question I've had myself a time or two.

But most likely, they've heard how desperate we're getting and want to remind us about our Non-Disclosure Agreements. I find the grand entrance of Winston and the ducklings no longer causes my heart to skip a beat. He strides across the room and gives me a strong hug, "Katherine! We're so glad to have you with us. What an ordeal!"

Maybe I'm more cynical than I used to be, or maybe I just don't care anymore, but he seems even more plastic and insincere than usual. I suppose if he was actually glad to see me, instead of just pleased to have this crisis winding down, he'd have visited me weeks ago.

Veronica glides in behind them, and gives me a small smile as she walks over and sets two folders in front of us.

I can't believe how much I used to crave this room and the power meetings that were held here. I'd walk past the windows and see Winston in here with some big celebrity, working deals, shaking hands. Now it seems like just about the most foolish way to make a living I can think of.

I take a quick peak at Matt to see how he's doing. He told me about the first morning he met Ken, and I think that's the last time he's been in here. He's got tiny beads of sweat on his forehead, so I imagine the answer to my question is not great.

Please help him, give him what he needs today.

I find it easier and easier to pray — it's as Becca said, just like breathing in and out.

I look past Matt and see Ken, giving me a reassuring smile as the three of us sit down. I'm so glad he's still here. I know how much Matt counts on him and I'm not too excited about his departure next week.

Besides, he's kind of a buffer these days. When he's not around, all Matt and I do is pick at one another. I've started thinking seriously about moving out — it'll be good for both of us, and I hope good for the survival of our friendship.

But the truth is, I'm heartbroken. Ever since I met Jesus Matt has thrown up a wall that never used to exist between us, and I stare at it every time we try to speak. We're broken in a way the kidnapping couldn't accomplish, and I can't figure out a way to fix us.

When I fell in love with Alex, Matt put up with me talking about her for hours — her virtues, her good looks, her sense of humor, her career and life goals that aligned with mine.

Sure, he'd roll his eyes repeatedly, and occasionally suggest we take a break from the Love Boat and watch a movie — but I knew he cared enough about me to listen to what I wanted to tell him.

It's not the same this time. I feel like I've fallen in love, but in a profound new way, in a way I've been waiting for all my life. I want to talk about God all the time — or about what I've been reading in the Bible Matt gave me, no less, tossing it at me and saying it's one Becca left behind last time she was here.

I read for hours, and every time he comes in the room and sees me he gets a look on his face that is some awful combination of dread, hate, pain and fear.

He says he's happy for me. He says he's glad I've found something that works for me, and is helping me through my recovery. But he doesn't want to talk about it.

Just when I thought we could get our conversational rhythm back, around a topic almost wholly unrelated to Becca and all the stories I can't tell, and he doesn't want to talk.

This morning he casually asked across the counter as we were eating breakfast after we'd exhausted the topic of what Winston might want, "So what, you're not gay anymore?"

I thought about it for a minute, and replied as honestly as I could, "I know it's important and I'll have to look at it eventually, but honestly I just don't think about it right now. I'm too intrigued by what I'm reading and learning about God and His love for me."

He'd gotten up abruptly, dumped his nearly full bowl of cereal into the sink and walked out. He didn't return until it was time to leave for the meeting.

Startled, I realize Winston is still talking and I've tuned him out completely. I used to hang on every word he said like it was wisdom from on high.

"...and we would just like to say again how happy we are to have you here with us, Katherine. We trust your recuperation is going well?"

"Yes, thank you," I say quietly, thankful I rejoined the conversation in time to hear his question.

"And thanks for joining us, Ken. We can't thank you and your company enough for all your assistance in getting our Katherine back for us."

Ken starts to reply, but Winston cuts him off as an unnecessary participant in his plans for the day. He signals to a lawyer who moves the mic to the center of the table and switches it on.

"We asked you here, Matthew and Katherine, because you are both valuable members of our family. It is important to us to do the right thing by our family members, even those who have left us, and we would like to offer a very small token of our appreciation for your work and sacrifice."

I'd been staring at a square of marble tile just to the right of Winston's head, wondering how much it cost, but my focus snapped back to him at that.

"Additionally, it has been heartbreaking for us to stand by and watch as we could only help with the negotiations for you, Katherine. We've followed your instructions to the letter, Ken, about not going public for Becca's safety."

Matt snorts and Winston looks a bit taken aback before continuing. "But we've figured out a way to come up with the money for the additional ransom out of our own house."

"We would like to offer each of you 1.5 million dollars, which we've been informed is the sum that is being asked of you for the return of Becca."

My heart rate spikes, and I can tell from Matt's intake of breath that he's as taken by surprise as I am.

"The only thing we are going to ask of you, and I'm sure you will find this completely reasonable, is that you continue to protect our family. We'll want you to sign something agreeing to not hold us liable for any of these events, and to keep the confidentiality you both know is so important in our business."

Matt nearly comes out of his seat by the end of this pretty speech, and I grab his knee and dig in hard. I can't believe the company I gave ten years of my life to, the company I trusted even though I decided to leave them, is stooping this low. Hush money that we have absolutely no choice but to take.

I can't imagine how Matt's feeling.

He told me how he did everything but get down on his knees in Winston's office, begging for this very outcome. How he offered to sign any contract they wanted, that he would work for free until he dropped dead. And all Winston did was offer platitudes and insincere apologies about how his hands were tied, before reminding him of the almighty NDA, and more meaningfully, Ken's advice not to go public.

But I can see now that they were just biding their time, waiting for the most auspicious moment before swooping in with a definitive action. It smells just like Winston.

When they know we are over an absolute barrel and have no other resources, they offer to buy our silence. They probably even billed Harry for it — a couple weeks' "work" for him.

I hear a squeak and look down, and see that Matt has bent the fragile arm of his chair. For my part, I can't feel the hand gripping his knee. I slowly release my grip, one finger at a time.

Matt is staring at the table, teeth gritted so hard it looks like he might break them off. So it's up to me then. I take a breath, and let it out slowly.

Please. Help.

And then I know just what to say to this snake.

"I think you can imagine our gratitude at this generosity, and of course we would not break our original NDA's, but if you feel it is a necessary step for us to sign something further, I hope you know we are certainly willing to do that."

My nails are digging into my palm, the only physical outlet I allow myself as my face remains smooth and earnest.

"Of course we would greatly appreciate expediting the settlement so that we can contact Amal as soon as possible and bring this ordeal to a close."

All the partners are nodding compassionately, and Winston continues quickly, "Of course, of course. We've actually got the checks right here."

He snaps his fingers at Veronica, hovering in the background, and she comes forward with two folders. He continues smoothly, "We've also got the documents for you to sign. And we want you to know that your counseling with Dr. Kolms is something we will continue to fund. We want you back to fighting form as soon as possible."

Winston laughs, then the rest of the partners give a series of small chuckles and smiles.

Part of me wants to climb up over the table and smack his smug face as hard as I can. He's pleased with himself because he's maneuvered this "situation" in a way that both benefits his client and pads his bank account. Quite a coup, when you consider what the situation involves.

But another part of me feels pity for him. What a terrible way to spend your life. I'm grateful that I was freed from this sinking ship a while ago. And I'm grateful that he's given us a way to get Becca back, finally.

I take another long breath, then look down and open my folder. The check stares up at me, and it might just as well be a picture of Becca's face, healthy and whole once again. I smile, and sign the new paperwork without even looking at it.

Chapter 30: Becca

"Becca."

I wake with a start, surprised by what sounded like my name. Groggily, uncharacteristically so, I realize I must have fallen into a deep sleep after the catharsis of last night. What a relief to sleep deeply after so many nights of desperate tossing and turning. I forget what woke me and start to drift off again when a stick hits me in the forehead.

"Becca!"

This time the hiss is louder and I turn my head, searching for the source in the darkness. Amal's face peering at me from fewer than two feet away startles me so badly I yelp and skitter away. I feel the opposite wall of the tent behind me, still trying to make sense of his face sticking through a hole that didn't exist when I fell asleep.

His words finally pierce my fog, but once I process what he's saying I realize I must still be dreaming.

"Becca, you must come with me. We are escaping."

What the?

I need a moment to think, but his eyes are just this side of wild and his arm has reached through the hole to try to grab my leg.

"Becca, I am going to help you escape, but we must go *now.*"

No way, no how, am I going anywhere with this man. He has clearly lost his mind.

He seems to sense the direction of my thoughts. Or maybe it's not sensing so much as seeing my fingers search for something to protect myself with.

He calms himself, looks right into my eyes, and I feel a familiar warmth come over me as he begins speaking.

"Jesus came to me just now and opened my eyes. He told me if I am to follow Him I must first get you out of here tonight. He told me that Oumar comes at dawn to take you away and you will not return. We must go now!"

And just like that, like saying abra cadabra, he has uttered the only words which will make me follow him — the man who has kidnapped, terrorized, and betrayed me — off into the pitch darkness of a wilderness from which there will be no return if he is lying.

....

A couple hours running through the brush like two people half-crazed, most of the time with him dragging me along as I try to make my battered body obey me once the first fit of adrenaline wears off, and suddenly we come to a barely outlined crossroad in the dirt. I stumble a few steps forward until I realize he's stopped.

I look back and hope he sees the question in my eyes because I can't catch my breath to speak.

I'm even more puzzled when he sits down and looks like he has all the time in the world. Finally, in exasperation, I gasp out, "Amal, what are you doing?"

"Jesus told me to bring you to the crossroad and wait. So I am preparing to wait."

Just like that. Unbelievable. Jesus has never told me anything like that, but that's clearly Who he's heard from. I've never seen him look so peaceful.

We wait for what seems like hours and I'm starting to get drowsy. Just as light begins to break the horizon we both notice a figure in the distance, running toward us. I grab Amal's hand to get up, but he says firmly, "He told me to wait."

Soon enough we can see that it's MJ, and he has a gun. I can feel Amal's stress building, but he doesn't move a muscle. We wait. MJ stops about five feet from us and casually slings his gun over his shoulder. He pulls a bag off his back and pulls out bread and water, then hands them to us.

He takes a moment to catch his breath, then breaks into a huge grin and starts talking. I feel the shock hit Amal and he turns to me. "He says Jesus came to him tonight and told him to meet us at the crossroads with food and water, and take us to his father's house."

MJ turns and starts walking, assuming we will follow.

Of course we do.

· · · · · · · · · ·

MJ walks ahead of us for about an hour until we reach his father's little village. It looks just like all the villages we've been staying in, several huts, women in front kneeling beside the fire, donkey, chickens.

His family looks at me oddly, but ushers us into the largest hut. Everyone gathers around, cramming inside those who fit, and those who don't sit on the ground in front and listen. Amal and MJ, or rather Tariq as his family calls him, begin to tell about their visions.

All of a sudden I realize I'm watching a scene out of Acts and shivers rip up and down my arms. We stay about an hour, then his mother takes me to her hut. She bathes me from a small bowl of water, the best she has to offer, carefully avoiding my many and various wounds. Then she pulls a colorful dress off the wall and wraps it around me, the first clean clothes I've had since this ordeal began. Looking at the dirty bandage taped over the remains of my ear, crusted over with dried blood, she clucks sadly, then hands me a headscarf to hide it.

When we emerge from her hut, the whole family escorts us to the bus station in the next village with a festival air. They wave us off as if we are family, off on a great journey. It is indescribably odd.

I find myself crammed into a seat between MJ and Amal, three people in a space that would normally hold one, maybe two skinny Americans. There was another man in our row leering at me and motioning for me to sit beside him, but Amal muscled his way in and MJ took the other side.

Again, I'm overtaken by a wave of how strange this all is. It felt just like a time when my brother and one of his friends protected me from some handsy guys at a college football game.

We barrel down the road, as I charitably call it, and I find myself focusing on the details in front of me rather than losing the thread of my mental health, something I fear is not so much a leap at this point as a brief hop.

The driver is bundled in a multi-colored ski coat and baby blue knit cap, though it has got to be at least 95 degrees. The windows are all closed, allowing us to revel in the smell of tightly-packed, unwashed bodies. I notice the smell, but not as I would have a couple months ago. I imagine without the intervention of MJ's mom, I

211

would have been holding my own in adding to the general raunchiness.

We roar down the road, headlights dimly stabbing into the darkness as we veer to avoid potholes, goats, men on bikes, women walking, and other cars not using their lights. It is Disneyland, Magic Mountain, NASCAR, and a really scary haunted house, reimagined by a maniac with no fear of liability lawsuits.

It is enough for now. A few hours in and even the driver's blaring music can't keep me awake. I'm so far gone I don't even recoil when I feel Amal take my bobbing head and direct it to his shoulder.

....

The only time I wake is when the bus causes my head to bounce and I bang the remains of my ear against Amal's shoulder. The pain jerks me awake and I barely contain the groan. The bandages Amal secured for me are dried now, fused to hair and skin. It's going to take a good long soak to get them off.

....

Our escape is not lithe, nor fast. It takes eighteen hours before we are finally rolling into the outskirts of Dakar. By then I have answered approximately 250 questions from Jesus' newest followers, from the mundanely trivial, to the highest heights of theological knots that people have argued about for two millennia.

I answer them as best I can, but at times it feels too surreal for words to be having this conversation. They both look at me oddly when I break out into loud cackles, not understanding that my mind is on the brink of cracking in two, or maybe a million, pieces.

I sleep a long time on the first bus, but then Amal wakes me and we change buses abruptly because "Jesus said to get off right now." It thrills me each time I hear Amal or MJ say it, while also flustering me. Again, I think, *what gives?* Jesus never speaks to me that way!

On the second bus I only sleep a couple hours before they wake me for questions. Their thirst is immense, and I find myself jealous as I always am when someone first meets Jesus. That first fire, unquenchable, insatiable; there is nothing like it.

As we reach the outskirts of Dakar their questions finally begin to slow, and they both fall silent for a time, then talk quietly with each other. I'm startled when I look over and see that MJ is crying.

"Becca," Amal begins, then stays silent so long I feel the need to prompt him.

"Yes?"

"We must ask you to forgive us. We know there is no reason for you to do so, but we must ask it. When we get you to the American Embassy there will be many questions and we will be taken away. We wish there was more time, but there is not. We are more sorry and filled with shame than we can convey, and we will not expect you to forgive us, but we must ask it."

I am so startled, even after the conversations we've been having, that my breath leaves me. Neither of them are looking at me, their faces locked in sync staring straight forward. But I see the silent tears trickling down.

And then it's like a film drops in front of them, and I see not only the now, but the innocent boys that were. The harm that was done to them. Evil over and over taking aim at their fragile hearts until they turned cold just to survive. I have had that same heart, and been forgiven of so much worse.

"Amal, Tariq. You may find this hard to believe, but with Allah's help I forgave you a long time ago. Allah showed me His love, and I now show it to you. I forgive you."

Just then the bus staggers to a halt. We were so caught up in our conversation, all of us crying and hugging, that we didn't see the checkpoint.

Soldiers surround the bus and several board quickly, guns raised. The driver starts yelling and points to us. MJ still has his gun propped up next to him, and for some reason he makes a move toward it. The soldier in front raises his gun and starts yelling, and I don't have time to think about it. I stand and try to shield MJ with my body while yelling that everything is okay. And then there's a light.

Chapter 31: Amal

I'm not sure where I am when I come slowly awake. My head aches and I reach my hand up to touch it, but the clink of chains stops me. I look down and see I'm bound hand and foot to a bed.

There is an ache in my shoulder and I can see that I'm bandaged there. I can see I only have one sandal on, and that my pants are ripped at my right knee.

There is one lightbulb in the ceiling above me, flickering just a little. It lets me see a little. I'm in some kind of small room, big enough for my bed alone. I see the bars that tell me it's a cell. There's water dripping from somewhere nearby and I crane my neck trying to see, but sudden pain blinds me.

There was something, something important. It's just at the tip of my mind. Something bad happened. I sit for a awhile, listening to the drip, when it comes back to me in a rush. Becca was wedged on top of me in the aisle of the bus, the warm blood gushing freely from her body onto mine. "No, no, no, no!" I'd yelled, but I couldn't move.

Two inches from my face, Tariq's vacant eyes stared at me. She didn't move, so I couldn't. I could hear the soldiers shouting, saw their feet move forward and drag Tariq's body roughly out of the bus. Half a minute later they returned for her, and with less care than I would have liked they pulled her off of me.

The second I was able to I hopped to my feet, and the guns were pointed at me immediately. "Is she alive? Is she dead? You've got to help her!" I yelled, swinging wildly, trying to get outside to where they'd dragged her. There was a large crowd standing around gawking. I could see two soldiers bent over her body, and when one shrugged to the other I went berserk.

215

Suddenly something hit me in the head, the world went dark, and I awoke here.

"Becca!" I yell, and the action causes a pain like death to shoot through my head. I yell her name again and again, for what seems like hours, until my throat is too raw to continue in more than a whisper.

After an eternity I hear footsteps coming down the hall. They approach, closer and closer, until finally I see a white man in a suit accompanied by a Senegalese soldier in uniform.

"Is your name Amal?" the man in the suit asks in badly-accented Wolof.

"Yes," I answer in English, "I am Amal. Please tell me, is Becca all right?"

"Do you have a full name Amal?" He switches to English, seeming relieved.

"Amal is all I remember. Please, I must know if Becca is alive!"

In my anxiety I try to raise off the bed and the soldier steps forward with his hand on his gun. The man with the suit waves him back.

He pulls a notepad out of his suit pocket, opens it up and says, "Alright then." He seems to study me for a moment, and I suddenly remember that I can ask Jesus for help. This memory calms me down considerably.

Please Jesus, I must know!

"I'm sorry Amal," the man continues, "but I'm not at liberty to share that information with you."

He says it meanly, like he takes pleasure in leaving me in the dark, and I close my eyes so that I don't have to see his expression.

There was so much blood, flooding down the side of my face from what seemed like a hundred holes in her body. She didn't even grunt when they picked her up so roughly.

I feel moisture sliding down my face, and try to reach my hand up to wipe the tears before the rattle of the chain reminds me that I cannot. How could this have happened? After everything.

Jesus, please. Please let her live.

And then I feel what can only be described as peace fall on me. My whole body relaxes and I feel my pulse lowering. And now the moisture at my eyes is more of a flood.

I don't know if she is alive or dead, but I know that it is going to be all right. I am going to be all right. And a void that has been cracked and dry and parched at the center of my chest all my life seems to be filling with water.

Am I crying because she's safe or because she's dead? Because I didn't get her killed, or because I did? Or just simple gratitude? I don't know. All I know is this is the first time in my entire life when I've felt whole.

When I open my eyes again I notice that the man is watching my reaction closely, but I don't care. When he sees he has my attention again he starts speaking.

"My name is Mario Hernandez. I work for the Federal Bureau of Investigation of the United States of America. I am here to formally advise you that you are being arrested for the kidnap and unlawful imprisonment of two US citizens, an international crime, over which we have jurisdiction.

"We have asked the Senegalese government to extradite you to the United States, where you will stand trial for your crimes. You have the right to an attorney when you arrive, and if you cannot afford an attorney, one will be provided for you. Do you understand these rights as I have explained them to you?"

After all this time, it looks like I'm actually going to the United States. What a joke. I start to laugh, and Mr. Hernandez looks at me like I'm a particularly nasty bug he'd like to squash underfoot.

Well, we'll see about that, Mario. Becca told me once that Allah works in mysterious ways and I didn't understand what she meant. Now I do.

"Would it be possible to get a Bible, Mr. Hernandez?"

He blinks once. Twice. Then asks, "seriously?"

Chapter 32: Matt

Kate has gone to her room to try to take a nap. Ken's gone back to his apartment to call his wife and tell her he's sticking around a little longer. He says there's not much we can do now but wait until Amal contacts us, then we can make the deal. Meanwhile he'll talk to some contacts and try to get our travel arrangements set up.

As soon as Winston dropped this on us I knew it was coming. I could feel it breathing down my neck. I'd gripped my chair as tight as possible, so as not to jump across and rip Winston's throat out. I nodded along, agreeing with anything, signing blindly, so that we could get out of there as soon as possible.

Now that the coast is clear, I let it out — the rage I haven't allowed myself to feel since I was sixteen years old and came home to find my father on top of Becca. I've worked ever since that night to keep it bottled up, but now it comes flying out full force.

I can't believe Winston did this. I can't believe this happened in the first place. I can't believe God allowed my father to represent him. I can't believe I purposely made best friends with a gay woman so that God could never get to her, and he did after all, and used me to do it. I can't believe.

There is no outlet suitable for this level of rage, but I put everything I have into it, and punch through the french door leading to my balcony.

. . . .

Kate comes rushing out wild-eyed, but when she sees the shattered glass at my feet and the blood gushing down my arm — me

219

just standing there with slumped shoulders letting it bleed, she doesn't say anything.

She wraps my hand up in a kitchen towel and walks me down the block to the clinic we visit for her check-ups every week. She handles everything, I just have to endure the repercussions of my actions — forty-three stitches and six bones fractured.

Each sting is somehow payment, and I endure them in silence. The only time I say a word is when the doctor suggests they have me stay the night for observation. I can tell he's worried I might do something more drastic, and I nip that idea in the bud, insisting I will be fine with Kate watching over me.

Somehow during the time we're back with the doctor, Kate manages to contact Ken, because he's sitting in the lobby when we walk out. He just looks at me, but doesn't say anything, and I feel about two-feet tall. He walks with us to my apartment, and without a word he and Kate start cleaning up the glass.

I lie down on the couch, elevate my throbbing arm, and close my eyes. How long do we have to wait? Is she already dead? Will this nightmare never end?

. . . .

We wait three days without word from Amal. I can tell Kate has gone back to thinking Becca might already be dead. I know I have. Ken made all the arrangements he could the first day, but keeps reiterating that this is very normal. They never leave me alone.

The two of them are moving around silently in the kitchen making dinner for us, something none of us are too interested in eating, when the doorbell rings. With my injury, I've been relegated to watching, so I get up and go to the door.

It's DHL, and I sign for it without thinking. I try to make out the return address as I walk back up the hall, calling to Kate "did you order anything?"

"No," she says, distracted by reading the recipe she's trying to follow.

"Who's it from," Ken asks.

I pull a knife out of the junk drawer and move to the other side of the counter. When I manage to wrestle the tracking slip out of its envelope, the address is smudged too much to make out.

"I can't tell," I mumble, and struggle to cut through the tape one-handed.

Ken and Kate laugh over something, but I feel a growing sense of dread as I rip off the last piece of tape and open the box.

There's a little card on top of a bunch of crumpled newspaper.

As I pick it up to try to read the small writing, I see there's a troubling red smear on the corner.

Last. Warning.

One of them asks again who it's from, but the roar in my ears makes it hard to define whose voice it was. I set the card down, then carefully lift off the crumpled paper.

It takes a moment to identify the thing at the bottom of the box, but when I do my knees buckle and I end up on all fours, retching.

....

My hands won't stop shaking. We've sat here on the couch for hours — three little Indians, three bumps on a log, three peas in a pod. A little strangled laugh escapes and Kate looks up quickly from the Bible she's reading, her eyes red and swollen.

"Sorry," I mumble, "it just came out."

"S'okay," she replies softly, "Becca always laughed at the most inappropriate times. She said it was her stress reaction. Must be a family trait."

She reaches over and grabs my good hand, holding on tight, then goes back to flipping through the book that never seems far from her side these days.

The phone rings and jolts us all, but I quickly realize it's Ken's phone. He apologizes, stands up, and walks a few feet away. He's been making and getting calls all night with his office and contacts. Trying to find out if there's any way we can track who sent the package. Doing whatever he can, like always.

"Can you repeat that?" He says abruptly, in a voice louder than we've used in hours. He steps through the empty doorframe out onto the balcony and Kate and I look at each other.

"What now?" she asks.

I wonder.

He's out there less than a minute, pacing and agitated, talking in a voice too low to make out. He hangs up and then dials again, and ends that call even quicker. Then he comes crashing back inside with a grin on his face entirely alien to the situation.

"She's alive! Becca's alive and in US custody!"

Kate jumps off the couch and bounces up and down, then leans down to give me a hug, but my head is already between my knees so she ends up hugging my back. I'm breathing for all I'm worth, trying to keep the black on the edges of my vision from encroaching any further.

Ken sits beside me on the couch and puts a hand on my back. "Breathe, buddy, it's true. She's alive. She's okay. She's gonna be okay."

A few minutes of steady breathing pushes back the darkness and I can see again. I sit up and ask, "Okay, start over please."

"That was a friend of mine from the State Department. He knew I was working this case, so he called to give me a head's up. The Senegalese police did a random bus search yesterday and found Becca with two of her captors. There was a firefight and Becca was shot multiple times in the cross-fire, but only a couple of them were serious. She was taken to the Embassy and triaged there, and they determined she could survive the flight to the same military hospital in Germany that received Kate.

"Her plane just took off, and when she arrives she'll go directly into surgery. I called a pilot friend of mine and he's getting a plane ready right now. It's not big enough to fly internationally, but he'll fly us to Chicago. My company has agreed to loan us the jet, so I need you to pack a bag, my friend. We're going to Germany!"

Chapter 33: Kate

We travel across the world much quicker than my initial trip, nearly nine months ago. Private jet is definitely the way to go, Matt and I decide. We are almost giddy with relief when we find out during our Chicago stop that Becca has made it to the hospital in Germany.

We end up stopping to pick up State Department Todd in New York, and after saying a quick hello, I fall asleep and don't wake up until Matt shakes me gently, telling me we're about to touch down. I can't believe I slept the whole way, but feel entirely refreshed.

When we get off the plane, Todd whisks us away like the VIPs we apparently are, and within minutes we're driving toward the hospital in a black Mercedes with tinted windows.

I recognize the man who greets us. It's the same kind doctor who took pity on me when I was here earlier, and explained his opinion of what Becca might be facing if she ever made it out. It turns out he was pretty much correct on all fronts, except that now she's missing an ear, and has additional bullet holes. Eight of them, causing varying degrees of havoc that will add months to her recovery. She has a long road ahead of her, but he assures us that she will be fine.

He leads us to her room, and we line up in front of the window gawking. She appears small and weak on a bed twice her size, surrounded by multiple machines and tubes attached everywhere.

At least she's not on a breathing tube, he says, so when she wakes up she'll be able to talk to us. One at a time, he reiterates, as if the three times he told us before wasn't enough.

A shiver goes through me at the thought of talking to her. I can still remember the look on her face, and now even stronger than the shame I felt over kissing her, I feel shame wash over me that I abandoned her to greater injury in pursuit of my own freedom.

What was I thinking, coming here? I should have stayed home. She won't want to see me. She'll never want to see me again.

I've just about convinced myself to turn around and leave when I hear Matt's intake of breath from where he stands beside me. I look up quickly, and see that her eyelids have started flickering.

He hugs me, then leans down and whispers, "ladies first."

Chapter 34: Becca

I have no idea where I am, but after a few moments of grogginess, I hear a kind of multi-symphonic beeping that starts to register.

I know this sound, I know it. Where am I?

Suddenly I realize I recognize the sound from my deep and abiding love for TV medical dramas — I'm in a hospital! My eyes fly open on their own, and I see that I was right, I'm surrounded by sleek machines and white walls.

I look down at my arms — the left is stuck with IV's, and the right is covered in the most pristine white wrapping I've seen in as long as I can remember, dangling from a band tied to the ceiling.

And it doesn't hurt! Nothing hurts, which is an entirely novel sensation. I must be extremely high, because all of a sudden I remember what happened last, and I should definitely be hurting more.

I'm trying to piece together how I could have gotten here, wherever here is, when the door opens and Kate enters. I'm so surprised to see her I don't say anything for a moment.

She looks wonderful! She's gotten her hair cut since Fatima hacked it, and it doesn't look half bad. Her cheeks have filled out, she's clean, and she's not wearing traditional North African dress. The change is a bit of a shock, really.

But more than all of that, there is something different in her eyes. A brightness, a peace, that is hard to look away from.

Meet your new sister.

Tears start leaking from my eyes and I let them go, unable to move either hand to wipe them away. She rushes toward me, but then stops abruptly at the side of my bed.

"I don't even know where to hug you!" she says in exasperation, but then slowly bends over and carefully places one hand on my cheek and the other on my shoulder. She lays her forehead gently against mine and our tears mingle.

Chapter 35: Amal

He says his name is Todd, and that if I help him, he'll put in a good word for me with the judge. I tell him I will help him any way I can, no matter what he does or does not do for me.

He brings me to a private jet in chains, with four guards watching my every move, but once onboard he has one of the guards unlock me. Two guards sit across the aisle from us, guns pointed at me the whole time, while the other two sit nearby.

He seems to understand that I need to begin at the beginning, and listens intently as I tell him about my parents and the *marabout*, and about my benefactors the Andersons. His right eye twitches when I say their name, and I wonder if he might have known them.

Then I begin to slowly and methodically unburden myself of every sordid detail from my time with the gang, listing off as many facts as I can dredge up. I tell him what I remember about how to get to Diadji's house, and every fact about his wide and varied criminal empire that I can remember. I list off all the names of members I've met, what their jobs are and where they might be found.

I tell him how to find Oumar, and where he keeps the girls before selling them to the buyers who come in from other countries. I feel a twinge of guilt, then decide Oumar has had his chance, and those girls deserve theirs.

I pick up each memory like a weight, examining it from all sides to make sure I've told them everything, and then chuck it, feeling lighter each time.

I talk for the entire flight, until my voice is hoarse and Todd has to lean forward to hear me. Finally, I get to the night before the escape. I tell him everything, how Jesus came to me and told me what to do, how we escaped, and how Becca had granted us forgiveness just before we were all shot.

Please sir, I ask again, can't you tell me if she survived? There was so much blood. I must know if she made it.

Todd looks at me for a long moment, and then nods.

Chapter 36: Matt

I watch Kate and Becca hug awkwardly and then cry together. I can't tell what they talk about, but apparently it doesn't involve a fight over who kissed whom.

After five minutes the doctor raps on the window. He says normal visiting hours will have to wait, and since he's the one in charge of patching Becca up, I decide to obey.

Kate stands up and lets go of Becca's hand reluctantly, then walks toward me. I don't know what was said, but I can see that the anxiety in Kate's eyes before she went in has vanished. She's glowing, and squeezes my shoulder on the way by.

I walk in and grab Becca's hand carefully around the bandaging. She's crying, and I feel the tears sliding down my face as well. I make no move to wipe them away since she can't.

I don't know what to say, so I say nothing. But as I stand there, I feel something immensely heavy I've been carrying fall off, and it feels like a kind of weightlessness to stand here only anchored to the ground by her hand.

I can see the question blazing through her eyes. It's the same one that's always there, and it tears at me somewhere deep inside that it intrudes even upon this sacred moment.

Even so, I'm bound to answer her.

"We made a pact, you and I. Do you remember?"

I know she's on heavy painkillers, I can see the fuzziness in her eyes, but I can also see that she knows exactly what I'm talking about.

"Not until then. I won't break it."

She nods ever so slightly and I watch another tear break off and slide down her cheek. It gets prematurely smothered in the bandage across where her ear should be. It's a body blow, but I contain the part of me that wants to howl in pain and lean down to kiss her cheek lightly.

"Sleep now, I'll be back later."

I just manage to not slam her door, but by the end of the hallway I'm running. I take the stairs, and five flights later I'm on the roof that I discovered when Kate was here. It looks out on the mountains, for some reason an image I always associate with God. My rage is all-encompassing.

"I know You're there," I shout, "and I will. Not. YIELD!"

Author's Note

If you made it this far, I want to thank you for taking this journey with me! I appreciate you investing the time — especially when you could be reading something much less heavy — and would love to hear your thoughts, either in a review or by email.

I also wanted to tell you that, while this *is* a work of complete fiction, my job as a videographer for an international NGO played a large part in the writing process. For five years I documented humanitarian projects, traveling to a number of different countries — some of which were less than ideal safety-wise — and during those travels the idea for this novel began taking shape.

While I never felt my life was in imminent danger, there were a few dicey moments where things could have gone rather quickly in an entirely different direction. When challenged about the different safety issues I sometimes faced, I always gave a stock answer — there is no safer place to be than in the palm of God's hand — and while I believed, and continue to believe, that to be true, I also believe His hand can take us places we'd never have gone if given the opportunity to choose.

I know Becca would not have chosen this particular journey, but I went with her there because I'm well aware that in this broken, evil world we're living in, things like this happen every day. And the good God both has His reasons, and never leaves us to face difficult situations alone.

Speaking from my own perspective, it has been at the bottom of some awful, endless, light-less craters—when I've been surrounded by fear, crying and alone—that I've experienced the most honest and life-changing moments of my life. And what profound, holy moments those are, when He comes to us, lends His hand, and obliterates the enemy.

I hope you've been able to experience one of these sacred moments in your own life. And I hope you enjoyed my novel. :)

Thank you to my cheerleaders, my team, my without-comparison husband, and our good, good God.

jc, Istanbul, 2016

As you might imagine, independent authors like myself don't have giant marketing budgets nor big publishers behind us. If you enjoyed this book, it's actually really helpful if you would mention it to one or two, or four or five ;-) of your friends. It also helps a lot if you'd be willing to take the time to write a short review on Amazon, Good Reads, or wherever else you yourself read reviews. I'd appreciate it a lot!

Made in the
USA
Middletown, DE